KIYA
MOTHER OF A KING
KATIE HAMSTEAD

A Division of **Whampa, LLC**
P.O. Box 2540
Dulles, VA 20101
Tel/Fax: 800-998-2509
http://curiosityquills.com

ISBN 978-1-62007-378-0 (ebook)
ISBN 978-1-62007-379-7 (paperback)
ISBN 978-1-62007-380-3 (hardcover)

TABLE OF CONTENTS

For Lilly, my little princess.

CHAPTER ONE

arkness surrounded me as I gazed around at our makeshift camp, lit only by the moonlight. The two camels Horemheb gave us dozed calmly on either side of us, with a canopy stretched between them for our shelter. I was unable to sleep because Horemheb's words resonated through my dreams. "Stay off the main roads and keep away from the river. If Nefertiti or Ay's spies see you, you will be done for..."

Between Malachi and me, under the canopy, were Tut, Itani and Hepsati, all still asleep, but Malachi was awake.

He must have heard me start, and shifted onto his elbow to look at me. "Naomi, what is it?"

"Bad dream," I said softly.

Those last moments in Amarna haunted me. Mordad's eyes gazing up at me as she begged me to take Hepsati with us, and her dying words of love, then Malachi rushing me to leave the city, Horemheb's desperate face when he stopped us and pleaded with me to let him guide and protect us on our flight. When I refused, he held back his emotions, but I saw the despair in his eyes. The memory of it gave me chills.

Malachi sat up and pulled the canopy back so he could see the sky. "We've slept long enough, anyway. We should get the camels packed and move on while it's dark." He stood and pulled the canopy down, then shoved it into the sack of the camel beside him.

I stood up and pulled my shawl over my head before I began waking the children. Hepsati folded her own blanket and gave it to Malachi, while I struggled with Tut, who found it amusing to toss his over his younger sister, Itani, who cried out every time. I snatched the blanket from him and threw it to Malachi before I strapped him up onto the camel. He fought me and protested the whole time, and even bit me as I tightened the band around his waist.

I slapped his cheek. "Tut! You know better than to bite!"

He wailed, which made Itani cry, also. With a sigh, I tried to ignore the screams. I picked up Itani, then tied her onto the camel. I turned to Malachi and found he had Hepsati up on the camel already; he brought it over so he could hold them both while I mounted behind her.

Malachi led the camels across the desert. The journey was considerably longer on foot than the times I had sailed from Thebes to Amarna on the Nile, and having to stay in the desert so we wouldn't be seen made it even longer and more dangerous.

We were careful with our water, and sipped only when we were almost desperate, which was hard on the children. I was still nursing Itani; that kept her strong and healthy, but drained me. Tut had not stopped complaining the whole time of being hungry, or thirsty, or tired, or just fed up.

Hepsati was quite the opposite. I could tell by how quiet she had been throughout the course of our journey that she understood what happened to her mother and felt deeply saddened by the loss. She leaned back, pressed her head against my chest, and sighed. I stroked her hair and kissed the top of her head. Her hand rested over mine wrapped around her waist, and she spoke. "Kiya, when we get to where we are going, will we be free like Mama always said I would be once I left the palace?"

Malachi looked back at us with his eyebrows furrowed. I squeezed her affectionately and said, "My father and brother will protect us, but you mustn't call me Kiya anymore, remember? It will make those bad people come after us. You must call me Naomi now."

"I know, I just forgot. I'll call you by that name over and over in my mind until I get it right."

"Oh Hepsati, you're a wonderful young lady. You are so brave."

The journey was tedious, and the land seemed endless and unchanging. I had no idea how Malachi led us the right way as there were no landmarks I could see to guide us. Eventually, the sun rose, so he paused to pull the shawl over Itani and tried to get Tut to put his on, but he just pulled it off

7

again. The rest of us covered our heads and faces to keep the sun away, and I watched my stubborn little son fight against the heat. Finally, he gave up, and begged Malachi to put the shawl over him.

Every now and then, we needed to stop so I could nurse Itani. The journey was hard on her, and she cried from the heat as I struggled to get her to latch on. While I nursed her, Malachi stood and unsheathed his sword while staring over the plains.

"What is it?" I asked him, alarmed.

"Lions." He caught Tut, tossed him onto the camel and asked Hepsati to sit with him. "We should move. You can nurse on the camel."

I pulled Itani off me, who screamed because she was not finished, and handed her to Malachi while I mounted the camel. Once I was situated, he handed her back to me and led out the camels as she latched back on.

The heat sapped my energy while I nursed. When Malachi looked up at me, he seemed worried. "Naomi, have something to drink."

"No, I'm fine…" I tried to protest, but when he raised the skin up to me, I couldn't stop my hand from wrapping around it. I sipped the water.

Itani soon fell asleep in my arms. I adjusted my clothing as I pulled her head out from under my tunic. I tied her in a sling around my body like Abi had shown me, and allowed my eyes to close. I must have dozed off, but awoke when the camels came to an abrupt halt.

"Are we going to set up camp?" I asked hopefully.

"No." Malachi spun, searching for something. "Naomi, no matter what happens, stay on the camel." He turned and handed me both of the lead ropes, then spoke to Hepsati. "Hold onto your brother and don't let him go."

She nodded and wrapped her arms tighter around the sleeping Tut.

Malachi pulled his sword out again, his gaze flicking from one place to another.

"What is it?" I asked, fearful that we had been discovered.

"The lions have been following us. We're surrounded."

I took a sharp breath in fear. Looking at Hepsati and I saw terror across her face. I pulled the knife out of my satchel on my belt, just in case I needed it.

Suddenly, the first lioness charged us. She came from my side and went to leap onto the camel's rump, but Malachi rushed over and stabbed her in the chest. She fell to the ground dead, but Hepsati screamed and the camel grunted in fear. Another lioness had jumped onto the camel and our beast kicked it off.

Both camels spooked and tried to run, but another lioness appeared in front of us and charged straight at us. She leaped up for my camel's throat; I stretched my knife forward and slashed her in the face. She pulled back just long enough for Malachi to come around and stab her in the side.

Hepsati screamed again, and so did Tut. The rope for their beast tore from my hand. The lioness jumped back onto the camel, and with the help of another, brought it down to the ground.

"Naomi!" Hepsati screamed.

"Mama!" Tut wailed and reached for me as I watched the animal hit the ground with them on top of it.

"Malachi!" I screamed in a panic.

He spun and rushed at them, his sword blazing. He sliced one who raised her paw to take Tut, then he snatched Tut away and handed him to me. But Hepsati struggled to free herself. I watched as a lioness sank her teeth into her arm and pulled her off. Her screeching rang in my ears as Malachi rushed to her and stabbed the lioness in the eye before pulling Hepsati free. He ran over to us and threw her up on the camel behind me. Then he took the rope and ran.

I looked back to see the lion pride tearing the bags off the camel as one held its throat, slowly suffocating it. I cried, realizing how close we had come to losing our lives. Then I felt a twinge of guilt and said softly, "I'm sorry, Horemheb. It was the beast or us."

The journey grew much harder with just one camel. We lost half our water and supplies, and there wasn't enough room for four of us to ride on its back. So I walked beside Malachi with Itani strapped to my chest. But my strength wavered, and eventually Malachi stopped and took Tut down to tie him on his back so I could rest on the camel.

Hepsati's wound soon began to fester. We needed to use precious water on it to flush it out before binding it up tightly. But she too started to weaken.

I watched her fade in and out of a daze and prayed desperately for her to pull through. I couldn't lose her after promising Mordad I would protect her.

I drifted in and out of consciousness until I passed out completely. The next thing I knew, I was pulled down off the camel and Malachi carried me through the streets of Thebes. I opened my eyes and became aware enough to notice people rushing to us. Malachi asked for my family. He fell to his knees and, looking down at me, smiled weakly. "We made it, Naomi. Everything will be all right now."

"The children..." I forced from my lips.

"All here," he answered, before his grip on me loosened and he collapsed.

I felt too weak to move, but Itani shifted on my chest and started to cry just as my brother Samuel's face appeared above me.

"Naomi, we're here, hold on."

His arms slid underneath me as Papa appeared beside him with tears in his eyes.

I passed out again.

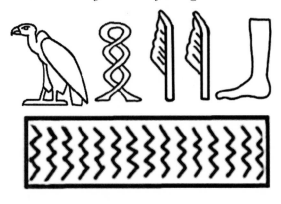

CHAPTER TWO

I awoke in the upper room of my father's house. I saw the dividing blanket pulled back. Sunlight poured through the windows. Itani slept beside me; Hepsati lay by the wall looking very pale, while my youngest sister Eliora patted her face with a damp cloth. I sat up and Hepsati's eyes flickered and look across at me.

She smiled. "Naomi, you're awake."

I scrambled across to her on my hands and knees, deeply worried. "Hepsati, how are you feeling?"

She lifted her arm to show me the bandages and smiled bravely. "It hurts, but I'm doing better."

"You're so brave." I gently stroked her cheek.

Eliora touched my shoulder. "Do you have the strength to walk?"

"I think so," I answered.

"Good because you need to eat something." She stood and offered me her hand.

I looked up at her and saw how much she had grown. She looked like a woman rather than the girl I had always known. I stood and noticed she was almost as tall as me now; her eyes nearly met mine, which made her taller than our sisters Adina and Rena.

As my legs wobbled under my weight, I glanced around the room. "Where are Tut and Malachi?" Fear rose within me as thoughts of them dying crossed my mind. "Are they—"

Eliora smiled at me and touched my shoulder again. "They're fine. They fared much better than you." Her eyes sparkled up at me. "Nursing without much to eat or drink is not wise, Naomi."

I smiled at her and laughed. "Thank you, Eliora. I will try to remember that next time I trek across the desert."

She held my arm and helped me downstairs, where her husband sat with their baby in his arms. He was an old childhood friend of mine, named Bilhan. We were about the same age, and it pleasantly surprised me to find he had grown very handsome. I was glad to know that my sister was in good hands. He smiled warmly at the sight of me, but didn't speak, so as not to wake the baby.

Eliora led me to where some bread and mutton sat by the stove. She cut me a slice of each and poured a cup of water.

I devoured them, feeling starved.

Eliora chuckled and sliced some more. "You have been asleep for several days, Naomi. We had to give you water by wetting your lips so we wouldn't drown you. Papa has been beside himself with worry and has spent every moment possible at your side."

She sighed and filled a small cup for herself. "The little girl, Hepsati, was very ill. I'm so glad you didn't see it. We had to cut the infection out of her arm. She screamed so loudly I think the heavens trembled. The guard, Malachi, held her through it all and wept with her. He's a good man."

I nodded. "I know. He was so brave and strong for us. He fought and killed three lions to protect us."

Her eyes widened with shock. "He didn't want to talk about what happened. He just said he pulled the children free from the camel and fled with all of you."

"He's a humble man," I said reverently. "But he's the bravest and strongest man I have ever met. My husband sent him with me for that reason, because he knew he would protect me at all costs."

Eliora caught my sleeve to pull me closer, a look of concern on her face. "The day before you arrived, Egyptian soldiers swept this sector searching for you. We thought you had been banished, that Pharaoh was displeased with you, that maybe he discovered you worshiping our God. But now you say he sent Malachi to protect you. What happened?"

I dropped my gaze. "Queen Nefertiti is after my life, and my son's. She's jealous of the love Pharaoh has for me, and she hates the boy for being named heir to the throne over her daughters. Pharaoh uncovered a plot for us to be killed the very night we fled. He saved me."

She let out a long breath as she gazed into my eyes. "Oh, Naomi, how I love you for the sacrifice you made for me. I wouldn't have survived as long as you have."

My emotions swelled up inside me. I wrapped my arms around her. "Dear Eliora, even now, I'd do it again."

Her arms tightened around me as she pressed her face against my shoulder.

Suddenly the door jolted open.

"Mama!" Tut's voice rang out as he flew across the room and into my arms. "You were asleep for a long time."

"I know." I giggled and stood up as he clung onto my neck, and looked toward the doorway. Malachi entered with his gaze fixed on me. For the first time I'd ever seen, he wore the robes of our people and had begun to grow his beard. He looked stronger and more handsome than ever.

My heart fluttered as he walked straight to me and smiled. "It's good to see you looking well again."

"And you, Malachi." I smiled back. I pried Tut from around my neck, handing him over to Malachi.

Slowly, all my sisters and brother arrived with their spouses and children. They each greeted me excitedly, and soon Hepsati came down the stairs to join in with us. I grasped her hand and held it tightly, which brought me an affectionate smile from her.

Once my siblings were all present, they sat me down and asked me to recount what happened to us. Malachi apparently had not been forthcoming, but wanted to allow me to tell them when I recovered.

I told them things I hadn't been able to in my letters—all the murders of the infant sons, Nefertiti's deep hatred for me, and Akhenaten's love. They listened closely to everything, fascinated by all the intrigues and plots within the royal family.

I told them of my flight from Amarna, and Mordad's death. As I spoke of Mordad, my grief filled me and I wept.

Hepsati pressed against me, also saddened by the memory of her mother's passing. Her tears fell on my arm, and I wrapped it around her to hold her close.

13

As I spoke of our escape, Malachi backed away into the corner. But when I told of how he fought off the lions, everyone turned and looked at him in awe. He bowed his head humbly.

Once I finished telling my tale, Samuel stood and walked across to Malachi. He embraced him with tears in his eyes. "Thank you for protecting my sister and bringing her back to us."

The door burst open again and Papa stood in the doorway. He scanned the room, his eyes first taking in all my siblings and in-laws, then they stopped on Samuel, who let go of Malachi.

"What is the meaning of all this?" Then, his eyes fell on me. He dropped the scrolls in his arms and rushed over. He lifted me up and held me tight, kissing my cheek over and over. "My dear, lovely, Naomi! How I have feared for you! But now you appear recovered, so we shall sing praises to God!"

Rena stood and faced us. "Papa, Naomi has just recounted her tales from Amarna—"

He let me go and snapped at her. "Hush, you selfish girl! You know we do not speak of that place in this house, especially you who should have been the one who had gone—"

I pushed Papa away from me. "Papa! Are you still blaming her for this? How many times must I tell you I made the choice?"

He sighed and looked mournfully into my eyes. "My precious Naomi, you are so brave. But who will have you now? You are no longer pure, and care for three children, one of whom isn't your own."

"They are all mine," I replied defiantly. "Hepsati is my husband's daughter and my beloved friend's cherished child—my friend who sacrificed her life for mine. I owe it to her, and my husband, to raise Hepsati."

Papa stepped back, his face growing red. "Your husband? He had you cast out, and yet you still remain loyal to him?"

"He didn't have me cast out!" I cried with annoyance. "He was protecting me!"

"Yes, Papa," Eliora interrupted. "The Great Queen wished her dead. You can even ask Malachi. He was sent to protect Naomi in her flight."

Papa turned to Malachi, whose gaze fell. "You know I am grateful to you for returning my daughter to me, but you have refused to speak of how you came to be here with her. Speak now, young man, and tell me the truth of things."

Malachi stepped forward and bowed his head to Papa as he answered. "As you know, my name is Malachi, but I have told you nothing more. First, I will give you my lineage. I am the fourth son of Reuben, son of Melek, from the tribe of Issachar."

Papa stood taller and said, "Your family has been employed as royal guards for several generations."

"We have, yes," Malachi answered humbly. "My family was taken to Amarna to continue our service as royal guards, and once I came of age, I too was expected to join. Three years later, I was given the assignment as escort to the wives and concubines of the Pharaoh—after the seventh guard in a row was found fornicating with one of them. About six months after that, I met Naomi, who was known as Kiya. She recognized my Hebrew lineage almost instantly and we became friends. My brothers and I helped her practice our faith in secret until she was finally discovered by Commander Horemheb and forbidden to practice with us.

"But I saw, and can attest to you, that Naomi was beloved by her husband the Pharaoh. He built her a temple and a tomb with his, to honor her and as a testament to his devotion. For a short while, no one was loved above her, but the great Queen Nefertiti was always jealous and so, upon failing to have the prince eliminated, she turned her focus onto his mother.

"The Pharaoh, knowing I am trustworthy, having served faithfully as his wives' escort for more than three years, beckoned me and gave me the final task of taking his beloved to protect her and his son from harm. He commanded me to stay with them and watch over them until the danger has passed, and so I am expected to remain here and send correspondence to the king regarding them."

Papa sat and pondered his words for several minutes. We all fell silent, waiting for his response. Finally, he looked at me and said softly, "So you have not been cast out?"

"No, Papa!" I rushed over, kneeling beside him. "My life and my son's life were, and still are, in danger. But my husband knows I am safer hidden here with my family to protect me."

He reached out and touched my short hair. "Will he ever call for you again?"

I clasped his arm and gazed into his eyes. "The Pharaoh has only a short time left to live. He grows sicker every day. I doubt he has enough strength or time left to subdue those who threaten me and have me return to him. I believe I will spend the rest of my days here."

He pulled me against him and sobbed onto my shoulder. "Oh, my Naomi! In my house you will remain, then. I will help you with the children and will arrange for the family to live close to us so we can all protect you from harm."

He held me tightly as he cried and stroked my hair, relieved by my safe return to him. When he released his grip, he looked at Malachi. "You will remain with us for your service, and so you can fulfill the orders given to you. You are obviously trustworthy, and we are greatly indebted to you."

I couldn't help smiling up at Malachi.

He seemed relieved as he answered, "Thank you. I was beginning to worry that I would have to live on the streets."

Papa stood and grasped his shoulder. "No man shall live on the streets under my watch, especially a man as noble as you." He embraced him.

Malachi blinked, surprised, but he willingly returned the gesture.

CHAPTER THREE

T ut loved going to the fields with his grandfather to watch the sheep. With Malachi assigned to duty as a daytime watchman, he would walk with Papa out to the fields with Tut on his shoulders.

I stayed at home to provide care for Hepsati and Itani while tending to the house.

Eliora and Bilhan lived with us for a while, as they lived with Papa to care for him, but with Malachi and me now living in the house, they soon purchased an apartment nearby and moved into it.

Papa quickly arranged for my siblings and their families to live within earshot of his house to keep us safe. I enjoyed it thoroughly; as I could visit with my sisters and sister-in-law easily during the day and have our children play together.

When Tut returned with Papa, he ran and chased his male cousins with delight, having only ever known sisters. Despite being younger than Adina's sons, he soon became their leader and took them on grand adventures, which often ended in destruction.

He rapidly became Papa's favorite. He loved the boy deeply and taught him of our ways by telling him stories about our ancestors.

But my life wasn't as easy. At home and with the family I felt loved and cared for, but out in the community was another matter entirely. Every few weeks, a part of our sector was swept by Nefertiti's men searching for Tut and me. It caused a great deal of fear among the people, who in turn, blamed me.

I also became viewed as a harlot. They saw me as an Egyptian more than as one of them, and more so, as an Egyptian queen who had been returned damaged and impure.

After several weeks passed, I went to do some trading with Rena. The whole time I felt like I was being watched.

Rena kept her arm tightly wrapped around mine as we walked. We approached a stall and she rested a blanket she had made on the table. "I would like to trade this for—"

The man turned, his eyes narrowing on me. "I don't trade with harlots."

My cheeks flushed.

Rena grabbed her blanket angrily and we moved on. "You're not a harlot, Naomi," she said. "They're just afraid of you now."

We came to another stall and the same thing happened. By the third stall, Rena had had enough and she yelled at the storekeeper.

"My sister is no harlot! Has everyone forgotten how she sacrificed herself to save me? She hasn't been cast out, but has returned to us to preserve her life from the evil queen who seeks to destroy it. Her husband still loves her, so you should all be ashamed of yourselves. None of you could ever come close to matching the bravery and nobility of my sister!"

She turned on her heel and marched us out of the marketplace.

This began to change their view of me, but although not openly scorned, I found many doors closed to me, and backs turned wherever I went.

Samuel walked with me out to the fields to collect Tut from Malachi. He kept me close, wary of what people had been saying about me.

I knew he felt concerned, so I tried to keep our conversation lighthearted. I made him laugh like I always had.

He wrapped his arm around my shoulder. "Naomi, I'm so glad that place didn't change you."

I sighed, knowing he wasn't entirely correct. "No, Samuel, it has. I don't think anyone could spend three years in that place without it having an effect on them. I just choose to not let it show, but secretly, I'm always thinking and watching and listening. I don't feel safe trusting people anymore, and the few I do, I feel like I need to fight to protect them, especially my children. You have no idea what it was like always having to worry about Tut's life."

"You have been exceedingly brave, dear sister." He smiled at me proudly.

Suddenly a fist sized stone hit me in the small of my back. Samuel and I both turned to see where it came from. A small group of men gathered behind us, all armed with stones of a similar size. Samuel pulled me in front of him to protect me, and hurried me away. But they followed us and called out to me, "Harlot!"

"Queen of the Whores!"

Another stone flew which skimmed off Samuel and hit me in the back of the head. He grabbed me tighter and we ran. They followed us to the fields where we saw Papa and Malachi with the sheep; Tut ran around in the grass. They both heard the commotion and turned to see us running. Papa stepped forward, while Malachi rushed over and caught a stone just before it hit me.

Papa stood tall and firm against them. "What is the meaning of this? Who gave you the right to stone my daughter?"

"She is a shame to your family!" one man called back. "She should be condemned for her idolatry and for being cast out by her husband!"

Malachi spun keeping me behind him. "She never worshiped the Aten in her heart! She was always true to our faith and our God!"

The small mob laughed and the same man responded, "From you, who is guilty of the same crime, we find that defense ludicrous!"

A stone flew at Malachi, which he again caught and threw back. It hit one of them; that startled the mob.

Papa took advantage of this, and spoke boldly. "Who has condemned my daughter? I don't believe any man has the right to say such things except me and her husband, and since neither have done so, there is no crime here."

His words made them stand down, but reluctantly. They turned away and departed from us.

Papa turned to me as the last few disappeared from view. "Finding you a husband is going to prove to be difficult."

I sighed, rubbing the back of my head where the stone had drawn blood. "I'm still married, Papa. I can't be given to another man."

Malachi kept his face turned from me as he walked over to catch Tut.

Papa shook his head sadly. "My dear daughter, this is not the life I had hoped for you. To be mocked and scorned at every turn because you were forced to flee from your husband? No, Naomi, you were supposed to be the joy of my life, to have married well and given me beautiful grandchildren to inspire and uplift me in my old age. But all this, it's too much."

I nodded sadly. My life could have been much easier, but I didn't regret any of the choices I had made.

"Papa," I said, "This is but a short trial; it will pass. We have come into this life to be tested and tried so that we may learn and grow closer to our Lord. My trials are just a little harder than most, but you have taught me to be strong, and so, I will bear this."

Tears blurred in his eyes a moment before he wrapped his arms around me and held me tight.

Malachi grunted in pain. Tut cried out. I pulled away and saw Malachi with an arrow in his shoulder and his arms wrapped around Tut. By the design of the arrow it had to be Egyptian, and I panicked.

"Run!" I tried to rush for Malachi and Tut, but Samuel grabbed me and pulled me away, just as another arrow shot passed where I had stood. Papa grabbed me as well. Malachi leapt to his feet with Tut held tightly in his arms.

We ran for the safety of a nearby shed. As Malachi rushed in behind us, another arrow shot in and skimmed my arm. I pulled back in fright, and held my arm as Samuel shut the door.

Malachi grabbed me and looked at my wound. "How bad did it get you?"

"It was nothing, just a scratch," I answered, but looked at the arrow protruding from his shoulder blade. "But you, Malachi—"

He reached back and yanked the arrow out. "It's nothing." He handed me Tut and grabbed the arrow that stuck into the wall.

"It's not nothing, Malachi. You're bleeding."

He turned to me and grabbed my shoulders. "Stay here, Naomi. I need to go and perform my duty."

"No!" I grabbed his forearms. "Don't go back out there!"

"I must, or he will come in here and kill you." He pulled away from me and disappeared through the door before I could react.

Arrows thumped, hitting the wall, then a few moments later, the sound of men fighting to the death resounded. I held Tut's ears and prayed for Malachi's life.

"I have to help him," Samuel said. The door rattled as he grasped the handle.

I spun on him. "No, Samuel! Stay in here! Malachi is a trained guard. He has amazing skills. I have seen them." I remembered how he had known exactly what Mordad was doing without even looking at her the day she took me to buy new wigs and fabric for dresses, and how he fought off the lions.

The fight came to an abrupt end, and it fell quiet outside. We held our breath as we listened for the outcome.

Something was dragged, then footsteps headed for the door. I pulled back so my body was between it and Tut. Suddenly, it flew open. Malachi stood there, covered in blood. He looked terribly beaten. He had another arrow in his leg, but he limped over to me and said, "Are you all right?"

"Yes, yes… Oh Malachi!" I put Tut down and threw my arms around him. "Don't do that again! I was so frightened!"

He trembled as he held onto me. "It's all right, Naomi. I will always keep you safe." He faltered from the loss of blood.

Papa and Samuel rushed forward to catch him.

"We must get him back and see to his wounds," Samuel said.

I nodded and snatched Tut up in my arms to follow them. As we headed out the door, Malachi looked at me. "Naomi, don't look to your left as you leave, and hold Tut so he cannot see either."

I clung to my son—despite his squirming and protests—as we passed by the body of the defeated assassin.

I brought the small jug of water up the stairs and knelt beside Malachi. He woke and turned to look at me with a smile. As I poured a little water into a dish and dipped a cloth in it, he spoke to me softly. "Are you all right?"

"Yes, Malachi. Tut and I are fine." I reached over and uncovered his thigh, where the arrow had been removed, and washed his wound. He didn't even flinch as he stared at me. When I finished, I bound it up again and rolled him onto his side to wash his wound on his shoulder blade.

"I'm sorry this happened to you," I said softly.

He sat up and caught my hand. "This isn't your fault. You must never apologize to me for such things again."

He gazed steadily into my eyes, then he leaned forward and softly kissed my lips.

I pulled back from him, startled, not by his gesture, but by the memory of my husband's commander, and my ally in protecting Tut, Horemheb, kissing me with all his passion. I touched Malachi's shoulder so he would turn his back to me, and I completed washing his wound. I then re-strapped it with clean bandages.

"How long do you think we will have to wait?" Malachi asked.

"I don't know," I answered, thinking again of Akhenaten's poor health. "I don't wish my husband to die."

"A letter came from him yesterday. He disguised it as a letter regarding livestock, but he was checking on your safe arrival. Nefertiti has resumed the position of first wife, with Mayati as her second."

He turned and faced me. "He said they are trying to blame you for Mordad's death. They claim you abducted Hepsati and are holding Tut for ransom. Obviously, none of the wives or concubines believe it, but the court is divided. You have your supporters, the Commander being your most fervent advocate, but Ay has taken Nefertiti's side and he has many followers. The king knows he is weakening, so he is relying very heavily on his advisers to assist him, which means he's relying on Ay and Nefertiti. Things are rapidly growing more contentious."

As much as my heart ached at the memory of Mordad's death, and feeling indignant about being blamed for it, I didn't want to let it show. I had to be strong. I reached forward and wiped the long gash across his chest. "It sounds like we escaped just in time."

He watched my hand as it brushed down his chest. "I worry for my mother and brothers. I hope they're safe."

"They are strong and careful. They will survive. But if you're concerned, write to Horemheb and ask him—"

His face darkened as he grabbed my hand. "No."

I fell silent and dropped my gaze. We hadn't talked about Horemheb since Malachi asked me if he was in love with me. It seemed to be a sore spot for him. He would have heard all the rumors of our alleged affair, so he was likely concerned that I may have feelings in return.

I patted his gash dry, then applied a small amount of honey and offered to help him stand.

He leaned heavily on me down the stairs as he struggled to put weight on his wounded leg.

Hepsati met us at the bottom, and wrapped her arms around him. Since we arrived, she had grown attached to him and followed him wherever she could. When she saw him badly wounded, she cried and asked me to teach her how to pray so she could pray for him to heal. I knew she loved him like a father, and I felt guilty for taking her away from her real father and denying him her devotion.

Itani cried out and Tut yelled, "Stop!"

I hurried over and broke up their fight, while Malachi sat at the table to wait for our meal to be served.

Papa entered carrying a head of lettuce from the garden. I handed him the last of the clean water in the jug for him to wash it, while I placed the fish on the table, along with some bread and cheese. Papa sat across from Malachi and examined all the food as he placed the lettuce down. "It looks like someone worked very hard today. Naomi, thank you."

"I had some help." I smiled and gestured to Hepsati. "She wanted to make sure Malachi ate well so he can be strong again."

Hepsati clung to Malachi's arm and blushed.

Papa laughed. "Well, thank you, Hepsati. This feast will definitely make him strong again, as well as help *me* grow fat."

I smiled as I brought Tut to the table and sat him beside Papa, then picked up Itani and held her on my lap. I felt glad Papa had finally warmed to Hepsati. At first, he hated her for being a foreign child in his home. He made statements about how she—a Persian *and* an Egyptian princess—would bring the wrath of two nations upon us, but when neither seemed to show any interest in retrieving her, he relaxed and slowly became charmed by her.

After our meal, I took Tut and Itani upstairs, then returned to assist Malachi.

Papa remained downstairs to clean up, and tell Hepsati stories about our forefathers.

I lowered Malachi onto the bed, just as Tut called for me.

Malachi let me go and nodded. "See to him."

I rushed over and coaxed Tut into lying back down, and as he dozed off, I pulled the blanket across which divided the room, then returned to Malachi. "How are you feeling?"

He sat up and pressed on his leg wound over the bandage. "Better, after that meal. I think I will heal quickly if I keep eating like that."

I giggled, which drew his gaze to my face.

"I hope your father includes this in some of my payment for you to be my wife. I don't know how else I can give him what I would owe for you. I have very little money, and you are without a doubt exceedingly valuable."

I sat back on my knees. "Let's not talk about that now. My husband is still alive."

"And it's only been three and a half years." He smiled.

I couldn't help chuckling at our running joke. I leaned forward and pressed on his shoulder to encourage him to lay back. "Sleep now, Malachi. You need your rest."

CHAPTER FOUR

I awoke, startled. My eyes shot around the dark room, unable to see anything that could have woken me. I looked across at Malachi, sleeping on the other side of the blanket, and felt reassured. Then, a soft scraping sounded. Malachi shot up and grasped the dagger he kept beside him at night. I reached over and pulled Tut closer to me, careful to not wake him. Malachi glanced at me and signaled for me to lie back down while he, too, lowered his head back onto his bed.

The latch on the door to the roof lifted, and it slowly and silently swung open. My tension rose as I watched the dark figure scan the inside of the room. He moved toward me while carefully pulling a vial from among his robes.

As he passed the blanket, Malachi leaped up behind him and grabbed him, holding the dagger against his neck. "Don't move!"

His voice woke Hepsati, Tut, and Itani. Hepsati grabbed Itani who began to cry, while I pulled Tut against me.

The man struggled to free himself from Malachi, but couldn't escape from his superior strength.

The noise awoke Papa. He ran to the window and called for Samuel and my brothers-in-law. They all rushed to the house and helped Malachi restrain the assassin.

"Who sent you?" Malachi demanded of him. He knew exactly who; the same person who had sent the last three—Nefertiti.

The assassin spat at his feet. "You filthy slave!"

Malachi pressed his dagger against his throat. "Do you know what happened to the last three assassins? Me! Two are dead and one is locked away in a dungeon and will probably never see the light of day again. So, I will give you the choice: will you choose death or a dungeon? Or if you swear to flee and never return, we will allow you to go."

The assassin's gaze shot to each of the men, before it dropped and locked on Tut and me. "So you're the treacherous queen and that is the filthy half-blood prince. You're not as fearsome as I was led to believe. I could easily just snap your neck—"

He thrust forward, but Malachi caught him. They wrestled until Malachi threw him against the wall and plunged the dagger into his chest.

The assassin gasped and laughed. "Hail to Aten! Hail to Queen Nefertiti, may she reign supreme…"

He slid, dead, onto the floor.

I reached over and pulled the blanket across so the children couldn't see his body being removed by the men.

Hepsati shuffled up beside me and clung to my arm with one hand, and held Itani tightly with the other. As she pressed her cheek against me, I felt her tremble in fear.

I looked down at Tut, who had buried his face into my chest, while Itani cried.

That attempt on our lives had been too close. None of the other assassins had entered our home. After the first one out in the fields, the second came while I collected water from the well with Hepsati. He grabbed me and tried to force me down the well, but Hepsati's scream drew attention, and although I fell in, Malachi arrived a moment later, killed him by slitting his throat, then helped me out of the well.

The third assassin stalked me through the marketplace, and when I noticed I was being followed, I rushed out to the fields to Malachi.

Malachi told me to lead the assassin away, and he sneaked around after I left, and snatched him up. He wrestled him down and bound him, then threw him in a dungeon.

But I knew this new attack meant that our residence had been discovered by Nefertiti's spies, and we now faced greater danger than ever.

I held the three children and kissed their heads, while trying to comfort them as they each cried from fright. It had to stop. I couldn't keep putting them through this. If it kept going, then either my life or Tut's would end.

I heard the men return upstairs and begin cleaning away the blood. Papa slipped through the curtain and sat beside me.

He stroked my hair and kissed my head. "Are you all right?"

I nodded. Then I had an idea. I handed him Tut, who protested at having to let go of me, and told Hepsati to stay with Papa. I stood and stepped onto the other side of the blanket.

Malachi and Samuel looked at me surprised as I walked straight to Malachi. "You must go to Amarna and take a message to the court."

He scowled at me. "No, Naomi. I must stay here with you in case this happens again—"

"You must go so this *won't* happen again," I said firmly. "Nefertiti will be waiting to hear from her assassin and spies to discover the outcome of this attempt on my life. So in the morning, the family must fake my death, and I'll hide away with Tut. Meanwhile, you will catch the first ship out of Thebes to Amarna and deliver the message that Tut and I are dead, but you killed the assassin while trying to protect me. This will satisfy Nefertiti and she will withdraw her spies and no longer send men to take our lives. Then, and most importantly, you must ask to speak with Pharaoh in private. There, you will deliver him a note from me explaining the scheme and informing him that his son and I are alive and well, so he does not grieve unnecessarily. I don't want him to be deceived by me. I will not be like Nefertiti."

"But what if he won't see me to deliver the note?" Malachi asked.

"Then go to Horemheb. He'll assist you and grant you access to the king."

Malachi's eyes narrowed at the mention of Horemheb, but he agreed.

At first light, I rushed downstairs, and while my family pretended to grieve, I wrote my note to Akhenaten to explain everything. I gave it to Malachi who hurried from our home and straight to the wharves where he caught a trade ship north to Amarna.

Keeping Tut inside over the next few weeks proved difficult. He tried to escape whenever he could, but luckily my sisters and sister-in-law, Dana, were more than willing to help by bringing him playmates. I felt grateful for their company, as I too became agitated by being stuck inside.

Finally, Malachi returned.

When he entered our home, my heart soared. "Malachi!"

A wide smile swept across his face. "It's good to see you, too, Naomi. And, I've brought a surprise for you."

He stepped aside. Leah, his mother, and his oldest brother, Tobiah, entered the house. It was so wonderful to see them again. We welcomed them into our home with open arms.

But they didn't stay with us for long. Leah explained that they owned some land on the border of our sector and that of the old Egyptian sector, and so would move in there.

Tobiah—being in his mid-thirties and never married—was eager to find himself a wife, and so sought advice from Papa for not only himself, but to send a wife each for his brothers who had not been released from service and remained in Amarna.

Malachi insisted on remaining with us so he could continue performing his duty. After his mother and brother left us, he took the children and me out to the fields to talk with me as we enjoyed the freedom of being out of the house.

Hepsati held Itani's hand to help her walk. Tut ran around trying to frighten the sheep, while Malachi and I hung back.

Malachi watched the children as they gained some distance from us, before he spoke in a low voice. "Naomi, the palace was in an uproar when I arrived. I was taken straight to the throne room where a great debate raged over what to do with the temple dedicated to you. When I entered the courtroom, Pharaoh stood and silenced the court, having recognized me immediately. He commanded me to speak, and I told him of how the assassin entered your father's house during the night and poisoned Tut and you in your sleep. I told him that the assassin woke me as he tried to escape, but when I saw what happened, I killed him.

"Nefertiti sat on her throne as I told the court. There was a satisfied gleam in her eyes, and when Ay stepped forward, feigning sorrow, I knew he too was pleased by the news."

Malachi took a deep breathe, shaking his head. "I wanted to blame them for everything right then. To announce it was their fault you'd been run out and killed, along with the heir. But I controlled my temper and focused on what needed to be done.

"So instead, I turned my focus onto the king. His head fell into his hands as he sobbed from grief. He then wailed for the court to be emptied.

As all the noblemen exited, he fell to his knees and wept loudly. I tried to ask him if I could stay, so I could speak to him, but he sent me away in a fit of rage."

Malachi paused and pursed his lips.

I watched him curiously, wondering what was going on in his mind. He seemed agitated, even angry as he continued. "So I went to the Commander as you suggested, and told him of the note and my need to see the king immediately.

"The Commander took me to the king's bedchambers, where he had retreated to mourn. After a loud argument, the Commander came back out and told me to enter.

"The king was lying face down on his bed, but when I pulled out the note, he sat up and took it. He read it slowly, his expression first showing shock, then relief, then delight. He looked to the Commander and declared, 'He lives! My son lives! Leave us, Horemheb. I must speak to this guard in private. He has done a grand deed in protecting my family, and he must be rewarded. But do not utter a word of what you have seen or heard here. If anyone were to hear of this cover-up, the protection it has granted will be nullified.'

"The Commander bowed and said, 'Of course, my lord,' and left.

"The Pharaoh then asked me about you. He wanted to know how you were, how you were being treated, and whether you were happy. I told him you were faring well, but decided to leave out how our people have been treating you. I knew that could cause unnecessary tension, another burden that he couldn't handle.

"Then I explained that you had grown tired of the assassination attempts, which was why you conjured this scheme. But, you were concerned for his health and didn't want him to be deceived by you. I explained that you remain loyal to him, so you made me promise I would deliver him your message personally."

Malachi stopped our stroll as Tut came screeching over and threw himself into his arms. Malachi laughed and lifted him onto his shoulders before he continued. "The Pharaoh turned the paper around in his hands before reading it again and kissing it. He said, 'She always wrote well. Her handwriting is so precise and her language is so clear. I would know this was her just by looking at it.' He then clasped the note to his chest as he said, 'I am greatly relieved. When you told me she had been killed, I felt as if my heart had been torn from my chest and that I would surely die. But she is clever, and she has tricked those who wish to harm her and my son. It seems she is the one having the last laugh.'

"He approached me and said in a whisper, 'I will prepare a false funeral for them, and have her tomb sealed. That will ensure there is no question in her adversaries' minds of her passing, and she will be left in peace. You will stay until the tomb is sealed, and then you will return to her so you may continue to watch over her for me. You shall be rewarded for your service. Is there anything you desire?'"

Malachi set Tut down; he ran off to chase Hepsati. Malachi watched with a somber expression.

"A false funeral," I said in a hushed voice. I felt relieved we would no longer be hunted, but also saddened for Akhenaten. His actions meant he'd never see me again, and quite likely Tut, too, which was a great sacrifice. But then I thought of the last thing Malachi had said. I touched his shoulder. "What did you ask for?"

He looked down at me and smiled. "I told him of my brothers and asked if they could all return with me to Thebes, so they could find themselves a bride each. He agreed, but upon discovering each of my brothers was loyal and diligent in their duties, he agreed to release only Tobiah. But I am allowed to send wives to Enoch and Jared.

"Pharaoh said that it was a selfless request, and wondered if there was anything I desired for myself." Malachi grinned. "I couldn't exactly say, 'Yes, I'd like permission to marry your wife,' so I simply told him I was wanting for nothing.

"But he insisted I take something, so he ordered a bag of gold to be brought to me. He said it was the least he could do to repay me for protecting his most precious possession.

"So I was given a sack of gold, and required to stay for a time, until your tomb was sealed. Tobiah was then released from duty, and he and I, along with our mother, traveled back here to Thebes."

"And what of Horemheb?" I asked. "How did he react?"

Malachi tensed and glanced away at the question, but I didn't care. Horemheb was dear to me and had sacrificed a great deal to help and assist me over the years.

"Horemheb?" He shrugged. "He was his normal, composed, unreadable self. I saw him flinch when I announced that both you and Tut had died, but that was the only sign of an emotional response he ever gave."

I nodded and watched my children playing together. I shouldn't have expected more. That was his way. I knew he showed only me his vulnerability, and even then, that was rare. But I had hoped he would react a little more than that.

I looked up at Malachi. "Thank you for doing that for me. It will ease my mind to know we aren't constantly being watched and hunted."

"You know, one day Tut will have to take his place as Pharaoh," he said. "What will you do then?"

I sighed. "I'll work that out when I get to it. For now, Kiya is dead, and shall remain dead. I will just be Naomi from now on."

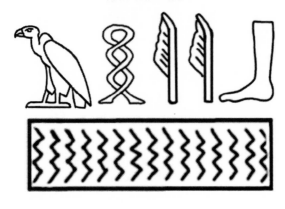

CHAPTER FIVE

I walked with Malachi, Tobiah, and Leah while Malachi held Tut's hand and I carried Itani. Tobiah watched the marketplace for maidens to be his and his brothers' wives. When he saw one who he thought might suit him or one of his brothers, he asked me about her. I gave him her family background and anything I knew. We had been searching for several days, and had inquired after a few girls, but none seemed to really catch his eye.

"Don't feel hurried," I told him. "There are plenty of maidens in this city. You will find one for each of your brothers and for yourself."

"But there will be none like you," he teased. "My brother has a fine catch. You have a good lineage, and you are a virtuous, caring wife and mother. When the day comes when he is finally able to take you as his wife, I shall sing praises to the Lord."

I blushed. "You would rejoice in my husband's death?"

"No, Naomi." He frowned. "I meant I would rejoice in my brother's happiness."

"I don't want to talk about this," I said. "I don't want to wish my husband ill. He's still alive and he is still our king. We should respect that."

Three young women walked in front of us, talking with their heads close together. Tobiah watched them closely and said, "Who are they?"

"They're the daughters of Laban, son of Micah from the tribe of Gad," I answered.

"They are very beautiful," he said, redirecting our course to follow them.

"They're charming young ladies, too, but their father drives a hard bargain for them. As you can tell, no man has been able to pay their bride price."

Tobiah turned to Malachi. "Malachi, you have that sack of gold. Help your brothers out by lending me some."

Malachi grunted. "Lend it to you? Just take whatever you need. I don't know what to do with it."

Tobiah grinned, delighted. "Naomi, take me to their father's house so I can offer a price for them."

I hesitated. "I can take you there, but it would be better for you if I'm not seen."

"Why is that?" he asked, looking concerned.

Malachi gently rested his hand on my elbow. "She's considered impure and idolatrous, so is shunned by most people."

Leah looked distressed. "You poor girl! That's terrible!"

I shrugged. I didn't want them to know it bothered me. "It's fine. My family understands and still loves me. I know what I did was right, so what others think of me is irrelevant."

I guided them to the house of Laban and paused by an alleyway. "I'll wait here with the children for you to make the offer."

"I'll wait with you," Malachi said.

I shook my head. "No, let them see you, so he knows you and your brothers are honorable."

He went reluctantly, while I backed down the alleyway. It didn't take long for them to return to me with excited expressions on their faces. Tobiah spoke first. "He has accepted my offer. I'm to return tomorrow and have the girls partake of the wine."

"That's wonderful!" I beamed. "I'm happy for you."

The next day, Malachi left me to be with his brother while the espousals were made. When they returned to our house, Tobiah glowed, beyond excited. "I will marry the oldest sister Miriam. She is exceedingly fair, and from what I saw, she is of a very level temperament. I hope my brothers find their wives as lovely as I have found mine."

"I'm sure they will." I smiled as I offered him some meat.

He sent word to his brothers to let them know they would be required to come down to Thebes to perform the marriage rituals a year hence. He promised he would prepare everything for them so they would need to stay for only a short while.

While he made the arrangements, I couldn't help but notice Malachi glance at me every so often. I knew exactly what he was thinking, and it made me uncomfortable. He must have wondered when we would be able to go through the same process together, but he knew he had to wait.

I, on the other hand, found myself feeling envious of the three girls. They came to me a few months after the espousals to ask for my help.

The oldest, Miriam, seemed in awe of me as she gazed up wide-eyed when I answered the door. "Naomi?"

"Yes?"

The three girls exchanged smiles. "Malachi speaks well of you. He says you are the maiden who saved us all from the Pharaoh."

I sighed, touched by Malachi's praise. "I would do anything for my sisters."

Miriam's eyes glistened. "We want you to help us. We need guidance with our preparations for marriage. Malachi said you are wise and well educated about our customs. We don't have a mother anymore, so we need someone to show us what to do."

I glanced up and down the street. Their father would not be pleased by that prospect. "Does your father know?"

They all shook their heads, and Miriam answered. "Our father…" she nodded inside. "May we?"

I stepped back and allowed them to enter.

They sat hip to hip and removed their veils. I found myself struck by how similar they looked.

"Our father does not want us associating with you," Miriam said. "He says it is unfortunate Malachi is honor bound to protect you according to Pharaoh's wishes."

I drew a sharp breath. I had not thought about how Malachi's association with me would affect him. I wondered if he resented me for being forced into such scandal.

"Don't worry," the middle sister said with a sweet smile. "Malachi is quite fond of you."

They giggled.

My cheeks warmed. "So, how can I help you if I cannot be seen with you?"

"Hepsati," Miriam said, motioning up the stairs. The sound of Hepsati's humming drifted down to us. "No one takes much notice of children running around the streets. You can write what we need to purchase and make, and we will send them to you with her for your approval. I think it will be a wonderful way to begin our bond as sisters."

"Sisters?"

Her sisters hushed her, but she smiled. "Yes, sisters."

I turned away from them, my heart pounding as I thought of Malachi. "I'm not related to your future husbands in anyway."

"Not yet."

"Miriam!" the younger two said in hushed voices.

Miriam chuckled. "Naomi, your selflessness will be rewarded. But for now, we must know, will you help us?"

I took a deep breath to control my emotions, then turned to her. "Of course I will. I will write all the things you will need and send Hepsati to you tomorrow."

Miriam leaped up and threw her arms around me. "I already love you."

The other two joined in.

Malachi entered.

The girls hurried to cover their faces as he swiveled around to avoid seeing them.

"We should go," Miriam said softly, and the three bustled out the door.

Malachi shut the door and looked at me. "What was that about?"

"They asked for some assistance." I turned away, blushing.

"I'm glad they took my advice." He walked up behind me. I felt him standing close, but he did not touch me. "It would be nice for you to know them better."

He touched my hair, but then he brushed by me. "Your father is bringing a ewe home. I will need to prepare it."

Hepsati rushed down the stairs. "Papa!"

My heart felt like it would rip open as she flung herself into his arms. I longed to be with Malachi.

One night, Laban came to our home in search of Malachi. He wasn't impressed to find me, but entered to wait for Malachi to return from the fields.

Papa returned home soon after he arrived, and, being old friends, they embraced affectionately. Papa gestured for him to sit, while he sent me to bring water and cheese for them. While I prepared the refreshments, I listened to their conversation.

"Laban," Papa said. "What brings you to my house?"

"I have come to speak with Malachi," Laban replied. "I have seen how he watches his brother with envy as he prepares for himself and the other brothers to take my daughters as wives, and so, I have come to make him an offer. I have a niece who has just come of age, and I want to see if he would like to take her as his wife."

I couldn't help gasping, and knocked the jug over. It broke in two when it hit the floor. I bent over to clean it up, and glanced across at Papa.

He watched me with a quizzical expression on his face.

I apologized for the interruption, and quickly stood to go fill a new jug from the storage jugs out back. As I left, I heard Laban whisper, "Jorem, why do you keep her in your house? Are you not ashamed?"

My heart sunk at his words, but Papa said, "No, Laban, she has done no wrong. She sacrificed everything for my younger daughters, and she has come back to us as virtuous as the day she left. She has known no man other than her husband and that's nothing to fault her for, even if he is an Egyptian. She has faced trials that many men would tremble before, and she has come back to us with more compassion than ever. Do not speak cruelly of her, Laban. She's a brave woman who deserves to be honored."

I smiled to myself as I filled the jug, feeling as if my father's love for me had returned completely, and he would stand by me to the bitter end.

I returned into the house and served them their food and drink, when Malachi entered. I couldn't help turning away from him. I felt embarrassed, as I knew what he was about to be asked.

Papa noticed my gesture, and reached for my hand. I looked down at him and our eyes met. In his, I saw him ask me what was wrong. As I pulled away so he couldn't see into my thoughts, his jaw fell as it dawned on him. He stood and waved at Malachi to take his place, then he followed me. When I reached the table and placed the empty dish on it, he whispered in my ear, "Say the word, Naomi, and I can head this off."

I shook my head. "No, Papa. He deserves to be happy. I have tortured him long enough. I don't wish to continue this way for an indefinite amount of time."

"You deserve your happiness, too, my child," he said, brushing back my shoulder-length hair. "You have given up so much already."

Suddenly, Laban spoke boldly. "So, Malachi, I have an offer for you. I have a niece who has just come of age and is as lovely as my own daughters. If you would like, I can make sure any offer you give for her is accepted, and you, too, can take a wife along with your brothers."

Malachi dropped his gaze and placed his cup down on his knee. He paused thoughtfully for several moments.

I held my breath as I waited for his response. Papa's hand pressed against the small of my back as he, too, waited in anticipation.

Finally, Malachi's gaze turned to Laban. "Your offer is generous, Laban, and I appreciate all you have done for my brothers. But I cannot accept. I already have my eyes set on a young woman whom I plan to take as my wife, when her time comes."

My heart skipped a beat at his words. I grasped for Papa's hand and clasped it tightly.

Malachi stood and took Laban's hand respectfully.

Laban stood, staring at him, surprised. "Dear young man, may I ask whom this maiden is?"

He shook his head. "I do not wish to expose my intentions for her prematurely. In due time, you will know."

Malachi walked Laban to the door, and Papa rushed forward to bid Laban farewell.

Once he was gone and the door was shut tight, Papa gazed up at Malachi. "You love my daughter."

They both looked across at me as Malachi answered, "I do, very much."

I flushed, feeling guilty, and rushed for the stairs.

Malachi hurried to me and caught my arm as I stepped onto the third rung. "Naomi…"

I turned to him, feeling my heart ache. "You should have taken the offer, Malachi. You could have been happy. You wouldn't have to wait any longer for something no one knows how long will take to become available."

"I have waited this long, Naomi, and I will continue to wait for as long as I need to. No one could ever make me as happy as you. You have my heart and nothing will ever change that."

Tears rose within me, and I pulled away from him, rushing up the stairs. I curled up by the window to cry my pain out. I didn't wish Akhenaten dead, but I desperately wanted to be free so I could finally be with Malachi, so I could finally end his suffering.

Papa's voice came up the stairs as he spoke softly to Malachi. "How long have you loved her?"

I held my tears so I could hear his reply.

"I have loved her from the moment she spoke to me in our tongue, the first night of her marriage."

"How did that come to be?"

He gave a melancholy sigh. "She had been completely shaved. She saw my hair under my military hat and pulled it off so she could touch it. She was convinced she would be put to death because she refused to lie with the king while he also had concubines in his bed."

Papa gave a horrified gasp. "He made her lie with other women?"

Malachi laughed softly. "No, not Naomi. She changed everything. She has a power over people. She had a power over him which no one else could fathom. He forgave her almost instantly and Nefertiti—fearing the power she had—gave her the job of making the conjugal visit assignments. She was supposed to fail, but Naomi seems unable to fail at anything. She changed it so each woman had one-on-one time with their husband and no one had to share a bed with another woman the whole time she oversaw the assignments. The king enjoyed it, also. He loved that he could spend time with each of his wives and know them better on a personal level.

"She did wonderful things in that place. Not a single wife or concubine ever spoke ill of her. They all admired and respected her—except, of course, Nefertiti, but she never spoke to me anyway. Oh, Jorem, I couldn't help loving her, even if she was married to my king."

Silence fell for a moment, before Papa spoke. "Malachi, I believe she loves you in return. I didn't see it until today, when Laban entered and told me what he wished to offer you. But can you wait for her? Who knows how long the king will continue to live? And even then, she has been known by another man before you. Can you live with that?"

"I know my time may be long, but as I tell her when she tries to tell me not to wait, Jacob waited for fourteen years for Rachel, so I can wait for her. As for her being known by another man? I escorted her to those evening meetings, and each time I saw her step out that door of the women's wing, my heart felt as if it was being torn from my chest. I know he knew her more than most. He found great pleasure in her, and although it pains me, I also know she was a faithful wife and he was the only man who knew her, and I respect her for that. So no, to me she will be a virgin, and through her I will

38

be blessed with strong and healthy sons whom I will be proud to raise up to the Lord, and we will all call her blessed."

Papa wept. "Oh Malachi, you are an answer to my prayers! How I have worried for my daughter and prayed for a man to take her as his wife despite her being a wife of Pharaoh first."

"Naomi is worth it," Malachi said softly.

I leaned back and clutched at my heart. I loved him so dearly, and he loved me despite my faults and impurity. I allowed my tears to fall again, as I gave thanks to God in my heart for blessing me so abundantly.

Malachi, Rena, and I searched through the hauls of the fishermen when a loud noise erupted from farther up the wharves. We looked across and saw the priests of Amun-Ra rejoicing.

"What do you think that's about?" I asked.

"I'll go find out," Malachi answered, giving me Tut's hand. "You stay here."

Rena and I watched him push through the crowd, until Tut distracted us by asking for dried fish to snack on. When Malachi returned, he seemed flustered, but I saw a slight smile in the corners of his mouth. "Nefertiti is dead."

"What?" I gasped in shock.

"Nefertiti is dead," he repeated. "A plague swept through the city and took many lives, including hers. The priests are rejoicing because she was an avid supporter of the new religion. They believe that since Pharaoh has lost his two favorite wives within a year, he will be greatly weakened. Naomi, you're finally safe, she cannot harm you anymore." But his face fell. "Oh, no, the king will want you back."

I shook my head. "No, there's still danger in the palace for me. Her daughters remain, and her father Ay. They would gladly kill my son and me if they discovered that we still live. They greatly desire the throne for themselves. Kiya will remain dead."

He looked down at Tut and touched his head. "It's hard to believe this little boy is destined to rule."

"I know." I sighed and smiled at Tut as he looked up at me and scrunched his nose with disgust at the affectionate attention being given to him.

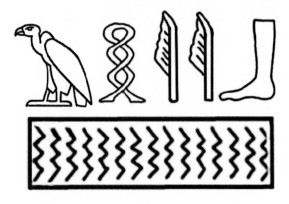

CHAPTER SIX

I made my way back to the house with my basket full of wet clothes and blankets. I saw a sight that caused my heart to skip with delight. Out in front of Samuel's house stood a tall, dark woman with three children—two daughters and a baby son—escorted by a tall, dark man. I looked down at Hepsati as I tightened my grasp on Itani, sitting on my hip. "Do you recognize them, Hepsati?"

Her eyes widened and a smile spread across her face. A short squeal of delight burst from her lips. She ran to them while I rushed to follow.

Abimbala turned at the sound of Hepsati rushing over, and looked down at her with a smile. Then she heard me approaching, and her eyes lifted. By the confused look in her eyes, I knew she didn't recognize me at first. I looked different in my Hebrew attire with my hair growing out and no makeup, but when she saw my face more clearly, her eyes widened and she gasped.

She handed her baby to her servant and rushed over, wrapping her arms around my shoulders as she held me in a tight embrace. "Kiya! I believed you dead! What a miracle to find you are in fact still alive and well."

I put down my basket and wrapped my arms around her waist. "How wonderful it is to see you again, Abi. But why are you here? Surely our husband hasn't banished you."

She leaned back to look into my face. "No, I have run away. Terrible things have started to happen in Amarna these past few months. It all began when the plague came through and killed so many people, including, and most significantly, Nefertiti. Our husband, although he caught it,

40

managed to survive. But he is greatly weakened, and many fear the illness has brought his death closer. He struggles to function each day. He's carried to and from his court and the temples, and without Nefertiti's assistance, he is desperate for help. He has turned to Ay, and Ay convinced him to bring back his brother, Smenkhkare to be co-regent."

"No!" I gasped in horror. "Surely after all Kare did, our husband wouldn't—"

"But he has. His mind isn't as clear as it once was. The Commander is struggling to remain in power against Ay and Smenkhkare, who both work to convince the king that he is disloyal, since he no longer has you to hold the king's heart for him. But, the Commander helped me flee when I was told I would be given to Smenkhkare as a wife, so I feel I must give him some of my allegiance. He gave me this spy, who had been hiding in the city for several years, to escort me back to our homeland. He told me that Prince Tutankhaten still lived and resided with your family, so I insisted on stopping to see him and the other children."

I glanced around, and noticed many people watching us as they listened to the scandalous news from the royal family. I took her arm and led her away. "Come, let's go somewhere more private."

I rushed her into my father's house along with the children and her servant. I sat her down and offered her food and water before we continued our conversation. "So you were to be given to Smenkhkare? But our husband favors you; surely he wouldn't agree to that."

She shook her head sadly. "He's not the man he was when you left. The plague devastated his house. Many of his wives and concubines died, as well as many of the young children. Mayati had a daughter who was killed by it, and Halima died from it also."

I grasped her hand. "Not Halima! Oh dear Halima!"

"Yes. Gerlind and I locked ourselves in your room to keep ourselves and our children safe and would accept food only when it was left outside the door. We survived, but every night, we heard the wails of women mourning as another died. By the end, there were only forty-two wives and one hundred sixty-five concubines remaining, not to mention all the children who passed. The scent of burning clothes filled the air, and bodies were thrown into shallow graves and unfinished tombs without embalming. It was horrible. Words cannot express the stench that filled the air for those weeks.

41

"When Gerlind and I finally emerged, we found our husband weak, and no longer on the edge of madness, but crossed over into it. With the sickness and being left alone with his night terrors, something inside him must have snapped. The conjugal visits restarted, but he was soon unable to lie with us. Gerlind was the last woman to fall pregnant by him; that's why she remains his and was not given to Smenkhkare.

"But more than half of the women have been given to him, and Mayati is his Great Royal Wife. She has usurped everything, including the temple which our husband built for you, and has removed your name and replaced it with her own. She's trying to erase you from memory. We aren't even allowed to speak of you."

Abi hung her head and looked at her hands. "These are turbulent times, and I fear they will only worsen once our husband dies. You have no idea how much of a relief it was when the Commander told me Tut still lived. He is the true heir and, being your child, he will be a good and decent man who will be strong enough to defeat the ravenous jackals who are trying to take over the courts.

"But I couldn't stay any longer, not to be with that man, not to watch my husband slowly die. So I'm returning to my homeland where, once they have heard the tales I have to tell, they will welcome me back, and will likely be furious that I was to be handed over to Smenkhkare when the agreement was for me to be Akhenaten's wife."

I sighed, feeling overwhelmingly grateful that I escaped when I did. The thought of all that suffering, all that death and sorrow, pained my heart. All those women who died, it must have shattered Akhenaten's heart knowing so many of his harem passed. He had always tried to love each of them. I knew he must have felt like his world was collapsing around him. I needed to send word to him, to try and comfort him, and let him know that I still supported him.

I stood and found some paper and wrote on it in Egyptian. Abi watched me curiously as I wrote, and when I finished, I sealed it and made it look like an official document from my father to be taken directly to Akhenaten.

I left it on the table and returned to Abi. "You were brave to leave. Allow me to give you food and a place to rest tonight before you continue up the Nile to your homeland."

A small smile swept across her face. "You are unchanged, Kiya. You're generous and caring, but you barely respond to my tales. The Commander did train you well, didn't he? So well that, even now, you remain cautious and guarded."

"As I must," I answered. "If anyone were to discover the truth, that my son and I still live, we would be in danger again. Only our husband knows, and apparently, Horemheb."

She reached up, took my hand, and kissed it. "I'm glad you live. Our husband was not the only one who grieved at the news. Gerlind and I wept for days, and many of the other women paid you a moving tribute, which enraged Nefertiti as I've never seen before. She told us your death was justice for killing Mordad."

Hepsati jumped at the mention of her mother and looked across at us.

"I didn't kill Mordad," I said to Abi in a soft voice.

"I know that, we all know that. There was no way you could kill anyone, especially her. You loved each other deeply."

I hung my head as a tear fell. I had loved her so much, and the mention of her brought back the feelings of loss.

Abi pulled me closer and rested my head on her shoulder, where I allowed my tears to fall silently. Hepsati pushed herself into my arms and climbed onto my lap. I looked down at her as she nuzzled up to me with tears in her eyes.

I stroked her hair as Abi said, "I'm so glad you took her from that place. No one could love Mordad's daughter like you."

I looked into Abi's eyes and smiled gratefully.

The door burst open. Tut came tearing through the house, pausing briefly at the sight of Abi's children. They didn't faze him in the slightest, and he instantly started bossing them around.

We looked back to see Malachi standing at the door, staring at us with a shocked expression. He quickly stepped inside and closed the door behind him.

Abi turned to me. "Is that Mehaleb?"

"It is. He was ordered to hide me—"

She cut me off. "He's a Hebrew?" Her eyes widened with delight. "Gerlind told me of you loving a Malachi. Is *he* Malachi?"

I couldn't help blushing. "His Hebrew name is Malachi, yes."

"Have you married him?" she asked excitedly.

I stared at her firmly. "No. I'm still married to the king."

Her face fell and she glanced up at Malachi. He dodged her look and walked out the back to wash up. "But Kiya is dead, and he looks incredible. He looks better as a Hebrew; he looks stronger and healthier."

"I think that's mine and Hepsati's cooking," I said with a slight smile as I stroked her hair. "This little girl loves him like a father."

"He's a good man. *I* always thought so anyway." She examined my face closely. "Why do you hesitate to marry him? He's so handsome; I would like to marry him! It can't just be because you think you're still married—"

"But I am still married."

"Is it because of Horemheb?"

I sat back, alarmed. "Why would you even suggest such a thing?"

"Gerlind and I were locked up for several weeks with just each other and our children for company. We talked about many things, and she told me things about him and you…"

A loud *bang* echoed around the room as Malachi dropped the firewood beside the stove.

I looked over as he pulled the door open roughly to feed the fire. I knew I needed to change the topic quickly. "Abi, you know those rumors were false. I don't want to dwell on them."

I saw Abi's eyes flick to Malachi, then she said to me, "I would very much like to meet these sisters of yours."

I smiled at her gratefully, and stood. "Then let's go see them."

I turned to Malachi. "Are you all right with watching the children for a short while?"

He nodded and beckoned for Hepsati to come to him.

My sisters lived in the houses around us, so we left Abi's servant behind as well and walked out into the street together, our arms entwined. Suddenly Abi spoke softly, but directly. "Gerlind told me Horemheb kissed you."

I took a sharp breath as the memory flooded into my mind.

"It's true, isn't it? She also told me that he confessed that he loved you."

"I don't want to talk about it," I said sharply.

"When did it happen? Was it before or after the rumors started?"

"Abi, please," I said in a low voice. "It was a long time after, a few weeks before I left. But I really don't want to talk about it. It's too confusing."

"Why? Because you love him too?"

44

"No, it's not that," I said, feeling her words pull at my heart. "He never followed through, except the night I left, when he tried to leave with us, but I told him to stay and watch over Tut's birthright. He has never once written to me or sent my father any word, not even condolences at my fake death. I think he was toying with me because he found out I'm in love with Malachi."

We reached Rena's house and I knocked on the door. "None of my family knows of this, so please don't mention it again. It's better forgotten, so that when the time comes, I can remarry without any scandal."

"All right," she said, as the door burst open and Rena smiled up at us.

That night, after the household had retired, I remained downstairs to clean while my mind flooded with thoughts. Abi brought back some memories and feelings I had tried to let go of, and I felt overwhelmed.

The thought of Smenkhkare returning to Amarna gave me chills. He was a horrible man, and with Mayati at his side, I knew my son's crown would be in great danger. But Tut was still young. He was only three years old, almost four; far from being a king. I wondered if Akhenaten would have handed me over to Smenkhkare if I had remained, and the thought filled me with dread. But I knew Akhenaten wouldn't have let me go; he wouldn't have willingly given *me* to anyone else. I tried to shake off the thought, feeling grateful for being spared the humiliation.

But, instead of thinking of more pleasant things, my mind turned to Horemheb and the day he kissed me. The same rush surged through me, and I froze, holding my belly. I shut my eyes and remembered how incredible that kiss felt, and the excitement it gave me as I ran through the moment in my mind.

A hand rested on my shoulder. I jumped, and swung around in fright to see Malachi looking at me with concern. "Naomi, are you all right?"

"Yes, I'm fine." I breathed deeply as I grasped at my chest, feeling my heart pound wildly at being caught. "Abi's presence has just brought back so many memories."

"Like what? Good ones, bad ones?"

"A little of both," I answered, as I stared into his eyes. "I was thinking about how many of the wives are being given to Smenkhkare and how awful that would be."

Malachi nodded and walked over to the stove; only embers remained to give the room a dim light. "I know many of the women were afraid of him."

"Malachi?" I said softly, feeling my heart yearn for him. He turned and looked at me and I couldn't help myself. I rushed to him and, wrapping my hand around the back of his head, I kissed him.

He reacted instantly. He wrapped his arms around me tightly as he kissed me back.

The same rush Horemheb had given me, surged through me and I grew excited. I could tell that, unlike Akhenaten and Horemheb, Malachi had never kissed anyone before, but it didn't matter, I knew he loved me.

But I remembered I was still married, and pulled away from him. "Oh, Malachi, I'm so sorry."

"Don't be sorry."

He reached for me, but I stepped back. "I just made an adulterer out of you. I can't keep doing this, it's so hard."

"Naomi, it won't be long now and we will be able to be together."

"Please don't talk like that. It makes this so much harder."

He came toward me and I backed away, but he continued after me until I found myself pressed against the wall. He ran his hand through my hair and whispered, "It does feel like mine, doesn't it?"

"Malachi, please, I shouldn't have started this."

He looked into my eyes. "Everything will be all right, Naomi, you'll see. The king doesn't have much time left to live now."

He backed away from me and returned upstairs.

I slid down onto the floor and cried into my hands tears of betrayal and complete and utter confusion.

CHAPTER SEVEN

My sisters, Dana, and I all went to the well, together with the children. Malachi's brothers, Enoch and Jared, arrived the day before, and we expected the taking of a wife to occur any night. We each felt very excited for it. Three all at once was rare, and the festivities would be rich with feasting and celebration for the unions. My father's house had been invited, so we would all be expected to attend.

As the five of us filled our water jugs, we sang and gossiped excitedly together. Suddenly, the sound of a mass of men approaching filled the square. We grabbed our children and rushed for cover. The instant we cleared the square, a large patrol of Egyptian infantry marched across it. I had Tut hold tighter to me, so I could pull my shawl in front of my face in case one of them recognized me. Then I wrapped my arms tighter around Itani and Tut, who sat on my hips while Hepsati clung to my robe.

Finally, the group passed, but one man appeared behind the rest who made me gasp. Horemheb wasn't paying much attention to anything, but stared at what appeared to be a map. He seemed to sense someone watching him, and his gaze shot across to our group. His pace slowed as he looked upon Hepsati, obviously recognizing her, before it lifted and lingered on Tut's face. But then, just as quickly, he returned his focus to his map and marched after his troops.

I wanted to rush after him, but I knew I couldn't without running the risk of being discovered alive. He must have known that, too, which was why he hadn't stopped to acknowledge us.

I stepped out from our cover, and couldn't help watching after him. Adina stepped up beside me and ask, "That was your friend Commander Horemheb, wasn't it?"

"Yes it was," I answered.

"Did he not recognize you?"

I looked down at her and saw her eyes filled with compassion. I smiled at her. "It doesn't matter if he did or not, he wouldn't run the risk of exposing me by approaching us."

We returned to the well where we finished filling our water and headed back to our homes.

Three trumpets blew. I shot up onto my feet and shook the children awake.

Malachi pulled the blanket back and grabbed Tut and Itani. "Hurry!" he exclaimed excitedly.

Papa lit three lamps for us as I pulled Hepsati to her feet, and we ran down the stairs into the street.

Outside, my siblings emerged, carrying their own lamps and children. We all hurried together to the house of Laban. There, Malachi handed me Itani, and Tut to my father, before he rushed to his brothers, and they all burst into the house together. A few moments later, they emerged with the three daughters of Laban, each veiled and adorned with beautiful jewelry, tunics, and robes.

We followed them through the city to the house of Malachi's family, where they rushed in ahead of us and entered their wedding chambers. Malachi stood by the doors while we feasted noisily together.

I moved through the room to fill my cup, when someone grabbed me and thrust me out the front door. I looked up and saw Laban glaring down at me.

"I don't want a harlot at the wedding of my daughters."

As he stepped back to shut the door, I saw Malachi watching at me with distress. I knew he couldn't help me because he had to stay where he was, in case his brothers called for him.

I stood to try and plead my case, but found the door slamming in my face. I stepped back and pulled on my veil, so if anyone had heard the disturbance they wouldn't be able to see me. Knocking would be pointless; no one would hear, so I sat against the wall in the dirt.

Then, an Egyptian man appeared out of the shadows and walked to the door. He didn't notice me, but I recognized him instantly and couldn't help feeling ashamed that he might see me that way. I pulled my veil closer to my face and kept my shawl over my eyes.

I watched Horemheb as he reached out and touched the door before he pressed his forehead against it. He remained completely unaware of my presence, not far to his left, as I watched him sigh and close his eyes. Pain crossed his face as a single tear fell, and I wondered at it. To see emotion from him was truly very strange. I couldn't help staring, trying to discern his thoughts.

As he slowly opened his eyes, he finally noticed me. He jumped back as I turned my face away. "What are you looking at? Are you a whore, waiting for the festivities to end?"

I didn't dare speak. I didn't want him to see me disgraced and cast out. If he knew I had been thrown out on the street and scorned, he would return to my husband and inform him of my shame, which would cause his wrath to befall my people for their cruelty.

"Speak, ignorant Hebrew!" he snarled.

I knew he had no idea who I was. There was no way he would dare speak to me like that, and I felt relieved.

He waited for me to respond, but when I refused to say a word, he unsheathed his sword. "Foul slave. One less Hebrew will do the world a favor."

My stare shot up to him in fear as I raised my hand. Just as I was about to speak, the door came open and Samuel stared at Horemheb in shock. "You!"

Horemheb lowered his sword and turned his attention to my brother. "You were Kiya's brother."

"Yes." He glanced at me quickly with confusion. "What are you here for? You're interrupting our celebration."

"I wish to see the boy," Horemheb answered, standing straighter.

Samuel looked alarmed. "He's too young."

"I have no desire to take him, he is safer here. I just wish to see that he is alive and well."

Samuel stepped back and gestured across the room.

Horemheb leaned forward to see.

"There he is," Samuel said with a snarl. "Now you've seen him, I ask that you leave."

Horemheb seemed to scan the room for a moment, and a hint of disappointment appeared in his eyes. "Thank you," he said, before his gaze fell to me. "I guess I could use some companionship tonight, even if it is just from a whore." He reached for me.

I pulled away, but Samuel grabbed his arm. "Leave, Commander. She is no whore."

He straightened and scoffed. "It's probably for the best. I wouldn't want to touch a Hebrew anyway." He replaced his sword. He turned, but then he paused and said, "Seven days, correct?"

"Yes," Samuel replied.

"All right. Tell them we will depart in eight. I have no desire to stay in this place longer than I need to." He marched away.

Once he left the street, Samuel pulled the door shut and fell on his knees beside me. "Naomi, I can't believe he spoke about you like that!"

I sighed. "He didn't recognize me. I'm not the queen I once was."

I hung my head and let my tears fall.

Samuel reached for me and wiped a tear from my cheek. "Naomi, come back inside. Laban is an ignorant and foolish man."

I shook my head. "No, he was right to have me removed. They are his daughters and I'm just..." My voice caught.

"Don't even think it!" Samuel grasped my face. "You are brave, and you are strong, and I swear to you that no matter what, your family will always stand by you because of all the things you've done for us."

I reached up and touched his face tenderly. "Dear Samuel, I thought for years you hated me for being loved by our father more than you, but you have become my truest friend."

He smiled and laughed. "I did hate you, Naomi. You were such a little know-it-all."

I laughed.

He took my hand and helped me to my feet. "Come inside, dear sister, and finish the festivities with us."

I nodded, and he wrapped his arm around my waist to lead me back in. Once inside, Laban scowled at me, but Samuel kept me within the heart of my family, so Laban didn't dare expel me again for fear of offending my father.

I looked across to Malachi, who watched me with concern in his eyes. I gave him a quick smile. His face lit up like it always had when I emerged from Akhenaten's bedchambers, and my heart fluttered. To distract myself, I sat with my children. I laughed and played with them, except Itani, who yawned and nuzzled my shoulder with heavy eyes.

Soon, I saw Malachi lean toward one of the doors and smile, then he called out, "It is done! The marriage has been made!"

A loud cheer arose. It didn't take long for Malachi to repeat the announcement for his other two brothers. After some final hurrahs, we all dispersed.

Papa and I were the last to leave. We waited for Malachi to set out food for his brothers and their new wives so they wouldn't have to leave their bedchambers before we returned the next day to continue the celebration. By the time we left, we each had to carry a child home and they fell asleep in our arms.

The seven days passed quickly and with great frivolity. Several times, Laban tried to put me out again, but Malachi and Samuel kept close to me to prevent it.

When the time came for the brothers and their new wives to emerge, we all sat around the couples and ate a great feast until we were so full, we felt we might burst.

None of the brothers departed for new homes as was customary; Enoch and Jared had to leave with the Egyptian infantry in the morning. So they remained at the house where Tobiah and his new wife would continue to reside.

Once the feast came to an end, we all departed, feeling contented with the outcome of the whole ceremony.

The next day, Malachi and I took my children and went to the house to bid his brothers farewell. I saw his sadness to see them go, but they all promised to send letters to keep in touch.

Malachi remained quiet on the way home, and stayed that way for several days. I didn't want to ask what bothered him. I believed he felt saddened by his brothers' departure, but I was wrong.

CHAPTER EIGHT

I returned home from the well and saw Papa and Malachi talking together. I smiled at them as I entered the house and glanced around. "Where are the children?"

"They're with Adina," Papa answered. "Naomi—"

"Oh! I better go collect them. Our meal smells like it might be done." I bustled out back and placed the water jugs down, then hurried back in to remove the bread and meat from the stove. As I pulled the food out, I felt their eyes on me. I placed the food down and I looked across at them. "What is it?"

"Naomi, come here," Papa said gently.

I approached with concern. Malachi's sack of gold sat on the floor beside Papa. I stared at it, confused for a moment, then noticed Papa holding a cup of wine. I gasped and leaped back, realizing what was going on. "Malachi, you can't—"

"I know what you are going to say, Naomi," Malachi interrupted, turning to me. "But hear me out. I know you are still married, but I wish to be espoused to you now so that when the king passes, I won't have to wait. I have waited so long already. I don't want to add an extra year onto it for the espousal period to pass."

"There's no crime in it, either," Papa said, stepping between us. "Your husband is an Egyptian and didn't marry you according to our customs. I know the laws well, Naomi, and I have found this as a loophole for you. So as long as Malachi doesn't know you before the forty days of mourning once the king has passed, there will be no adultery committed."

I stared between the two, feeling ambushed and unable to speak.

"Naomi," Papa continued. "Malachi has given me a very generous price for you, but even without it, I would have been more than happy to give you to him for all the sacrifices he has made for you. This union would please me above all those of my other children. He has even purchased land to build a house for you and to start a small farm."

I dropped my gaze and sank onto a stool in shock. When had he found the time to do all of that? I thought of Akhenaten and felt overwhelmed with guilt. He still loved me, he still thought of me and trusted in me; I couldn't betray him.

"But what of my husband?" I said. "He may not die for years, and this would be such a betrayal."

"No, it wouldn't." Malachi rushed over and knelt in front of me. "He is sickly. He doesn't even know what's going on most of the time. Naomi, the man you once knew as your husband is gone. Only a shell remains. He always said how he wanted you to be happy. Now is your chance. I will always love you, and I swear to you that I will always take care of you and provide for you. Please, Naomi. I cannot bear the thought of waiting longer than I need to."

I looked into his eyes and saw his sincerity. I wanted to go along with his plan, so I felt my resolve falter.

He stood and walked over to Papa. He took the cup from his hand and sipped from it. I stared at him, completely overwhelmed and shocked. He handed it back to Papa, who walked over to me and motioned for me to stand.

As I stood, he held the cup out for me to sip. I hesitated, feeling conflicted. I wanted so badly to accept, but my guilt remained so strong. I glanced across at Malachi, who stared at me intensely, knowing I could easily reject him. I didn't want to reject him, I loved him so much. So I shut my eyes, took the cup from my father, and sipped.

Malachi moved in with Tobiah to begin the betrothal customs. Tobiah gave him a room to prepare for our wedding chambers; my sisters helped me with my own preparations. I had some jewelry left over from when I fled Amarna, and they took me out to buy cosmetics and new fine fabrics to make a tunic, shawl, and veil. But, because I was still married, the espousal was kept quiet, and my face was not veiled.

We had no idea how long it would last.

Meanwhile, Tut flourished. When his fifth birthday arrived, I couldn't help feeling amazed by how quickly the time had passed.

I went out to meet him and Malachi in the fields, but they were nowhere in sight. I checked the marketplace and my siblings' homes. Finally, I headed to Tobiah's house and heard voices inside. I paused when I heard Tut laugh.

"Boy, mind your manners," Malachi said.

"But Uncle Tobiah is so old," Tut responded.

"To you maybe." Tobiah snorted.

"I can help much better than him. Look at my huge muscles!" Malachi laughed.

"Don't indulge him," Tobiah said in a scolding tone.

"Anyway, I am a prince," Tut responded with a haughty voice. "I will be king someday."

"And who told you that?" Tobiah asked.

"Mama, and Mama knows everything. She's the smartest person in the world."

Malachi laughed again.

"He's going to be trouble," Tobiah said with a sigh. "He's spoiled."

"I am not."

"You are… why am I arguing with a five year old?"

Malachi laughed again.

"Malachi, stop laughing."

"I'm sorry," Malachi said. "He's just so like Naomi. Those poor Egyptians."

"Poor Egyptians? We have to raise him!"

"We?" Malachi chuckled. "Naomi and I will raise him, not you."

I rested my hand over my heart, touched by his love for my children. I tapped on the door and their conversation came to an abrupt end.

Miriam answered and smiled. "Naomi! Come in."

As I stepped in, I saw Malachi and Tobiah sat facing each other with Tut climbing Malachi's back.

"Tut! Get down."

Tut pouted and jumped onto the floor. "Why are you here?"

"Don't be rude to your mother," Malachi said, sliding something behind his chair.

Tobiah stood, and nudged it with his foot out of the room.

Leah appeared and took my hand. "How are you, my dear?"

Tut tugged at my skirt. "Mama, Papa says I have to start lessons with Grandpapa now. Tell him he's wrong."

I grabbed his hand. "But he's right."

He slumped. "Why? I want to be a shepherd."

"But you know you will be Pharaoh someday."

"Ah!" Tobiah burst back into the room. "Why do you tell him that? He uses it against everyone. Maybe you should wait until he's a little older."

I looked down at Tut, pressing my hands against my hips. "Tut, you know that's a secret. If too many people know you could be in danger."

"You can keep a secret, can't you?" Malachi said.

Tut turned to Malachi. A wide grin swept across his face. "I can. I'm the best secret keeper."

"Good boy. Now keep that secret too."

Tut nodded.

"Too?" My eyes narrowed on Malachi. "What are you hiding?"

"Mama!" Tut grabbed my skirt again. "It's a secret. Don't ask."

Malachi laughed.

Hepsati's humming always calmed me. We'd just dropped lunch off for my father and Tut, and I'd argued with my father again.

"Hepsati?" I said with a sigh.

"Yes, Mama?"

"I'm glad you are a reasonable child."

She giggled. "What did Tut do this time?"

I huffed. "You know Tut. For months he has run your grandpapa ragged during these lessons. The second he turns his back, Tut is out the door."

Hepsati grasped my hand. "Tut says he is bored in his lessons."

I looked down into her beautiful, dark eyes and saw Mordad gazing up at me. I touched her cheek, longing for my dear friend. "I can't believe you are ten years old now. Did you know every day you look more and more like your mother?"

Her face lit up. "Really?"

I nodded. "Mostly your eyes. You look at me like she did."

"That's because I love you." Hepsati's arm wrapped around my waist. "And my mother loved you more than just about anyone."

"Not you."

She giggled. "I said just about."

I kissed her head. "You keep me sane."

She laughed. "Tut will be fine. I'll talk to him."

I looked down at her, surprised. "He listens to you?"

She shrugged. "Sometimes. It's usually when I tell him he made you cry. He hates that."

"He does?"

She nodded. "He loves you more than anyone."

The waiting seemed endless as the weeks turned into months. I sensed Malachi's growing frustration. He'd see me, his eyes full of love, but he'd turn away and vanish for days on end.

"He's building the farm," Hepsati told me as we prepared dinner one night. "Although, he finished the main house months ago. He works on making it comfortable, adding extra luxuries and preparing the riverbank for crops. I heard Aunt Adina say he works when he is upset that he still can't marry you even though the espousal period has passed."

I let out a long breath, feeling that same frustration. Akhenaten had sent a letter to my father for me on Itani's fourth birthday. He rambled about his visions and dreams, making no sense. But he did express jealousy for Horemheb. He said he wished he could be strong and handsome like Horemheb so I would crave and desire him in the same way.

I burned the message immediately, hoping my father and Malachi had not read it.

The door burst open, making Hepsati and me jump. Itani yelped, jumping up from her game on the floor.

Malachi marched right at me, his eyes ablaze. "How is that man still alive?"

"What?"

He grabbed his hair, pacing the room. "He's so weak and sickly. His mind is gone. Why does he keep fighting?" He snickered. "Probably because he doesn't want the commander to have you."

"Malachi!" I hurried to shut the door. "Don't say things like that in front of the children."

Malachi looked down at Itani, frowning.

Hepsati rushed over and grabbed Itani's arm. "Let's go visit Aunt Rena."

"I don't want—"

Hepsati cut Itani off as she tugged her out the door.

Malachi glanced at the stairs. "Where's Tut?"

"With Papa."

"Good." He rushed at me and kissed me.

I pushed him off. "Stop. You're not even supposed to see me under normal circumstances."

"These aren't normal circumstances." He clasped my face and kissed me again.

I moaned, enjoying the kiss. His love flowed into me through that forbidden kiss.

I pushed him back again. "Malachi—"

"I love you, Naomi. It has been almost seven years since I vowed to wait for you. Seven wonderful years, but seven years of yearning, seven years of watching you from a distance, forbidden to touch you." He clasped my face, stroking my cheeks with his thumbs. "When will it end?"

"I don't know," I said breathlessly.

"Everything is ready for us to be married. The wait is torture... and don't you dare tell me to stop waiting."

I couldn't help smiling.

He kissed my forehead. "Tell me you love me."

"I love you."

He let out a shuddering sigh. "That will get me through for now."

He stepped away from me, and hurried out the door without looking back.

It wasn't long after that Laban discovered our betrothal. Then, late one evening after the children had gone to bed, he burst into the house with Tobiah hurrying after him. He pointed at Malachi and snarled, "You will not marry that harlot!"

I backed into the garden so he wouldn't notice me as I listened.

"I will not have her associated with my daughters!" he hissed. "This betrothal is shameful and I demand you call it off immediately."

"I won't," Malachi answered in a steady, calm voice.

"You will!" Laban snarled. "My daughters will not be associated with that... that filth!"

"Laban," Tobiah said in a deep, strong voice. "Naomi is no harlot, and as the patriarch over my brothers and thus their wives, I insist you set your feelings aside and accept that Naomi is going to marry Malachi and will be an honorable sister to your daughters."

"Honorable?" He snarled. "She has three children and no husband to show for it! I will not stand for this!"

"Laban," Papa said. "You would disrespect me by insulting my daughter?"

"Jorem, she is no longer your daughter. You should forget your love for her and see her for what she is!"

The door slammed.

I peeked around the corner to see Father, Malachi, and Tobiah exchange concerned looks. Itani started to cry from the commotion, and I rushed upstairs, keeping my eyes low.

"Naomi, everything will be all right," Malachi said softly as I climbed the stairs.

But a few days later, as Hepsati and I returned home from the well, a mob cornered us. I handed Itani to her as she clenched Tut's hand. "Hepsati..."

The mob closed in, trapping us in an alley.

"Mama." Hepsati's soft voice quivered.

"Run."

She rushed with Tut and Itani through a small doorway, but someone caught me by the robe. He yanked me backward and tossed me to the ground.

The first stone hit me in the chest, and the second on the face. I scrambled to my feet and threw up my hands to protect myself as the stones rained down on me amidst sneers and foul accusations. I tried to break free and run several times, but the mob was too large, and thrust me back against the wall.

Blood poured down my arms as I fell to me knees, fearing that I would finally be about to face my end. "Please!" I begged.

"Harlot!" Laban's voice hissed.

I looked up and saw him standing over me with a large stone clenched in his hand. "Cast-out wife of an idolatrous king!"

"No! Please, it's not—" As he hand came down, I screamed.

"Naomi!"

Laban's hand barely grazed my head as Malachi leaped between us and threw him back.

Samuel lifted me into his arms and shoved through the crowd, with Malachi rushing behind us. The mob followed us through the streets, stones still flying and hitting both Samuel and Malachi as they shielded me from harm.

We burst into my father's house, and Malachi held the door closed as the mob yelled from the street. After a few minutes, Tobiah's voice arose from the confusion. "Disperse, I say! Laban, you shame me!"

We listened as the crowd broke up, and I looked upstairs to see my children cowering together as they watched me.

Samuel set me down on a chair and called for Hepsati. "You were very brave," he said to her. "Now I need you to run and find your aunts."

She nodded and rushed out the door.

Malachi knelt in front of me, looking at my arms and face in distress. His head fell as he wept into my lap. "This is my fault!"

"No, it isn't. Malachi, please don't blame yourself for their ignorance," I said, touching his hair.

My sisters burst in and each gasped at the sight of me. Adina rushed out back to warm some water, while Rena and Eliora hurried to find rags and clean clothes for me.

Papa returned to see how badly beaten I was, and stared at my injuries with horror.

"Oh, Naomi," he said on a sigh, as he knelt beside Malachi and wrapped his arm around his shoulder. "Come, we will bless her, and while her sisters take her into the wash shed to see to her injuries, we will pray together for this to end. You have both been tried enough. Surely the Lord sees that and is waiting for us to come to him in faith so he can end this suffering."

Malachi nodded, and Papa helped him to his feet, then motioned Samuel to come forward. They blessed me.

My sisters took me out and removed my clothes to examine the rest of my injuries. I looked down at my body and saw myself covered with red welts, with grazes and deep gashes on my arms where I had tried to shield my face and head.

I found myself secretly longing for the palace in Amarna and the days of joy I had experienced there. I missed Akhenaten and how he showered me with his devotion. I missed Abi, Gerlind, and Halima, along with the other women, and I missed Mordad most of all. I thought of Horemheb and I knew I missed him, too. He had been more constant than my husband, and he had always been good company.

I looked at my sisters and my love for them grew. I had sacrificed so much for them and now they were doing the same for me. When they finished and helped me redress, I reached for them, and held them in my arms. "I love you all, I hope you know that."

"Of course we do," Rena answered and squeezed me tighter. "No one has ever done more for us than you."

We returned to the house, and found Tobiah and his wife waiting for us. Upon seeing me, she rushed over, crying. "Naomi, this is my fault. I believed my father no longer thought badly of you, and I told him in confidence of your betrothal to Malachi. He asked me repeatedly why Malachi was still unwed when he is starting to grow so old, so I finally told him everything. I honestly thought he would understand. I didn't know he would do this. I am so sorry."

Her gaze fell. She saw my hands, which made her sob more loudly.

I gently wrapped my arms around her and kissed her head. "Please don't blame yourself."

As she slowly cried herself out, Papa brought us all around him and we fell to our knees in prayer.

Samuel burst into the house and grabbed Tut by the arm. "Naomi, come to the courthouse, quickly. An Egyptian ambassador is there to make an announcement and he would like as many people present as possible."

I lifted Itani onto my hip, while Hepsati rushed out the door after him.

We made it to the courthouse in a matter of minutes. Seeing that I didn't recognize the ambassador, I moved to the front of the crowd with the rest of my family.

After a few minutes, he raised his hand for silence and all fell quiet to listen. He cleared his throat and spoke loudly in Egyptian.

"Seventeen days ago, our mighty Lord, leader and living god, the great Akhenaten, was taken from this Earth to return to his father the Aten. For the next twenty-three days you will observe the appropriate mourning practices until the Pharaoh is resting in his tomb."

The ambassador then bowed, and left the courthouse.

Murmuring filled the air as people hurriedly translated the message while I stood, stunned. Samuel grabbed me and said something to me excitedly, but it didn't register in my mind. I thought about Akhenaten, and how suddenly, he was gone. It seemed surreal, unbelievable.

My eyes fell to my three children. I knew only Hepsati understood what it meant to them. She hung her head reverently, while Tut stared up at us, confused. I then realized he was next in line. His turn had arrived to take the crown. But he was only six years old; he was much too young. I bent down and looked into his eyes.

"Tut, do you understand what this means?"

"No," he answered.

"This means your real father has died. Do you understand that?"

"My real father who I don't see who isn't Malachi?"

"Yes, him."

He looked up at Hepsati, unsure why the information should affect him, then I saw something click in his mind. "Does this mean I get to be king now?"

I grabbed his mouth and glanced around to make sure no one heard him before I answered. "Not yet, Tut. You need to be a little older first."

I released his mouth and a huge grin split across his face. "How old? Like as old as Hepsati?"

"Older than that."

"Like as old as you?"

"That would be a much better age, yes."

He looked noticeably disappointed. "That's forever away. I'll never get that old."

I sighed at his boyhood shortsightedness. "One day you will, Tut, just be patient."

Samuel bent down to me and whispered, "Naomi, hurry, let's get home. We must talk about this."

He plucked up Itani and led the way back through the crowd.

Soon after we arrived at the house, the whole family filed in, including Tobiah; they talked excitedly about how finally, Malachi would be able to take me as his wife. Then, Malachi burst in and all eyes turned to him. But he scanned the faces for me.

I stepped forward and our eyes met.

He rushed to me and held me in a tight embrace as we both cried. They were tears of mixed emotions; relief that we could finally be together, but also sorrow, because we both knew the king well for several years.

"Naomi," he said in a hushed voice. "You know I have been looking forward to this for many years, but I do feel grief for him."

"As do I, Malachi." I squeezed him tighter.

He let me go, looked around at the family, and said, "We will mourn his passing. He was the father of Hepsati, Tutankhaten, and Itani, husband of Naomi, and our king. He deserves our respect. So we will not speak of me taking Naomi as my wife until the appropriate time passes."

Everyone bowed their heads and agreed.

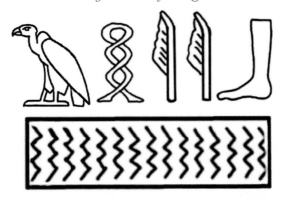

CHAPTER NINE

They were the slowest twenty-three days I ever remember. I went to the temple of Aten to pay Akhenaten tribute, and found I was the only one who thought to do so.

I took my children with me so they could know something of their father. As we entered the abandoned temple, Itani grasped my skirts and looked frightened. She had grown up in our religion and had learned to fear the Egyptian gods, but Tut was curious. He ran up to the altar and tried to climb up on top of it. It took me several minutes of struggling with him to get him to stop. Instead, he ran around the room examining the reliefs on the walls while Hepsati tried to help me by watching over him.

I made my way through the temple to find something to show them of their father. Then, in a small room, I found a bust of him. He looked very young, maybe even younger than I was. I examined his face closely, having not known him until he had reached his thirties. I touched the painted stone, remembering him and the love he gave me, and felt grateful for the children we shared. I let my tears fall for him and for the tortured life he led, especially at the end, when he must have felt so alone. Despite everything, I did miss him and I felt a twinge of guilt for never being able to love him as he had loved me.

Hepsati soon entered with Tut, and she stared up at her father's face. I knew she recognized him, but Tut pointed and said, "Who's that?"

"That's our father," Hepsati said softly.

"That looks nothing like Papa," Tut answered, shriveling up his nose.

My heart wrenched at his words, knowing Akhenaten loved Tut so dearly, but Tut didn't even recognize him.

"Not Malachi," Hepsati said. "Our real father, the king."

"The one I never see who died?"

"Yes, Tut," I answered looking down at him. "This is your real father. He loved you very much."

I tried to lift the bust, but it was quite heavy and I knew I wouldn't be able to slip it unnoticed back through the city.

"He looks funny," Tut said. "His face is too long."

I spun and snapped at him. "Tut, don't talk about your father like that! He loved you and it would break his heart if he heard you say such a thing."

Tut stared up at me, wide eyed and frightened by my uncharacteristic outburst and backed away, clasping Hepsati's hand. "I'm sorry, Mama."

I sighed, feeling guilty for yelling at him. He didn't know how sensitive Akhenaten had been about his appearance. Tut was just a normal six-year-old boy who said whatever came into his mind.

I squatted down and stretched my arms out for him. "It's all right, Tut. I shouldn't have yelled at you."

He rushed forward into my arms and wrapped them around my neck. I squeezed him, before I let go and stood to look at the bust again. I had nothing to give as tribute for him, until I remembered how he told me he liked my Hebrew hair. I pulled the knife out that I still carried on me, and took hold of a tuft of my hair. I sliced it off, near my scalp, and laid it down in front of the bust.

"There, Akhenaten. You always liked my hair."

I lifted Itani and had her kiss the bust, followed by Tut and Hepsati. As we turned to leave, I glanced back one last time and said a silent prayer for him to finally be free and happy.

Over a week had passed since the days of mourning, and everyone waited in anticipation for the night Malachi would come and take me as his wife. My guilt had finally subsided and, knowing Eliora would watch my children for the seven days, I grew anxious with anticipation.

One day, as I returned from doing the laundry by the river with my sisters, I saw Malachi returning from the fields with Tut. We stayed back so they wouldn't notice us and I whispered, "What's taking so long? I thought after seven years of waiting he would be eager for us to be wed."

Eliora giggled. "Oh, he is. It's Tobiah who holds him up. He says he wants the taking of the bride to be a surprise, just like any other marriage celebration. But, I doubt he will hold on too long, I'm sure Malachi is growing very frustrated with him."

Two nights later, we heard the trumpet sound. My sisters, who had been sleeping at the house with us, were on their feet in an instant to finalize the last details before I was veiled.

Only moments later, a great noise arose out in the street as Malachi and his groomsmen stormed the house. I heard them charge up the stairs as Papa reached my side and smiled at me. "I love you, Naomi. You have always made me so proud."

I threw my arms around him, but Malachi tore me away and rushed me down the stairs, with my sisters close behind.

Outside, in front of the house, the crowd of wedding guests gathered to watch. As Malachi burst out with me in tow, a cheer arose and the crowd parted to let the wedding party pass. We rushed through the streets to Tobiah's house where our wedding chambers had been prepared. My excitement rose and my heart pounded in my chest. I couldn't believe it was finally happening; after seven years of waiting it seemed like a dream.

We arrived at the house. He led me into the room Enoch used for his chambers, and shut the door behind us. He paused for a moment to listen to the guests enter the house, then we heard the front door shut. Tobiah announced the beginning of festivities before he sat to wait by the door.

Malachi looked me over, and slowly walked toward me. My heart pounded harder, and my breathing quickened as I gazed up at him. He reached out to remove my veil and smiled when he saw my face. "Naomi! Seven years felt like a lifetime, but now I'm here it *does* feel like but a day."

I couldn't help blushing as he caught my chin. I gazed up into his eyes as he pulled off my shawl and ran his fingers through my hair. I smiled and stepped closer, feeling incredibly attracted to him. He looked so different from Akhenaten. Akhenaten had looked almost feminine, with his wide hips, narrow shoulders, and soft skin, whereas Malachi stood tall and broad shouldered, and had a thick, dark beard. He was the epitome of masculinity, and I found for the first time, I looked forward to having intimate relations.

He pulled off his robe and mine. I began to tremble as we stood in our tunics, staring at each other. I reached up and touched his face, feeling a deep affection for him. But I saw in his eyes something that surprised me—he was worried.

"What's wrong, Malachi?" I asked.

He appeared embarrassed as he answered softly, "I don't want to disappoint you."

I blushed and giggled. "No, Malachi, you won't. I love you, remember?"

To reassure him of my affection I untied his belt and pulled open his tunic. I hadn't seen him bare-chested since we left Amarna, and it surprised me to find hair on it. I knew he gave up shaving, since he wasn't among the Egyptians anymore, but it surprised me how different it made him look and, along with several years of age and being well-fed, he was much thicker and more heavily built than I remembered.

As my hand ran up his chest, he rested his fingers on top of mine and watched for my reaction. He wrapped his other arm around my waist and pulled me against him. I looked up at him, pleasantly surprised, before he bent down and kissed me.

He lowered me onto the bed and made love to me slowly, passionately, lovingly. It was the first time I had ever enjoyed it so completely and my love for him grew even deeper.

We lay on the bed, staring at the ceiling; he breathed, "That was…"

"Worth the wait." I smiled contentedly.

He rolled on his side and pulled me in for a kiss. "You're my wife now, Naomi."

I touched his cheek affectionately. "All those years in the palace, I always wished to be your wife, but never dared believe it could one day be true. But here we are, and I am so happy."

He brushed my hair back from my face and smiled down at me. "I'm glad you're happy. That's all I've ever wanted. I knew you didn't love him, I knew you weren't happy with him, but you are so strong and you persevered. It was such torture for me to watch you go in to him, but now you're with me and those memories just feel like a bad dream."

"Let's pretend that's all they are, dreams, and we never had anything between us. But, my dear Malachi, if I hadn't been his queen, I never would have met you, so I cannot regret that time because it brought me to you and it gave me my beautiful children."

"*Our* beautiful children," he corrected me. "From now on, I will officially call them my own. They already call me father, so I will proclaim it to be true to all who ask."

Suddenly, he shot to his feet and rushed to the door.

"Almost forgot." He smiled back at me before he leaned against the door and whispered for Tobiah. He received acknowledgment and said, "I have taken myself a wife."

"I know, I heard," Tobiah answered through the door before his voice rang out to our guests. "The deed is done! Let us rejoice!"

Cheering arose as Malachi returned to the bed and wrapped his arms around me. "Oh, if only I would never have to let you go again."

Our seven days in the bedchamber felt like a dream. I had never been so blissfully happy, and each day I fell more and more in love with my new husband. I couldn't help comparing him to the king because he was so different. He was always gentle with me, he never raised his voice, or hit me, or made me feel frightened in any way.

We spent hours curled up together just talking and laughing. We had spent so many years being worried we would never be together and hiding away for my safety, that I'd forgotten how funny he could be.

He loved to make me laugh. He said I had grown so serious from being forced to fight for myself and my son that he enjoyed hearing my laugh. I realized in those seven days how weighed down we had become from all our burdens, and I worked hard to let it all go so we could start fresh. My prayers were answered in that room, and I found myself constantly sending up gratitude to the heavens.

Eventually, the time came for us to emerge and join our guests at the feast. We felt reluctant to leave the room. We had enjoyed our time together, completely isolated from the rest of the world, immensely. Our love had grown stronger and so had our relationship. But, we dressed and stood for a moment by the door as Malachi looked down at me.

"Well, my beautiful wife, are you ready to face the world again?"

"No," I answered honestly. "But I will, because I must."

He laughed. "We will do it together." He lifted his hand for me, and I smiled, taking it tightly in mine.

He pushed the door open.

Cheers and loud celebration met us as we stepped through. Tobiah greeted us first. He embraced his brother before gently kissing my hand. Then, three smaller bodies wrapped their arms around me. I bent down to kiss each of my children.

"I missed you, Mama," Itani said.

"I missed you too, my little darling." I beamed, feeling touched.

Tut soon tried to climb Malachi, who lifted him up and sat him on his shoulders. Hepsati's hand wrapped around mine as she spoke softly in my ear. "Is Malachi our father now?"

"He wants to be," I answered. "If *you* want him to be."

Her face lit up. "Of course! I've always wanted him to be."

I touched her cheek, and saw in her eyes Mordad looking back at me proudly; I had fulfilled her last wish for me, to choose Malachi.

We were guided by the crowd to the center of the table and the feast began. Malachi and I ate our fill quickly, and sat back to watch the antics of our family and friends who remained overly exuberant from seven days of festivities.

As Bilhan stood and told a very long joke, Malachi leaned closer to me and whispered in my ear. "We will be alone again tonight. The children won't be moving to the house until tomorrow."

He stroked my leg, and my gaze fell as my cheeks warmed.

Suddenly Laban stood and hollered, "I can't do this any longer! Malachi, you have made a foolish choice in taking a known harlot for a wife after I offered you a woman of unquestionable virtue! And now you have brought shame to my family by associating my daughters with *her*."

"Stop it, Laban," Samuel snarled.

"I won't! This woman needs to be done away with, not celebrated."

Fear rose in me as I remembered how, only months earlier, he had brought a mob together and tried to stone me to death.

Malachi stood. All eyes turned to him.

"I will not allow you to speak about my wife like that."

"*Your* wife?" He laughed loudly. "She's the cast-out whore of a Pharaoh."

I gritted my teeth, enraged. I felt tired of being wrongfully accused, and I no longer wanted to hear it. I stood and stared Laban in the eyes. "I am no whore."

All eyes turned to me and Malachi grabbed my arm. "Naomi, let me—"

"No, Malachi. I have listened to these lies for long enough."

"How dare you speak out of turn!" Laban yelled at me. "Learn your place, woman."

I sneered. "I know my place perfectly well. I was a *wife* to the late Pharaoh, nothing less, and he didn't cast me out, he loved me dearly. He sent me away to protect me from the wrath of the jealous queen Nefertiti and her scheming father Ay who wished to take my life and that of my son to ensure their rights to the crown."

Malachi sat down beside me and watched me proudly as I continued.

"I am not below you, Laban. I am well above you in status, so I will hold my tongue no more. Don't you think it strange that not long after I returned to this city, Queen Kiya, much beloved and favored by Pharaoh, died along with her son, the *only* heir? Have you never put two and two together and seen that the great Queen Kiya is me? I am not a harlot. I am a Queen of Egypt, and mother of the heir to the throne."

Laban leaned back, alarmed, as my family stared at me proudly. I knew that they believed my outburst had been a long time coming. I felt courageous again like I had when I stood in the courthouse and stepped forward to take Rena's place.

"Bow before your queen, Laban," Malachi said from beside me.

Laban's gaze shot to Malachi. "You knew?"

"Of course I knew. I was the one who brought her here, remember? I was the escort for the royal wives and concubines. I have known all along. Why do you think I paid such a high price for her?"

I could see Laban was humiliated and he began grasping for straws. "But as the Queen Kiya she is obviously idolatrous—"

"No, she isn't," Tobiah said. Laban looked to his son-in-law, his jaw hanging, as Tobiah hurried on. "You forget I knew her then, also. I administered to her in secret. She may have appeared to worship Aten, just as all of us had to do to survive, but she stayed true throughout."

"Papa," Miriam said softly. "Naomi brought husbands for me and my sisters who are goodly men and you love as your own sons. Why won't you see she is a blessing? Have you forgotten that terrible day when the Egyptian soldiers came and began searching houses for girls to offer up as a wife for Pharaoh? That day, Naomi stepped up and volunteered herself to save us all, even if she thought she was only saving her sisters."

That surprised me. I hadn't known the Egyptians had searched the city. I had been out playing games with my sisters instead of at home where we were supposed to be. Horemheb never said anything about that. I knew he planned on taking one of my sisters or me. It must have been a ruse, or some kind of scare tactic to remind us that the Egyptians remained in charge.

Once Miriam finished speaking, Laban looked me over and slowly bent forward into a bow. "Your highness."

He sunk into his seat, flushed with embarrassment and clenching his jaw.

Malachi shot to his feet beside me and raised his cup. "Come, let us drink and be merry. We are all friends and family here, so let's celebrate my taking such a wonderful wife."

"To Naomi!" Samuel called out and everyone else followed.

Malachi motioned for me to take my seat. As we both sat back down, I saw Papa watching with pride and tears in his eyes. He saw the woman he wanted me to be, the woman he raised me to be, and my heart swelled with love for him. I waited for eye contact from him and mouthed, *I love you.*

He sat up straighter, and stuck his chest out as he filled with pride, and mouthed back, *I love you too.*

As the feast wound down, Malachi took my hand to stand. "I believe it's time for us to leave."

Everyone nodded as he continued. "We are grateful for all your love and support through these past few years, and we look forward to strengthening our family relations with each and every one of you. But for now, it's time for us to bid you farewell and for me to take my wife to our new home."

He led me around the table, and among cheers and congratulations, we left Tobiah's house.

Outside, it felt oddly quiet after all the noise of the feast, and the evening air had a chill to it. I shuddered and pulled my shawl and robe closer around me.

Malachi looked down at me and asked, "Are you cold, my dear?"

I smiled up at him. "A little, but nothing I can't handle."

He wrapped his arm around my shoulders and pulled me against him. "It never ceases to amaze me how it can be so hot during the day, and then get so cold at night."

He led me into a brisk walk through the city to the outskirts of our sector where the farmland began. The grass and plants were green from all the irrigation, making the scene quite beautiful. Eventually, we reached a small house which overlooked the flooded riverbank.

I grabbed his arm to stop so I could look it over in awe. "Malachi, it's beautiful! How did you manage to get such prime land?"

"The late Pharaoh gave me a sack of gold. It seemed to go a very long way around here." He smiled down at me and rubbed my arm. "I'm glad you like it."

"I love it." I rushed toward the house. I touched the walls and found them sturdy and well made from mud brick and solid wood.

He pushed the door ajar and pointed to the frame. "I installed a latch, to help keep the children in, or out, if that's what you would prefer."

I laughed and grasped tighter onto his arm as he led me inside. The first thing I saw was a wide room with a stove, a table and chairs, which would be well lit by several windows facing north. To the back of the room was a wooden doorway that led to a small washroom, and to the left were two doorways with blankets draped over them.

"My sisters wove those." I hurried forward to touch one of them.

Malachi walked up beside me and pulled the blanket back to reveal a small room with another blanket, to divide it, pulled back, and two beds set up on either side. "This room is for the children," he said. "One side for the girls, and the other for the boys."

"Boys?" I beamed up at him.

He nodded. "Of course. I have every intention of having more than one son. I may call Tut mine, but he will not inherit the firstborn birthright; he has his own birthright to fulfill."

He leaned over and softly kissed my cheek. "I know we will have many children together. You're a strong woman and a wonderful mother."

I smiled, flattered by his words. He wrapped his arm around my waist and led me to the other room. He pulled the blanket back to reveal a smaller room with one bed. "And this is our room."

I turned and smiled up at him. "This is a large house, Malachi, and very well built. You honor me greatly with this."

He chuckled. "I did have a lot of time to work on it."

He pushed me back into the room, and kissed me.

71

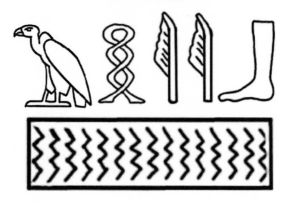

CHAPTER TEN

I climbed out of bed and dressed as Malachi rolled over to continue sleeping. It would be a lazy day, but I wanted to explore my new home and make sure it was ready for my children when they arrived that afternoon. I made sure everything was clean and tidy, and removed a scorpion from the girls' bed, before I went outside to find the kindling and wood for the stove.

While I was out, I saw, tucked away, a small hut. It held some empty pottery and jugs. There were also dishes of dates and figs, with a small jug of water left for us the day before. I picked them up and brought them inside before returning to collect the firewood. While I brought the fire to life, Malachi rose and came out to join me. He sat at the table and started playing with the food. "We should get some food and water today."

"I know," I moved and sat across from him. "I found the storage hut outside. You thought of everything."

He smiled proudly. "I had a lot of time to prepare, and your father watched me every step of the way."

I chuckled. "I don't doubt that for one second."

He tossed a date in his mouth and smiled. "Tut loves this place. He loves how close it is to the river."

"You've brought my children here?" I asked surprised.

He shook his head. "Just Tut. He would come down with your father or after we had finished in the fields."

"He never said a word, which is rather remarkable."

Malachi laughed. "I swore him to secrecy, but I didn't think it would actually work." He slid the dates toward me. "Eat up, Naomi. We need to go to the markets."

I stared at the dates, feeling uneasy. "I don't go into the market anymore."

He looked confused. "How did you keep your father's house so well supplied?"

I sighed and picked up a date, turning it over in my hand. "I sent Hepsati with one of my sisters. It was always hard to get them to trade with me, but after the last attempted stoning, no one will even look at me."

Malachi slammed his fist on the table. "Why didn't you tell me?"

"I didn't want to worry you. You were already so distracted with everything else."

"Oh, Naomi." He huffed. "Come on; let me take care of this." He stood, grabbed a few more dates, and offered me his hand.

We packed a small cart full of baskets and pottery and walked into town together. As we approached the marketplace, I grasped the cart handle, feeling nervous as the memory of my last assault flooded into my mind. Malachi looked down at my hand and shifted his over it. I looked up at him, and he smiled at me reassuringly.

We turned a corner and came face to face with the marketplace. At first, there seemed to be no reaction to our presence, but as we approached a stall to buy grain, the storekeeper turned away from us.

"Storekeeper," Malachi snapped. "Will you not sell us your goods?"

The storekeeper glared at him and pointed at me accusingly. "Not after you married that harlot."

Malachi grew angry. I grabbed his arm. "Leave it, Malachi," I whispered. "We can try somewhere else."

"No, Naomi," he said sternly. "You're not a harlot. I'm growing weary of everyone saying you are." He turned back to the storekeeper. "My wife is no harlot. I would appreciate it if you refrained from insulting me by saying such things."

"You deserve to be insulted for making such a poor decision in a wife. If she's not a harlot, then why does she have three children?"

Malachi went to raise his fist, but I caught it. "Stop, Malachi. Please—"

"What is the meaning of this?" We swung around to see Laban behind us, Tobiah at his side. Laban stepped toward the storekeeper and said, "Trade with this man. His wife has done no wrong."

I stared at him, my jaw hanging. I couldn't believe my own ears.

Malachi straightened and turned to Laban, also taken aback.

Laban rested a hand on his shoulder before speaking to the storekeeper again. "Let it be known among all the trader's that the daughter of Jorem, who is the wife of Malachi, is no harlot. I have repented of the things I have said in the past after being humbled by the truth. She is virtuous and beyond reproach, and any man who doubts it should come and see me so I can correct their errors."

He looked across at me as I grabbed Malachi's elbow. "Dear Naomi, I feel I have wronged you greatly and I must make amends for my mistakes. You saved many daughters in this city with your courage to face those evil men, and you came back unscathed and stronger than ever. I'm sorry for all I did and I will go about with you both now to mend the damage I helped create."

He turned to the storekeeper and tossed down some coins. "Give them that grain."

The storekeeper obeyed, and we filled up our storage jug. Laban and Tobiah walked with us as we went through the marketplace and bought all that we needed. If any of the storekeepers had misgivings with us, Laban was quick to correct them, which brought about quite a stir.

We finished purchasing what we needed, and headed back to the house. On the way, we stopped at the well so I could fill our water storage jug. I quickly drew a cup for each of the men before I began drawing to fill the jug.

The men talked quietly so as to avoid me hearing, but I listened carefully, having had Horemheb train me to keep my senses sharp to avoid foul play. Laban began the conversation. "Malachi, I'm sorry for what I have done. I didn't want to know the facts."

Malachi responded solemnly. "You can't begin to imagine all she has been through. The palace was terrifying and I was just a guard."

"How did she become the Greatly Beloved?"

A hesitant pause hung in the air. I glanced across to see Malachi clench his fists as Tobiah answered, "She was trained and tutored by Commander Horemheb himself. He pushed her upward and encouraged her to use her feminine charms and clever mind to make the king love her above all the other wives. She was also his eyes and ears in the women's wing, where Nefertiti ruled supreme until Naomi came along and dared to defy her."

Laban looked at Malachi, his eyes narrowing. "Why does this bother you, Malachi? Surely her status saved her from humiliation and grief, and with bearing the heir, she was able to free herself from being forced to marry Smenkhkare."

Tobiah answered for him in a hushed voice. "The Commander loves her. Malachi fears that he will come back and steal her away—"

"Like the high-bred Egyptians are so fond of doing," Malachi snarled. "They have no respect for another man's property, they just take what they want, especially *him*."

I felt angry at Malachi for calling me his property. Even if, in society, that was all I was, I thought him better than that. My grip loosened on the rope as I turned to glare at him and it slid, burning my hands. I winced and let it go. It fell with a loud splash into the well, which drew their attention to me. I looked at my hands to see the damaged skin as Malachi rushed over. He grabbed my hands to look at them but I pulled away.

"Property, Malachi?" I hissed under my breath.

His face fell. "Naomi—"

"Don't talk to me right now." I leaned over the side of the well to see the wooden bucket floating on the surface. "How am I going to get that back?"

"I'll climb down and get it." Malachi rushed back to the cart and pulled out a rope. I took a small piece of cloth and dipped it in water, then dabbed at my hands.

Tobiah took another cloth and wet it before tying it around my left hand. He then tied the piece I held around my right hand and whispered, "Naomi, was this reaction because we mentioned the Commander?"

"I don't like what you are insinuating, Tobiah," I snarled at him. "I love my husband. I chose him, didn't I?"

I pulled away from him, feeling annoyed that the Horemheb issue still seemed to be alive after so long. I walked over to the well to watch Malachi retrieve the bucket.

Once he grabbed it, he tossed the rope back up. I caught it and he climbed out. I began drawing water again and he said, "No, Naomi, you don't need to draw anymore today—"

"Yes, I do."

He wrapped his arm around my waist to whisper in my ear, "Stop being so stubborn. Laban is still with us."

I looked up at Malachi as he gently took the rope from my hands. I sighed, relenting, and allowed him to pull up the last bucketful and empty it into the jug in the cart. He then turned to me and lifted my wrists to look at my hands. "Have Hepsati draw for a while until your hands heal."

I nodded, and saw Laban smiling at us. "Ah, it's been a while since I have seen such a fine couple."

"Thank you," I responded, knowing he was trying to be kind to me to make up for all the trouble he had caused. I didn't want to let him feel like I didn't appreciate it.

Back at the house, Tobiah and Laban helped Malachi take the filled pottery and baskets into the storage hut before they left. While they unpacked, I took some grain to grind down, enjoying having something to take my anger out on, even if it did hurt my burned hands. By the time Malachi came in, the grain was a smooth flour and I was about to add some oil in it to begin making bread. He walked over and knelt beside me. "Naomi—"

"I can't believe you called me property," I said in a hushed voice. "I thought you were better than that."

He sighed and pulled my shawl off my head to touch my hair. "I know. I'm sorry."

I stopped mixing and looked into his eyes. "Why would you even say that?"

I saw him clench his jaw as his eyes flashed with rage. "It's the Commander. The very thought of him makes me angry. He would take you if he could, and I have always been afraid that maybe you wouldn't fight it. That you would let him…"

I clasped his face. "No, Malachi, I want to be with you. No matter how he felt, I married you."

Malachi sighed and took my hands to unwrap them. He looked at the burns and softly kissed them. "I'm sorry, Naomi. It's not like he has come for you, anyway. I shouldn't let it bother me."

A twinge of pain shot in my heart at his words, but I didn't allow it to grow into more than that. Malachi made me happy. He was a good man with a kind heart and gentle spirit, but Horemheb was clever and cunning and a fierce soldier, feared by the kingdom and most of its enemies. I had to force the minute feelings I did have for him aside and let my feelings for Malachi grow in their place.

I leaned forward and kissed Malachi quickly before I smiled at him. "Feed the fire for me?"

He smiled back at me and stood to go collect the wood.

A few hours later, the children arrived. Itani dragged Hepsati around behind her as she explored her new home, while Tut talked on and on about how much his cousin annoyed him and how when he was king he would make him pay for it. I turned my back from him to hide my smile as I snapped at him for being unkind.

CHAPTER ELEVEN

I left the midwife feeling elated. With Itani now more than four years old, I felt that it had been a long while since I last carried a child. I smiled down at Hepsati, who seemed more excited than me about the news. She almost dragged me to the fields to meet up with Malachi and Papa to tell them, while I held back so Itani could keep up with us.

When we reached the fields, we scanned for them quickly. When Hepsati saw them in the middle of the herd, she ran over, calling for Malachi.

Tut's head appeared from among the sheep and stared at her as she ran, while Papa rushed toward me. Hepsati flew passed him and jumped into Malachi's arms. "Hurry, Papa! Mama wants to tell you something!"

Papa reached me and lifted Itani as she pulled on his robe. "Is everything all right, my dear?"

I smiled at him. "Oh yes, everything is wonderful."

Hepsati dragged Malachi over to me and grasped my hand, grinning from ear to ear.

I looked up into Malachi's eyes as he watched me quizzically. I smiled at him in anticipation and said, "I just went to visit the midwife and she confirmed that I'm with child."

Hepsati squealed with delight and tugged Malachi's arm. "Isn't it wonderful, Papa? A new brother or sister! I'm so excited!"

Papa wrapped his arms around me and laughed. "Oh, Naomi! Praises be to the Lord! I have waited for this day to come!"

As Papa let me go, I looked up at Malachi. He had a dazed look on his face, but I could see a small smile curling at the corners of his mouth.

"Malachi." I smiled up at him. "What are you thinking?" I reached out for his hand, but he caught my arm and, forgetting all decorum, he pulled me up against him and kissed me.

"Ugh!" Tut grunted while I heard Papa laughing.

When Malachi let me go, he looked down at me adoringly. "Finally, this one is mine," he said softly.

I tilted my head and said teasingly, "I thought they were all yours."

He smiled and shook his head. "You know what I mean."

I laughed and rested my head on his chest, feeling grateful this one *was* his, and feeling excited to begin carrying his children and raising a family for him.

I entered the courthouse to collect Tut, who spent the day with Papa learning how to read and write. I entered, and saw a group of Egyptian courtiers stood in the center of the room, which surprised me. Seeing that I recognized them, I quickly covered my face and dropped my eyes. I looked down at Hepsati and pulled her shawl around her.

"Don't let them see you," I said quietly as we hurried by them to Papa's office.

They didn't even notice us as we passed. Once we reached the corridor, I breathed a sigh of relief.

I turned to hurry to meet Papa, but he burst out of his room. Upon seeing me, he rushed over and took Hepsati's hand. "Hurry, hide in here with Tut."

He led us into his office and shut the door.

"What is it, Papa?" I asked with concern.

He gazed at me, then his eyes fell to Tut as he answered, "The Egyptians are starting to move back. They intend to abandon Amarna."

"What?" I gasped.

He nodded, still staring at Tut. "The new Pharaoh is not fond of the city, and the courts are pushing for a movement back to the old religion. The people will slowly make their way down here when they can, but Pharaoh and his household will be back in the palace by the end of the month."

I glanced down at Tut. "What does that mean for him?" I asked in a hushed voice.

Papa shook his head solemnly. "I don't know. He is so young still, he just barely turned seven. Surely the commander will leave him until he at least comes of age."

"I hope so," I whispered. "Thank goodness he doesn't look much like his father."

Papa grasped my shoulder. "What about you, Naomi? What if you are discovered? Will they have you put to death, or worse, make you marry the new Pharaoh?"

I shuddered at the thought of being given to Smenkhkare. "I'll have to avoid being discovered. Luckily I look very different as a Hebrew than how I did as queen. Hopefully, no one will be able to recognize me simply for that reason."

I looked down at Hepsati, who bore a striking resemblance to Mordad. "But we will have to hide Hepsati's face whenever Egyptians are around. She looks too much like her mother for anyone to miss."

Hepsati blushed and dropped her eyes.

Papa sighed as he, too, stared at her. "She's twelve years old and will come of age soon. When she does, we will arrange for her to marry as soon as we can. That will help to protect her."

I stared down at Hepsati, wondering where the little four-year-old who had climbed out from under the table in Amarna had gone. I touched her face tenderly. "Hepsati, what say you? Would you be happy to marry soon?"

She nodded. "I would if it stopped my uncle from taking me as his wife."

I smiled at her, seeing Mordad's defiance in her eyes. "All right, Hepsati. Your grandfather will help Papa start looking for you. They will find you a nice, gentle man to protect you."

During that month, many ships lined the wharves and the river as the first wave of Egyptians flooded back into the city. When the royal family arrived, they paraded through the streets, which caught me off guard while out with my sisters in the marketplace. I grabbed Hepsati and pulled her behind some boxes just as Smenkhkare and Meritaten's chariot approached. I ducked my eyes and covered my face. Thankfully they didn't see me, but I saw them clearly.

Mayati had grown into a woman of twenty years, and easily as beautiful as her mother, even with the slight disfigurement she inherited from her father.

Smenkhkare was larger in stature than when I last saw him. He stood tall and strong beside his Great Wife.

Following them was Ay, who held his head up and refused to acknowledge the "slave race." He was obviously disgusted even to be in our sector.

After him came a string of wives and concubines, most of whom I recognized, except the younger ones. Their numbers were greatly depleted from what I remembered. I counted twenty-eight wives, and could tell there were less than a hundred concubines.

Then I saw a slender, pale-skinned woman with two small daughters. She hung her head and looked broken, but I knew immediately she was Gerlind. I gasped at the sight of her, and tried to follow her to catch her attention, but Adina caught my arm. "Where are you going? Are you *trying* to get caught?"

"It's Gerlind," I said in a hushed voice. "I have to see her."

"Not now you don't," she said fiercely. "Have some sense, Naomi."

I stepped back, knowing she was right. I couldn't approach Gerlind. But it was enough for me to know she lived, and I hoped I would eventually have the chance to see her again.

The procession drew to an end; the royal guard followed up the rear with their families. I held my breath, until finally, I saw Enoch and Jared with their wives and a small child each. I smiled and grabbed Adina's arm, but then I saw a sight that made my heart skip a beat. Both the wives showed signs of being with child again. I remembered how devastated Miriam had been when she heard I was with child. It wasn't that she was unhappy for me, but she had been married for three years and had not yet conceived. I knew I had to get to her immediately. The sight of her sisters both on their second child would break her heart, so I wanted her to be forewarned.

I squeezed Adina's arm once the procession passed and the crowd filled the street again. "We must hurry to Tobiah's house. I must warn my dear sister-in-law of her sisters both being with child. This is going to be a terrible blow for her. She already fears she is barren."

My three sisters all turned to me and agreed, so we scooped up our children and hurried to Tobiah's house.

Miriam stood outside beating the dust out of a blanket. As she saw us coming, she quickly finished and pulled down the blanket, smiling at us. "What a pleasant surprise! I didn't expect to see all of you today."

I gently took her arm. "Let's go inside and talk."

She opened her house to us and we greeted my mother-in-law Leah—who sat weaving a blanket—affectionately before I turned to Miriam. "We have news for you, dear sister."

"What is it?" She smiled at me eagerly.

"Our brothers-in-law have returned from Amarna with your sisters."

She clapped her hands with delight. "Oh, how wonderful! I have missed them so much! I'm excited to see my two nephews!"

I smiled at her and rested my hand on her shoulder. "We saw them with the royal guard as the royal family entered the city. They both look well..." I paused as I watched her face, wanting to be gentle with her. "And they are both in the family way."

Her eyes widened and her face fell. She stepped back and sank onto a stool. "They're both having a second child. And I have been unable to conceive one," she said softly.

I knelt in front of her and grasped her hands. "Dear sister, you are young yet. You're only nineteen, and sometimes youth can prevent conception, or even be dangerous. I saw it in the king's house; even the princess was killed from bearing a child too young—"

"My sisters are younger than me." A tear rolled down her cheek. "And we all shared the same wedding night. My husband will have me put out, I am a disappointment—"

"Oh, no, he would never do that!" Eliora gasped. "Tobiah is a good and patient man."

"But he's the oldest son and he needs a son to continue his line." She dropped her face into her hands. "I have failed him! He married the wrong sister."

Leah looked at us with concern in her eyes. "Dear child, sometimes these things just take time. My son will not be angry with you because of it."

I gently took her hands away from her face so I could look into her eyes. "Listen to me. Sometimes we are given trials to teach us patience and to rely on the Lord. Let us fast and pray with you so that you may conceive."

"I have fasted and prayed many times," she whispered. "But still nothing. God has forgotten me."

"No, never even think such things!" I gasped. "Sometimes His plan for us is just different from those around us. We may not be able to see it right away, but in the future, it will be clear. I look back at my life and I can see how the Lord has guided it so I could help and protect those I love, and even through the hard times, He never abandoned me. I had to wait and persevere through many things to get where I am, and although at times I feared for my life, or wondered how I could ever get through the day because my heart felt so heavy, I still made it, because the Lord brought me through.

"I know that you fear you may never bear a child, but think of Sarah, who was in her old age when she bore Isaac. You are still young and have many years left to conceive a child for your husband. Have faith, and tomorrow we will all fast together for you."

She stared into my eyes as tears streamed down her face. "I don't know if I can ever be as strong as you, but I'm grateful to have you as a sister so that you can hold me up when I'm weak." She threw her arms around me and wept onto my shoulder.

Several days passed before Malachi's brothers and their families could visit with us. When they did, I felt so proud of Miriam, who kept her smile the whole time and remained focused on being excited to see her sisters again.

On our way home from visiting with them, I felt the child within me drop and I paused, feeling uncomfortable, and held my belly while the child shifted inside me.

Malachi rushed to me and grabbed my arm. "What's wrong?"

I smiled at him. "It's nothing. This is normal. It means I'm drawing close to the delivery."

Hepsati and Tut's hands flew across to touch my belly as they saw it move from the right to the left. Itani clung to Malachi's leg, staring up at it with wide eyes. I giggled at my children, loving how much they enjoyed watching their new sibling grow within me.

But Malachi, out of concern, wouldn't let me walk on my own the rest of the way home, and back at the house he made me sit and rest while he put together some food for the family.

After the meal, Hepsati ducked outside while the rest of the family cleaned up and started to play games together. Suddenly, we heard a shriek and Hepsati burst back into the house sobbing uncontrollably. "I'm going to die! Something is wrong with me!"

Malachi spun alarmed and I sat up. "Hepsati, what happened?"

"I'm bleeding from... from... I'm dying, aren't I?" She sobbed harder and couldn't say another word.

I sank back, feeling relieved, and I glanced over at Malachi who turned away, trying to avoid the situation as his cheeks flushed. I stood up and took her hand. "You're not going to die. Come with me."

I took her out of the house and led her to the place of seclusion. "You have come of age now, Hepsati, and you will need to start going into seclusion for a few days, like you have seen me and your aunts do. Your Aunt Eliora is there right now and will watch over you and guide you."

She held my hand tightly as she stared at her feet while we walked. "Why does this happen?"

I glanced down at her. "It's part of the curse and gift we have been given as women. When Eve partook of the fruit in the garden, she broke the Lord's commandment, so she was cursed to travail in childbearing. But, by breaking the commandment, she also made it possible to fulfill another, higher commandment, which was to multiply and replenish the Earth. So, although we suffer pain and bleeding, we are given the great gift of rearing children, which brings us joy beyond compare. The bleeding is a sign for us; to show we are not with child. So when it doesn't come it's a sign that we may be carrying a child within us."

Her eyes lifted and she gazed up at me in awe. She then turned her eyes forward and whispered, "So Papa will arrange a husband for me now."

I took a sharp breath and looked down at her. It had come too soon. I still saw her as a little girl, my beloved Mordad's innocent child. I gently touched her dark hair, feeling a deep melancholy. "Yes, my dear, he will."

Her eyes fixed ahead. "Good. I don't want my uncle to find me and come after me. He always harassed my mother. He thought she was my father's most beautiful wife, and I remember my mother fighting him off.

Whenever he came to visit, she would sleep by the door to keep him from entering."

My heart sunk. I hadn't known that and it made me feel sick for poor Mordad, and so grateful I had sent her to Akhenaten the night he had been at the palace.

"I'm surprised you remember that," I said softly.

"I remember many things." Her gaze dropped to her feet. "I remember you grabbing Nefertiti by the neck when she tried to strangle me. I was terrified of you for several weeks after that because you had looked so ferocious. I couldn't understand why my mother loved you so much." She wrapped her arm around mine and she leaned against me. "But I do now."

I leaned down and kissed her head. "I love you, Hepsati."

We arrived at the place of seclusion and I knocked on the door. A woman answered and beckoned for us to enter, but I shook my head.

"Not me." I touched my belly and the woman nodded and stretched her hand out for Hepsati. Hepsati drew back shyly. I sighed and asked the woman to bring out Eliora.

A few moments later, Eliora came to the door with a wide grin across her face. "Hepsati! How wonderful! You and I will have time to bond for the next few days. Won't that be nice?"

Hepsati stepped toward Eliora. "Yes. Nothing bad is going to happen, will it? I have seen women give birth and they seem to hurt a great deal. Will this be painful?"

Eliora and I both giggled and I answered, "No Hepsati, you'll be fine."

I encouraged her forward, and Eliora wrapped her arm around Hepsati's shoulders, then shut the door.

I turned and headed for a well. I drew some water and cleansed myself. On my way back to the house, I came across Bilhan with his three children. He smiled, relieved to see me. I lifted his daughter onto my hip and paddled his older son for being rude.

"I was just heading your way," he said. "These seven days are near impossible for me. I don't know how she takes care of these three day in and day out."

I chuckled as we turned and walked toward the house.

"So what brings you out here by yourself?" he asked, looking concerned.

I shrugged. "Hepsati has joined Eliora."

"Oh." He flushed, and quickly changed the subject. "I remember running down this street when we were children. You were taller than all of us boys back then, and much stronger, too. I remember you humiliated Liam by beating him in a wrestling match." He laughed to himself, as we remembered his cousin—who married Rena—being pinned in the dirt by me. "You were positively terrifying to us. I remember when you pinned him, Samuel found you and was furious. He pulled you off by the hair and dragged you screaming back to your father."

I chuckled. "Oh, yes, Samuel really had it in for me back then."

"I'm certain he was jealous because you were so smart and everyone thought you were something special. He must have hated you being beloved above him."

I hung my head. "He did."

"But I remember, one day, it suddenly changed." He shifted the baby in his arms. "I've always wondered what happened."

I looked across at him and sighed. "I'll only tell you if you promise to never repeat it to anyone."

He seemed surprised, but agreed.

"I was fourteen," I began. "And a young man came to Papa to offer a price for me. He was the first, and Papa refused him. He told him that I was too clever and would be troublesome for him, but his second daughter, Adina, had a pleasant disposition and was much prettier. They discussed it in great lengths, going to and fro, but Papa was adamant that he would not give me as a wife. So the man accepted Adina.

"The whole while, Samuel was present and listened silently. He knew how insulting it would be for Adina to marry before me, and for the first time, he felt bad for my favor with our father. He saw that Papa would keep a tight grasp on me and prevent me from being given to any man.

"When I discovered Adina was espoused, I was distraught. I couldn't understand why Papa would allow her to be given before me, and so I went up onto the roof that night and cried. Samuel came and found me, and told me all that had happened. He began looking out for me then. He swore to me that he would ensure I married well, despite Papa's best efforts to keep me by his side. After that night, we quickly became close friends."

"So," Bilhan said. "Uriyah wanted to marry you?"

I nodded. "But Adina does not know that. We kept it from her to save her feelings. She and Uriyah have come to love each other very much, and so it doesn't need to be mentioned."

A smirk spread across his face. "That does explain why he always seems to size Malachi up when we are together."

I laughed. "No one could size Malachi up. He's very large in stature."

"Except his brothers, of course."

"Of course." I smiled.

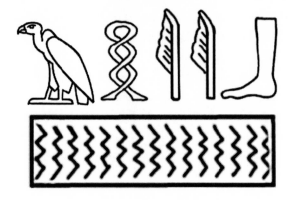

CHAPTER TWELVE

I awoke to a great gush. I sat up in fright. That wasn't how it usually happened. I had felt pains during the day, but nothing that concerned me. A severe cramp hit me and I wailed in agony. Malachi shot up beside me and grabbed my shoulders.

"Naomi, are you…?"

"Go get my sisters," I ordered. "And take Tut with you."

He leaped to his feet and rushed into the next room to collect Tut; I saw him dash out of the house with the sleeping boy on his shoulder. Hepsati appeared at my side within moments and grabbed my hand. "Mama, is the baby coming?"

I tried to smile, but another wave came upon me and I moaned in pain. When it subsided, I answered her. "Yes, Hepsati, the time is drawing near."

"Should I stay with you?"

I looked into her face and saw Mordad staring at me while I had delivered Tut and Itani. "Yes, oh yes, Mordad, stay," I muttered before another cramp rose up. As it subsided, I saw Hepsati stroking my belly with tears streaming down her face. "What is it?"

"You called me by my mother's name," she said in a hushed voice. "She was with you when you had Tut and Itani, and you wish she was here now, don't you?"

"Oh, Hepsati…"

She smiled at me. "It's all right, I know you loved her. I wish she was here, too."

As another pain arose, Itani rushed into the room at the sound of my wailing. She scrambled to my side and started to cry, not understanding what was going on.

"Hepsati, take your sister away," I ordered.

"But you—" she began to protest.

I cut her off. "Your aunts will be here soon. I'll be fine, but your sister is frightened. Take her to Papa."

She stood and lifted Itani from me, who screamed at being torn away while I was in pain. They headed for the door and a click sounded as it shut behind them. I glanced around the dark room and suddenly felt frightened. I found myself completely alone and I could tell the baby was coming quickly. As another wave of pain came, I screamed and started to sob as my fear rose with it. I worried I would have to deliver the child on my own, and I remembered how I had passed out from blood loss after delivering Tut. I became terrified of them rushing in a moment after the child had come and finding me unconscious in a pool of blood.

"Oh, God," I wailed to the heavens. "Let my sisters arrive in time. I'm so afraid."

Another cramp came, and then another and another. They rapidly drew closer together as I sobbed in fear. I rolled onto my side and curled up my legs as another hit me. It subsided, and I saw three of the most wonderful faces appear above me. My heart soared as Adina took my arm.

"Adina, I was so frightened."

"We're here now, dear Naomi." She smiled as Eliora took my other arm. Rena came behind me to help lift me onto the stool they brought into the room with them. "Rena, take those blankets away. They're soiled and are beginning to smell."

Rena rushed to obey, and soon returned with the midwife at her side and Hepsati behind her. That meant Malachi was outside, so with that knowledge, and my sisters with me, I relaxed and said a silent prayer of gratitude that I wouldn't be left alone to deliver my child.

It wasn't long after that the child came screaming into the world. Rena wrapped it in swaddling and began cleaning it, with a huge smile. "It's a son, Naomi."

Smiling to myself, I allowed my sisters to lower me back onto the bed as Rena wiped him clean. She then handed him to me so he could nurse. I chuckled as he latched on greedily, sighing with contentment. I looked up at my sisters. "Tell Malachi he has a son and to give him a name."

Eliora rushed out the door, and a few moments later she returned. "He wants to see him before he can name him."

I nodded. "All right; I will need a few moments."

We all waited while the infant nursed, then quickly fell asleep. Eliora gently lifted him from my arms and took him out to Malachi.

While she was gone, Hepsati crawled onto the bed beside me and snuggled up under my arm. "I'll stay with you until the time of isolation passes."

I smiled at her. "Don't you want to go stay with your Papa and grandfather?"

She shook her head and scowled. "No, I want to stay here with you and the baby."

I kissed her forehead. "You're a good girl, Hepsati."

Eliora returned and handed my son back to me. "Malachi says his name will be Zakkai."

Two months passed. I took Hepsati and Itani with me to help me do laundry by the river. I strapped Zakkai to my chest, but Hepsati did most of the work while I tried to keep track of Itani. Malachi and Tut were back at the house; we could see them planting seeds in a small garden. I grabbed hold of Itani's arm and lifted her out from among the reeds, and as I turned, I looked up toward the house and saw Papa approaching with a young man. I stared, wondering what he was doing.

As he approached, Malachi turned to him. Papa motioned to the young man, to introduce him.

I suddenly realized what was going on. I looked at Hepsati.

"Hepsati, come dry off. We should return to the house."

She leaped out of the water and dried quickly before we rushed up and stood by the windows to listen.

"You know she's an Egyptian *and* a Persian princess," I heard Malachi say. "And my wife relies on her a great deal to help with the children. I expect a high price for her."

"I understand," a new voice, the voice of the young man, said. "And I believe I can give you what she is worth."

We heard a sack of coins jingle before he continued.

"I will also help with planting your crops on the flood plains, when the water recedes, for five seasons. I am able to purchase land not far from here, so she can visit with her mother whenever she wants, and, being away from the main city, will keep her out of sight of any of the royal family who may recognize her."

"Hmm." Malachi grunted, and I carefully glanced in the window to see what was happening. He opened the pouch and looked into it, apparently counting the money.

Hepsati peeked around as well and gasped quietly before pulling her head back. She tugged at my sleeve.

"Mama, he is very handsome," she said softly. "Do you know who he is?"

I quickly examined the young man, who looked to be about eighteen and was indeed very handsome. He wasn't as tall as Malachi or Papa, but he had a strong build and a gentle face. However, I didn't recognize him.

"No, my dear," I answered.

Malachi's gaze shot up. He tossed the coins onto the table. "I will accept your offer."

He began walking to the door. I pulled Hepsati back to make it look like we were just coming up from the river.

Malachi opened the door, smiled excitedly at us and motioned for us to come inside. Hepsati placed the wet laundry by the door and took a deep breath before stepping in.

As we entered, the young man's eyes turned to her and he looked her over, catching his breath. He had obviously never seen Hepsati before, and was stunned by her beauty.

Hepsati blushed, her eyes lowered, and I wondered how Mordad would feel if she saw the exchange. I hoped she would be happy.

"Hepsati." Malachi motioned for her to approach him. She stepped forward and he placed his hand on her shoulder, then motioned to the young man with the other. "This is Joshua, son of Obadiah, from the tribe of Naphtali. He wishes to take you as his wife. Are you agreeable?"

Hepsati looked at him again and blushed even more. I glanced at him and saw him gazing at her with a small smile and a gleam in his eyes. I knew Papa had managed to find a wealthy family who would listen to and heed his requirements for Hepsati, and be able accept that she was not our race.

He must have told Joshua that she was lovely, but Joshua had not anticipated how beautiful she would be, and found himself mesmerized.

Hepsati glanced up at Malachi. "I am, Papa."

Joshua's face lit up and he looked up at Papa with excitement as Papa pulled the cup out for them both to drink. I rushed out and grabbed a bottle of wine and poured it into the cup before Papa handed it to Malachi. Malachi offered it to Joshua, who sipped before he offered it to Hepsati. She smiled and blushed again before she, too, sipped. Papa then led Joshua from our house, and as he left, he glanced back to get a last look at his future wife.

As more and more Egyptians arrived in the city, I felt grateful that Hepsati would spend the next year veiled in public. I had to be more careful, even though it seemed the story of Kiya's death was believed by all, and none assumed that a humble Hebrew woman could possibly be the once highly regarded Queen of Egypt.

About halfway through Hepsati's time of espousal, we were surprised by Tobiah rushing to our house and pounding on our door.

Malachi answered and invited his excited brother in. Tobiah smiled at the eight-month-old Zakkai and blurted out, "My wife is with child."

Malachi embraced his brother. "Tobiah, that is wonderful news!"

"Isn't it? She has been so desperate. She even began talking about finding a handmaiden to give to me as a second wife, so I could have a child. But I have been refusing, hoping she would eventually conceive. I guess my patience has paid off."

"I must go to her!" I exclaimed with delight. "She must be overwhelmed with joy."

"We will all go." Malachi grinned and embraced Tobiah again. "This is something we should all rejoice in together."

We collected the children and rushed to Tobiah and Mirian's house. I sat with Miriam and we talked together excitedly. As she spoke, I stared at Zakkai and I realized something. I had begun to be in the ways of women again, but it had only been once, almost two months earlier.

On the way back to the house, I spoke softly to Malachi so the children wouldn't hear. "I think I need to visit the midwife."

He looked down at me and raised his eyebrow. "Are you just saying that because...?"

I glared up at him. "No. I went into seclusion once, but it has been two months since. I'm not sure what to make of it."

He gently lifted Zakkai from me and tilted his head in the direction of the midwife's house. "Take Hepsati and go see her now. I'll take the children and buy them a toy each."

I took Hepsati and departed from Malachi to see the midwife. She checked me and declared that I was definitely with child again. I stood up, feeling stunned that it had happened so quickly, but Hepsati was just as excited as when we found out about Zakkai.

When we met back up with Malachi and I told him, he laughed. "Oh my dear Naomi, you are truly blessed!"

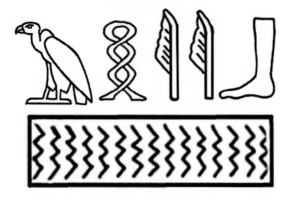

CHAPTER THIRTEEN

We ran through the streets, chasing after Joshua and Hepsati to his father's house. I struggled, being more than halfway through my pregnancy, but felt grateful for Miriam—who was just as slow as I was—to keep me company as we trailed behind the group. Our husbands both returned every so often to help us along. The two of us laughed, knowing they wouldn't dare close the door without the mother-of-the-bride present, but amused by our husbands growing more and more frustrated with our slower pace.

As we rounded the last corner, we saw the door open for us, and the party all inside. I laughed again as I saw Tobiah's head appear and call to Miriam in frustration. We entered, and the door shut tightly behind us. The celebrations then began with loud laughing and singing.

Suddenly, the door burst open and a patrol of Egyptian soldiers forced their way into the house.

Malachi grabbed Tut and shielded him and me from view, then checked that Itani was safe with her grandfather.

"Taxes!" the captain called out with a sneer. I knew he had not come for taxes, as he grabbed a girl sitting close to the door. Her father pulled her free and handed the man some money before the soldiers ransacked the place for anything they wanted.

I looked across to Itani and saw Papa pull his robe around her and struggle to pull a pouch of coins from his pocket. I then looked to the closed door which hid Hepsati and her new husband, and prayed the soldiers would not try to enter and discover her.

But, I had no such luck. Once they seemed satisfied they had found everything of worth among our party, a man turned to the door.

"Let's see what's behind there!" he called out.

Malachi rushed forward to block the doorway and spoke to them in Egyptian.

"This is a wedding. You will leave this place now; you have collected what you came for."

Several of the soldiers seemed to have their interest piqued by the knowledge of the gathering being a wedding celebration, and I saw lust glimmer in their eyes as they advanced on Malachi.

All his brothers rushed forward, and so did Samuel and my brothers-in-law, to protect the sanctity of the marriage chambers. A tussle started, and I felt frightened for my family as the soldiers drew their swords.

"Enough!" a loud voice bellowed from the doorway.

All eyes turned to see Horemheb standing there, looking more terrifying than I had ever seen him. I couldn't help gasping at the sight of him, which drew Malachi's eyes to me, but he didn't dare move.

Horemheb looked so much stronger, more powerful, and just as strikingly handsome, with his strong set jaw and dark, stern eyes that stared directly at Malachi.

"Get out, you swine!" he hollered at the soldiers. They all rushed for the door. Once every last one was out, he gave Malachi another stern look before he slammed the door shut.

"He's back," I said softly to myself, in shock.

Tut looked up at me confused. "Who, Mama?"

I looked deeply into Tut's eyes, feeling worried for him, but doubting Horemheb would come for an eight-year-old boy.

"An old friend from when we lived in the palace."

Malachi rushed at me and grabbed my shoulders, staring at me intently.

"Naomi, don't go looking for him."

I could hear tension in his voice, anger, fear.

"Why would I do that?" I asked.

He clenched his jaw. "Just promise me you won't."

"I won't," I answered earnestly.

His eyes narrowed on me for a moment, then his gaze dropped to Zakkai and my pregnant belly. "You love me, don't you?"

"Of course I do, Malachi!" I said in a hushed voice. "You never need to doubt that. I love you completely. You're my husband."

He touched my face, then kissed me. "It's still nice to hear it. I love you so much, Naomi."

The festive feeling seemed to fade after that, and didn't get back to the same level as before the intrusion. Eventually the call came—"Joshua has taken himself a wife!"—and there was cheering and brief rejoicing, but the celebration ended right after, and we all headed home.

The seven days passed. I helped Hepsati settle into her new home built not far from ours. She was so excited about her new husband, and told me everything she could about him. He was a kind and affectionate young man who could not stop telling her how beautiful she was, which delighted her immensely.

Tut came with me, but I'd left Itani and Zakkai with Malachi, who was working around the house and farm that day. Tut was excited to meet his new brother-in-law and found him a great deal of fun to taunt. He brought up, to my dismay, that he was the heir to the Egyptian throne. Joshua didn't believe him at first, but when Hepsati confirmed it, he became uneasy—which was exactly what Tut had hoped for. He spouted off orders and demands until I slapped him across the behind and told him to leave Joshua alone. He grumbled under his breath, which earned him another slap.

We finished visiting. I kissed Hepsati goodbye, feeling grateful she wouldn't be too far away. As we headed toward our house, it surprised me to find Malachi not in sight.

"Do you see your father, Tut?"

He looked around and shook his head. "No. Maybe he's getting something to eat, or putting Zakkai down for a nap."

"Maybe," I responded and wrapped my arm around his shoulders. He wrapped his arm around my waist and looked at my belly. "I hope it's another brother. Sisters are a pain."

I laughed. "You love Hepsati."

He grunted. "Only sometimes. But Itani drives me crazy."

I laughed. The door to our house flew open and Itani sprinted toward us looking frightened. "Mama!" she called. "There's a bad man in the house and he's yelling at Papa."

I hurried to the house feeling worried for Malachi. As we approached, I heard him yelling in Egyptian, "No, you can leave and never come back! I don't want you anywhere near my family!"

Tut pulled the door open before I could reach it and rushed inside. As I entered, I saw Horemheb turn and look at Tut.

"Is this the boy?"

Tut pulled up short, stunned that suddenly the attention had turned on him. Malachi gestured for me to leave, but before I could react, Horemheb's eyes lifted to me and he froze. We found ourselves at a standstill. No one spoke, and no one moved. The tension in the air grew so thick, it was suffocating.

"Kiya!" Horemheb whispered, his eyes widening on me.

"Horemheb," I replied softly.

His eyes dropped to my belly. I saw rage flare up in him and he spun on Malachi. "You told me she was dead! You told me only the boy survived!"

"It was for the best," Malachi snarled.

"For the best?" Horemheb said with a growl. "For all these years I believed she was dead and you say it was for the best? You just wanted to steal her away and hide her so you could keep her for yourself, and now look at her, carrying your filthy slave child. I should have you executed for your deceit, you miserable traitor!"

He reached for his sword.

I panicked and rushed forward without thinking. I grabbed his hand. "Horemheb, no!"

He froze again. He looked down at my hand for a moment before he grabbed it.

"She's coming with me as well. She is a Queen of Egypt, and as the mother of the true king, she will be highly respected."

Malachi rushed forward and pulled my arm away from him.

"Don't you ever touch my wife again!"

Horemheb sneered. "*Your* wife? Kiya is a Queen of Egypt—"

"Kiya is dead!" I yelled. "She died during the reign of Akhenaten. I'm Naomi now, a simple Hebrew woman."

Horemheb's eyes fell to my face as he took it all in. I watch his expression change and soften, until suddenly Malachi covered my head and pulled me behind him.

"Leave!"

"Not without the boy!" Horemheb growled.

"I don't want to go with you!" Tut spoke up defiantly. "You've been unkind to my father—"

Horemheb turned on Tut and said in a hushed voice, "*He* is not your father—"

"Yes, he is." Tut raised his chin. "He may not be my real father, but in my heart, he is."

Horemheb composed himself. As he turned, I saw the powerful, controlled man I had always known. "Kiya, you made me stay behind to protect the boy's birthright and crown. Now it is time for him to step forward and take his place as Pharaoh."

I moved to step around Malachi, but he held me back and hissed, "You promised me you wouldn't go to him!"

"I'm not going to him!" I snarled back. "I just need to talk to him. He wants to take Tut away, Malachi. I need to see what he intends for him."

I tried to step around him again, but he continued to block me.

"Malachi, please!" I said. "I need to watch over my son."

"*Our* son," Malachi growled.

"He's not *your* son," Horemheb corrected.

Malachi filled with rage and lunged forward. I leaped in front of him to block his assault and gazed up at him. "Malachi, you knew this day would come."

Malachi glared at Horemheb as he muttered, "Stay in sight of the house." He then let go of me.

I turned to Horemheb and motioned him to step outside.

We walked silently to the edge of the river where we stood for several moments. It felt horribly awkward between us. I glanced at him, as he stared out across the river, and took in his face. He still looked essentially the same, but it had been six years since I last looked at him that closely. He had aged well and looked very powerful. At thirty-one, the youthful appearance of his face was completely gone, and he looked like a full-grown man with rough skin where he shaved his face. He had a large, muscular chest and shoulders, which made him look stronger than Malachi, even if he wasn't as tall.

He turned to me.

I glanced away, feeling embarrassed for staring.

"Why do you want to take Tut now?" I asked gently. "Surely he's too young, and Smenkhkare—"

"Why didn't you send word to me?" he interrupted.

I paused, thrown off guard. "I thought you knew. I wrote the note to Akhenaten explaining what I had done, and Malachi had gone to you to seek an audience to deliver it—"

"He said it was from your brother." He turned to face me. "That wedding with all his brothers, that was you as well, wasn't it?"

I shook my head. "I was still married, I couldn't—"

"Of course you couldn't, you are a good and faithful wife." He laughed sarcastically. "I don't understand, Kiya—"

"Please, I am Naomi. Kiya is dead."

His eyebrow twitched as he continued. "I don't understand, Naomi, I thought you understood my intentions for you, I thought..."

He sighed and rubbed his eyes. "I thought you were dead."

"I'm sorry, Horemheb. I truly did believe you had been told."

He stared at me again, his eyes lingering over my face, before his hand came up and touched a lock of my hair that hung out from under my shawl. It made me start, as my own feelings bubbled to the surface at his touch. I stepped back from him and pushed away his hand, which seemed to frustrate him, but he held it in as he always had.

"Tell me what your plans are for my son," I said, trying to redirect the conversation.

"I will take him and give him his crown, as I promised you I would."

"But he is too young," I said softly. "He is only eight years old—"

"Don't make my sacrifice a waste, Naomi!" he yelled. "I gave you up for that boy, so you had better not keep him from me."

I stepped back, startled, no longer accustomed to dealing with Egyptians and their manipulative ways.

Horemheb turned and towered over me.

"I will take the boy, as promised." He stepped closer to me and growled, "It didn't take you long to remarry, did it? And now you are on your second child and the king has been dead just over two years. You were always

99

fertile, but for the king and *that* guard to both love you that well and that often, you must be something else in bed…"

I slapped him hard across the face. "Don't you dare talk to me like that!"

He caught my arm and pulled me closer. "You've hurt me, Naomi. Do you have any idea the pain I felt when I heard you were dead? I didn't even know I had a heart to break until that day. I wept in secret for months until I finally drew my focus to your son, thinking that since I couldn't save you, maybe I could protect him instead."

"I told you, I thought you knew." I pulled my arm free from him.

"Then why did you never send word to me? That day we kissed has haunted me all these years. The memory of it still burns hot in my mind. I should have taken it further, I should have—"

"No, Horemheb," I said firmly. "We went too far as it was."

He took a deep breath and smirked. "You are still so strong and honest. You have no idea how refreshing that is. But tell me, Naomi, did that day mean anything to you?"

I dropped my gaze and folded my arms uncomfortably, remembering how I had kissed him back and enjoyed it, and how afterward, I felt conflicted by my feelings for him and Malachi.

"I don't think—"

"Answer me, Naomi."

I looked up into his eyes. "It did mean something, but that feeling has passed. I'm completely devoted to Malachi. I love him with my whole heart."

He scoffed and looked away.

"Very well. Let's talk about your son." He turned away from me and folded his arms. "If you are concerned, then we will wait for his next birthday. That will give you time to prepare him and to say your goodbyes. Does that sound fair?"

"It does, yes," I answered flatly.

"Good. I will come back to collect him the day after. Good day to you." He turned and, without looking back, headed up the street toward the city.

I looked to the house where I knew Malachi was watching and sighed. A deep pain tugged at my heart, and I didn't know why.

CHAPTER FOURTEEN

I reentered the house and found Malachi standing by the window with his arms folded and his eyes narrowed, watching me. I couldn't help feeling angry with him for lying to Horemheb, and for making me believe he knew I lived. I knew if we didn't have it out right then, it would linger between us for days, keeping us apart. So I turned to Tut and said, "Tut, take Itani and Zakkai to visit Hepsati."

He understood what that meant, so he quickly picked Zakkai from the floor and pulled Itani out the door behind him.

Malachi watched them go from the window before he snarled, "Does he still intend to take you?"

My anger fizzled as I clenched my fists. "It doesn't matter if he intends to or not, I won't be going anywhere. But why did you lie to him? Surely you knew he would come for Tut one day. It has made everything more complicated than it needed to be."

"Why? Because you have feelings for him?" he bellowed.

I threw my hands in the air in frustration. "Malachi, I married *you*, I chose *you*—"

"Because I made sure of it by keeping *him* away."

"No, Malachi, I would have chosen you either way. I have loved you since I met you. You know that. How could you doubt me?"

He sneered and shook his head, turning away from the window and walking toward the table. "He always had a way of dragging you away. He had this power over you."

"Of course he did; he was my tutor and royally appointed guardian."

"But it was more than that!" he yelled. "You always turned to him and he always turned to you. Those rumors didn't start and travel so quickly without fuel for their flames. Even the king saw it, and told me when I came to him and passed on your message, that I shouldn't tell the Commander because he would come looking for you."

I caught my breath surprised. "He knew?"

"Of course he knew, Naomi!" Malachi swung around and stood over me. "He knew his subjects well, especially those closest to him. Which was why Horemheb began to lose favor; the king grew jealous of him. Come on, Naomi, you're supposed to be smart; surely you would have worked that out."

I placed my hands on my hips and glared at him. "Don't insult me, Malachi."

He laughed sarcastically. "How about you, then, my dear wife? You insult me by saying there was nothing between you and him when I know there was. I could see the way you looked at him. You were in complete awe of him because he challenged and flattered you. It made me sick with jealousy."

His words stung as they resonated within me. I rushed forward and pointed at his chest.

"So what if it was true? It isn't anymore! That was another place and time. Everything was so different there. Most of the time, I was afraid for my and my son's lives and I took any ally I could to help protect us. Horemheb offered to be an ally from the very beginning, and yes, because we spent a great deal of time together I grew fond of him, but it was nothing compared to how I feel about you."

Hot tears burned in my eyes. I stepped back from him to try to compose myself taking several deep breaths. He stood stiffly, waiting for me to continue. I wiped my eyes and spoke gently.

"He has come for Tut, and that's all he's going to get. Anything that may have been between us is done, because I love you. My children are yours, my heart is yours."

He sighed deeply and sank down onto a stool, rubbing his eyes. When he looked back up at me, I saw him fighting tears. I knelt before him, quickly kissing his cheek. He caught my hand, and encouraged me to sit on his lap. He wrapped his arms around me and pulled my head against his chest.

"Oh, Naomi, I love you more than anything," he said. "That man frightens me, he always has, but I know that I need to trust you."

I clung to him, enjoying his arms around me and feeling his love for me. "It will always be you, Malachi."

He pulled off my shawl and softly kissed the top of my head. We fell silent for a short while as we simply basked in each other's love. Finally, he whispered, "When will we have to give up Tut?"

I sighed sadly, wondering, like I had with Hepsati, where the time had gone. "The day after his ninth birthday."

"That's a few months away yet," he said softly and kissed my head again.

"I know, but I have to make sure he is prepared. I will have to tell Papa to increase his lessons so he can be fluent with the hieroglyphics. An illiterate king would be a serious problem." I sighed again and clung tighter to him. "I don't think I'm ready to let him go. He's still just a boy, and that place can be so cruel and unforgiving."

Malachi stroked my hair as we fell silent, and my heart ached for my dear, beloved Tut.

I stopped at the courthouse to bring Papa and Tut some food. Papa looked up and smiled at me as I entered, while Tut stared fixedly at the papyrus as he tried to decipher what it said. I placed the food on the table and looked over Tut's shoulder.

"The beginning of Amun, Papa? Don't you think that's a little scandalous, with so many Egyptians around?"

He shook his head. "They're opening all the old temples. The Pharaoh and Lord Ay have kept Aten as the supreme god, but the people have been pressing for religious freedom. So, I felt it would be important for young Tut to learn the ways of the people he will be leading soon."

"What are you stuck on?" I asked Tut. He pointed at the papyrus and I read it quickly before asking him, "What do you think it says?"

"'Life breath,' maybe?" Tut muttered.

"Close. It says 'breathing life into.'"

He pulled it closer to his face and grunted. "I'm never going to get this."

"Yes, you will." I patted his shoulder as I straightened back up. "Just be patient."

"Of course you'll get it." Papa grinned. "You are just like your mother and have a gift for languages."

Tut muttered something under his breath and I flicked his ear. "Tut, what have I told you about doing that?"

"Ouch, Mama!" he grumbled.

I broke some bread and handed it to him. "Eat, Tut."

He took the bread from me and nibbled on it as I stepped around and kissed Papa on the head. "You too, Papa."

He grinned at me and kissed my hand, then took a piece of bread for himself. "You take good care of me, Naomi."

"Someone has to," I teased before kissing his head again. I returned to Tut and kissed him on the head, also, before leaving.

Outside, I met Rena who handed me Zakkai. "How is he doing?" she asked.

I sighed and we turned to walk to the well. "I've been cursed with a child who is just like me."

She giggled. "Oh, Naomi."

We both took our time drawing water, as she too was with child, but nowhere near as far along as I was. Once we had filled our jugs, we both leaned back against the well to catch our breath while the children played.

"I can't believe this is number five," Rena groaned. "I feel like if I don't have a baby, my husband is trying to put one in me. It's exhausting."

I laughed. "They have no idea, do they?"

She smiled. "Not in the slightest. I don't know how Adina does it! Six seems impossible."

"I don't know how she copes with the two she lost," I said reverently.

Rena looked down and stroked her belly. "I've lost three."

I looked up at her surprised. "You never said anything."

She shrugged. "They were all very early in my pregnancies, so I didn't want to share it and cause too much grief. Plus, I've always seemed to fall pregnant again right away, afterward."

I smiled to myself. "We do seem to be blessed with being fruitful."

She laughed heartily. "Except little Eliora, who seems to be able to hold off between children."

I grinned. "Yes, how has she managed to only have three?"

I heard someone desperately call my name. We both stood up and glanced around. A moment later, Tut came tearing around the corner looking frantic, with Rena's husband, Liam, right behind him.

"Tut, what are you—?"

He flung himself into my arms and gasped, "Mama, hurry! Grandpapa has fainted!"

Liam grabbed Rena's arm. "Hurry, dear. Samuel believes it's his heart and he is dying."

Rena and I both gasped. We scooped up our smallest children while Tut and Liam collected the others. We hurried through the streets, and as we approached the courthouse, Adina appeared up ahead with her children trailing behind her as she rushed through the doors.

We burst in after her, and a moment later, Eliora and Dana arrived behind us. My sisters and I ran together to Papa's office, where we saw Samuel on the floor holding Papa's head in his lap. They both looked across as we entered. I felt relieved to find Papa still alive, but by the tears that streamed down Samuel's face, I knew he didn't have much longer.

"My beautiful girls," Papa said breathlessly.

We rushed to his side and knelt around him. He touched my sisters' faces lovingly before he gazed up at me and became choked up with emotion.

"My dear Naomi." His hand lifted and touched my hair. "I hated when I heard they cut this off. I'm so glad it's all grown back now."

He sighed and glanced at my sisters again. "I have such beautiful children."

His gaze fixed on Samuel as he clenched at his chest in pain.

We all leaned forward, grabbing at his robe and arms to try and comfort him. He began to breathe heavily as he gazed up at Samuel and gasped, "Watch over the family, Samuel."

"Of course, Papa," Samuel whispered.

"I've given you all the blessings of the birthright, so you are ready."

"I know."

Papa's gaze turned to me again. "Naomi, my brave, clever daughter. I'm so glad you found Malachi in that horrible place. Seeing you start a family with a man of the covenant people is my greatest joy, and to have seen you bear him a son made me so proud." He winced in pain again before he continued. "Kiss me, dear child, let me know you love me as I do, you."

105

I leaned over and kissed his forehead. He held my arm so he could whisper to me, "Never let them beat you, Naomi. How I feared for you while you were gone, but their wickedness will only grow. Tut is our only hope for freedom in this place. You, my Naomi, have given me that hope. You were always meant for greatness. I saw in you the bold spirit of our great ancestors, and like Jacob favored Joseph, I couldn't help favoring you."

He released his grip on me, and I leaned back.

We watched as his eyes darted among us, then, a warm smile spread across his face and he whispered, "Ziva…" as his breath of life left him.

We stared at him, stunned that he was gone, and startled by hearing him say our mother's name after he had refused to utter it since she died delivering Eliora.

We slowly looked to Samuel, who stared at Papa with tears streaming down his face. He glanced up and whispered, "Is this real? Please tell me I'm dreaming."

"It's real, Samuel," I answered gently.

He sobbed as he pulled Papa up against his chest and wept into his gray hair. I felt Eliora's hand grasp at my shoulder. I looked at her to see she was crying, too. I reached for her and she fell into my arms while Adina and Rena turned to each other.

Malachi and Laban burst into the room and stared down at Papa in shock. Malachi fell to his knees while Laban came forward and squeezed Samuel's shoulders.

"Samuel, let me help you prepare the body for burial."

Samuel nodded as Laban knelt down beside him and helped him lift our father. Malachi rushed forward to assist, while calling out for his brothers and our brothers-in-law. They all came in to help carry him, while Samuel covered his face.

We buried Papa, and most of our people came to pay him tribute. Each of my siblings and I were given gifts of condolences, and we felt greatly honored to know our father had been so well respected in our community.

As we departed from the place of burial, I saw standing back—almost out of sight—Horemheb, with his head bowed. I glanced at Malachi to see if he had seen him, but he was preoccupied with comforting Hepsati and Tut.

I looked back across and saw Horemheb staring directly at me. I nodded to him to acknowledge my gratitude for his sign of respect, and he nodded back.

Samuel began tutoring Tut in Papa's stead. I was returning to the farm with Tut, as he talked about what he had learned, but I wasn't paying much attention. I was trying to remember the last time I felt my baby move. I couldn't recall it moving all day, and I touched my belly, feeling worried.

Tut looked up at me and said, "What's wrong, Mama?"

I gave him a quick smile. "It's probably nothing. Keep telling me your story."

He looked concerned and touched my belly. "Is there something wrong with the baby?"

"Tut, it's nothing, I promise."

He didn't believe me, so he wrapped his arm through mine before he continued talking. We reached the river and I suddenly felt a wet, sticky feeling between my legs. I paused and caught my breath, looking down.

Tut turned to me, looking more concerned than before. "Mama, there *is* something wrong, isn't there?"

"Maybe." A sickening sensation crawled through me as I started to cramp. I held my abdomen and gasped.

Tut grabbed my arm to support me and he grew more worried. "Mama…"

"Tut," I said breathlessly. "Run ahead and find Papa."

He stepped back from me, and as he did, his gaze fell. He gasped, which cause me to look down. Blood soaked through my tunic. Fear wove through me, and I looked at Tut desperately.

"Find Papa, Tut, as fast as you can."

"No, I can't—"

"Tut, hurry!" I snapped at him as my cramping worsened.

He turned and ran down the street toward our house. I tried to stumble after him, but the cramps intensified, and I soon fell to my knees in pain. I knew something was terribly wrong with the baby. I began to sob.

Suddenly, I was lifted up off the ground. I looked up, surprised to find Horemheb carrying me in his arms. "Horemheb! You shouldn't, I'm impure right now. I'm covered in blood."

He smiled at me. "Naomi, do you think that's something I'm not accustomed to?"

"But this is different."

"I don't care."

He tried to carry me toward the house, but my cramps grew stronger and pressure built between my legs. I wailed in pain and begged him to put me down. He gently placed me on the ground. I felt the baby coming.

"You have to find one of my sisters or a midwife!" I begged him.

"I'm staying right here with you," he said defiantly as he grabbed my knee.

"No, you can't, the baby's coming."

"Then I definitely can't leave you alone."

I stared at him, stunned, as I tried to control my breathing. "You can't deliver a baby! You've probably never seen a birth before."

"Ah, I have, actually." He tried to smile at me. "It may not have been human, but…"

I wailed as I felt the child pressing down on me. I felt terrified. I couldn't believe he compared me to one of his beasts delivering in the field or stables, so my wailing also came from being annoyed with him. "You can't uncover me, Horemheb!"

"Who else will, Naomi?" He met my eyes and pulled up my skirts.

Shame washed through me, but I couldn't look away as he quickly examined the situation. He pulled off my shawl to wipe away the blood. He glanced at me. "I see feet."

"Oh no!" I gasped. "It's coming out the wrong way!"

"Can I turn it?" he asked, trying to stay as calm as possible.

"No, no! Just try gently pulling!"

I felt the child slide lower as he grabbed hold. I screamed in pain, but a few moments later he held it, rubbing its back. "He's not breathing."

I tried to sit up, but felt too weak. I fell back as I watched him working intently on the child. "What are you doing?"

"I've seen my servants do this with animals that are born without breath," he muttered.

"Horemheb." I gasped breathlessly. "He's dead, that's why he came so early." I gasped as the after-birth passed, and felt very weak. "Horemheb, I need you."

108

I rested my head back, feeling faint. Just as I began to pass out, I saw him place the infant down and turn to me with a worried expression.

I awoke in my bed feeling dazed and confused. Then I remembered what happened. I touched my belly. I ran my hands over my diminished abdomen and cried. I had lost my baby. I felt as if my heart had been torn from my chest.

Malachi must have heard me. He burst into the room and knelt down at my side, reaching for me.

I pushed him back. "Malachi, I'm still bleeding—"

"It doesn't matter, Naomi. Not now." He pulled my head against his chest.

Feeling the security of his body, I allowed myself to sob loudly in grief. The pain ran so deep, I thought I would never recover. Malachi climbed up on the bed and held me tightly in his arms while I clung to him in a desperate attempt to ease the pain.

We stayed that way for more than an hour, until I finally regained some control over myself. My tears subsided, but my grief did not, so I continued to cling to Malachi as I listened to what was going on in the house. I heard Tut talking quietly, before I heard Hepsati's voice; then I heard a man's soft chuckle. My eyes widened in surprise as I realized it was Horemheb. I looked up at Malachi, who stared off, his mind elsewhere.

"Malachi?" I said softly.

He took a sharp breath as he came back to reality and looked down at me. "Naomi."

"Where is the baby?"

"He has been taken to be prepared for burial."

I rubbed at my eyes. "How long have I been unconscious?"

"A few hours," he answered as he stroked my hair.

Tut made a loud groaning sound and Horemheb laughed.

"Tut likes him," Malachi said. "I guess that's a good thing if he will be watching over him once he goes to the palace."

"I can't believe you let him in the house."

He scoffed. "I couldn't exactly stop him. He was carrying you and you were both covered in blood. I had barely come back in from the fields and Tut came running to me frantically. He told me what happened and I ran inside to grab some cloth for you, when *he* came in with you in his arms and the baby wrapped up in your lap. I was so shocked; all I could do was step over and pull the blanket aside so he could put you down in here."

I rolled away from him to examine myself. "I've been washed and changed..."

"That was your sisters," he responded. "I sent Tut out to bring them here. Right now they're with Tobiah, burning your clothes and the remnants of the birth."

I turned back to him and touched his face. "You are so calm; how are you doing it? I feel like I'm about to be torn apart from the inside out."

He rolled so he leaned over me, before he kissed me quickly and said, "I wasn't, before. I was terrified I would to lose you. You have no idea how much blood there was. When your sisters arrived to clean you up, I held the baby and wept over him, and prayed that you wouldn't soon follow. The Commander came back in then, after washing and changing, and sat beside me. He never said a word, and I couldn't send him away, not after what he had done." He looked down at me with concern. "Tell me, Naomi, and be honest; did he uncover you?"

I blushed. "He did. But there was no other way; we had to get the child out."

His face turned stone cold as he pulled me up against his chest. "I know."

When my sisters and Miriam returned, I insisted on getting out of bed to see my child and eat something. As I stepped out of my room, Horemheb turned to me. I couldn't help staring at the sight of him in Hebrew clothes and without a hat on, exposing his short, dark hair.

"Still not going bald, Horemheb?" I tried to say lightly as I passed him.

"No. Call me unconventional, but I like my hair."

I smiled at him, but then my eyes fell upon a tiny bundle, and my heart sank. I reached out and lifted the tightly swaddled infant, who looked underdeveloped. I wondered what I had done wrong, which only made me feel heartsick, and my tears fell again.

Horemheb stood beside me, but Malachi pushed through and pulled me away from him. This action seemed to cause everyone to hold their breath as they watched tensely.

"Malachi," I said softly. I looked up at him as he stared fiercely at Horemheb, who rested his hand on his sword. "Our child just died. Now is not the time for this madness."

I looked across to Miriam, who held her belly, looking very pale. I knew what she was thinking. Being only a few weeks ahead of what I had been, she was afraid of losing her child after she had prayed and waited for so long.

I looked away from her, feeling envious and grieving even more for the loss of my child's life.

I walked slowly to my room again while stroking my son's cheek. I rested on the bed with my baby beside me, and snuggled him while staring into his tiny face. I soon heard the hushed voices of Malachi and Horemheb arguing.

"You should leave," Malachi demanded. "You know she's well now, so you have worn out your welcome."

"Excuse me," Horemheb said with a low growl. "I saved her life!"

"Because you have been following her since you came here several weeks ago!" Malachi snarled.

"I haven't been following her, I just check on her. She's still under my guardianship as appointed by the late king."

"I can't believe you are still using that excuse."

"You obnoxious slave!" Horemheb's voice rose slightly. "I saved your wife's life and this is how you treat me? You don't deserve to have Kiya."

"And you do? You murderous—"

"Enough!" Tobiah growled.

"He uncovered her!" Malachi hissed.

"How else was I going to get the child out?" Horemheb said defensively. "I could have just left her to die, if you would have preferred."

"It would have been better than having *you* see her."

"Malachi!" Tobiah gasped, horrified.

Rena slipped into the room with me and rushed to kneel beside me.

"Don't listen, Naomi," she whispered. "Malachi doesn't mean what he's saying."

She climbed up on the bed and wrapped her arms around me. I sighed as I heard them continue to argue, while I stared at my baby.

Rena stroked my hair back from my face before she kissed my cheek. "Naomi, you never told us that the Commander was in love with you."

"He isn't," I responded, trying to convince myself as well. "He's trying to do something; I'm not sure exactly what. Maybe use my status as mother of the heir to his advantage or something like that."

"No, Naomi, he really does, I'm not blind. Why else would Malachi be so jealous? Why else would he have helped you when men should flee? Why else would he insist on staying now?"

"Because that's what he does, Rena," I whispered, feeling my heart ache at her words. "He's a master manipulator and his intentions are never clear."

"I don't believe it," she said firmly.

"That's why I survived in that palace and you wouldn't have."

I felt her pull away from me, and I knew I had hurt her. "You're in pain, Naomi. I'll leave you alone to grieve."

She left me in the room, and I heard that the arguing had stopped.

My son was buried beside my father. I stared at the two graves after the rest of the family departed, my grief growing deeper and more mournful. Within a month, I had suffered from two deaths and two heartbreaks and I struggled within myself to keep going.

Malachi rested his hands on my waist as he stood patiently behind me. I grabbed for his hands, feeling grateful for his strength. He had not once fallen apart, and stepped up to fill my place when I became so overcome with sorrow, I stopped functioning. I even stopped eating, feeling like there was no point, so he and Tut had forced food into me.

"Come, Naomi," he said gently. "You need to eat something."

I nodded and turned as he guided me home. I hung my head most of the way, feeling heavyhearted and not wanting to look at the world around me, until Itani grabbed onto my skirt and said, "Mama, Benoni is in heaven now right?"

I started at her words, thinking about my sweet little baby. "Yes, Itani, he is."

"Then he will be fine. Grandpapa will take care of him, and so will Yahweh."

I grabbed at Malachi's robe, feeling as if a great weight had slammed into my chest. My faith had wavered, but her simple, child-like faith impacted me instantly. My baby wasn't dead, neither was my father, they were just doing the Lord's work elsewhere, and my father would indeed be watching over my child, as well as my nieces and nephews who had been lost. "Yes, Itani, they will watch over him. He is very blessed."

She smiled at me. "Then I am happy."

I reached down and touched her hand. She let go of my robe to hold mine. I smiled down at her, feeling my grief lift, knowing her words were true. I looked at Tut, who carried Zakkai, and realized how blessed I was. I had three wonderful children of my own, as well as Mordad's beautiful daughter, and I was still young enough to give my husband more. No, Benoni wasn't to be my last, and he definitely wasn't my only child. I needed to pull my chin up and keep going. In a few months, Tut would leave for the palace and I needed to be strong for him.

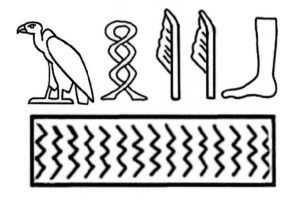

CHAPTER FIFTEEN

We feasted on Tut's favorite foods: roasted lamb, barley bread, eggs, figs, and pomegranates. We laughed and talked loudly together, enjoying our time as a family for probably the last time. I felt reassured that Tut was ready, but I still felt afraid for him. I knew Smenkhkare would not take kindly to a newcomer who had more right to the crown than he did, especially because Tut was supposed to be dead.

The next day, the sun had barely risen when I awoke to a knock on the door. Malachi hurriedly dressed to answer it, and while I pulled my clothes on, Tut burst into the room and leaped into my arms.

"Mama, I'm so afraid."

I stroked his brown curls, knowing by the end of the day they would be gone for good. "There's no need to be afraid, Tut. This is what you were born to do. Horemheb will watch over you."

"But I want to stay here with you." His grip tightened around me.

I glanced up as Malachi pulled the blanket back and looked down at us with a pained expression.

I sighed sadly. "Tut, it's time to go."

"No!" He pushed harder against me and held on as tightly as he could.

I glanced to the doorway and saw Horemheb standing behind Malachi, watching us. I suddenly had an idea.

"Why don't I come with you today to help you with the transition?"

Horemheb's face fell and he shook his head.

"Could you, Mama?" Tut looked up at me with hope in his eyes.

114

"Yes, I—"

"No you can't, Naomi," Horemheb said. "It's too dangerous for you, since you don't want to take your place among the royals."

Tut glared at him. "I *want* her to come."

He clenched his jaw before he pointed at me. "I blame you for his obstinate attitude. His father never had an ounce of it."

"Yes, he did," I said simply.

He shook his head. "Fine, but since you're supposed to be dead, we will need to make up a story for your presence. There's a good chance no one will recognize you as a Hebrew because you look so different, but having a Hebrew woman with him may raise questions. You will be my servant who cared for him after Kiya died. I chose you because his mother was a Hebrew and I wanted someone who would raise him like she would have."

"I can do that," I responded.

"Naomi." Malachi stepped toward me and grabbed my shoulder. "I'm not sure if this is a good idea. You have other children who also need you, and if you're caught—"

"I won't get caught," I said. "Tut needs me, Malachi."

He sighed, knowing it wasn't a battle he could win. "All right, but please be careful. You know I'm going to spend the whole day worrying about you."

I gently encouraged Tut to let go of me so I could kiss Malachi. "I know you will, and I appreciate it."

He chuckled and shook his head. "Go! Get this day over and done with."

I took Tut's hand and we followed Horemheb out the door. As we walked up the street, my sisters hurried toward us.

"We didn't want to miss saying goodbye," Adina said, breathless from the brisk walk.

They each held Tut tightly.

"Your cousins will miss you," Eliora told him.

His face fell and he answered solemnly, "I will miss them, too."

"Tut!" a voice called from behind us. We turned and saw Hepsati running up the road. She threw herself at him. "You can't go without saying goodbye to me, little brother."

He wrapped his arms around her. "Hepsati, you tell Joshua if he doesn't take care of you, I will have him thrown into a pit of lions."

We all laughed as she pulled away. "I will, Tut."

I saw her unconsciously rub her arm where she still bore a scar from the lioness' bite.

"Come, Tut, come, Naomi," Horemheb said, gesturing for us to leave.

"You're going, too?" Adina gasped, grabbing my arm.

"Yes, Tut is feeling a little nervous—"

"Then we are going as well," Rena interrupted me.

Horemheb groaned. "No, one of you is bad enough—"

"Yes, we will all go," Rena snapped at him.

"I can't say you *all* raised him."

"Actually, you can," I said, as a new excuse for our presence came to mind. "It was fairly common knowledge I had sisters, but I never specified how many. Four sisters would be believable for a Hebrew family, and since we all look similar, no one would pick me out as his mother, they would just believe I am another sister. You can say we are his aunts who raised him."

"No, Naomi. It's too dangerous. What if Smenkhkare decides he likes the look of you and tries to steal you all away as concubines? Your sisters are beautiful women."

"We are all married and have children," I answered. "That would deter him, and you can protect us."

He huffed. "This was what I meant when I said I blamed you for his obstinate attitude. Very well, they can all come. Having four would draw attention away from you."

"Five," Hepsati interrupted. "I'm coming too."

"No!" Both Horemheb and I snapped at her.

She took a step back with alarm. "Why not? He's my brother and I'm married as well!"

"You look too much like Mordad," Horemheb said firmly. "Smenkhkare always coveted her, and finding you would be too wonderful for him to pass up. He wouldn't care that you are married."

"But I—"

"Stay here, Hepsati," I commanded her. "I don't want to see you taken back to that family. Your mother wanted you free of them, so don't risk being caught and forced to be his wife."

She huffed and folded her arms. "Fine. I'll stay, but only if Tut promises me he will visit."

116

"Of course I will," Tut answered, looking alarmed. "Why wouldn't I?"

I glanced at Horemheb, who scowled. He reached for Tut's arm and said, "We will definitely try."

He looked at me again, and I knew the chances for Tut to visit us would be very limited.

Horemheb led us through our sector of the city, which brought many confused stares. While we walked, I gave my sisters a rundown of what would be expected of us as we entered the Egyptian sector and the palace.

"We must remain three paces behind Tut and Horemheb at all times, and we must be in order of seniority. I will go first, so you can follow me and do as I do. We should also cover our faces, and not reveal ourselves unless Horemheb commands it. We must make it look like he is our master, or we will be treated with contempt and possibly attacked. When we enter the palace, keep your eyes low at all times, and when we are taken before the king, we must sink to our knees and stay there, unless told otherwise."

They all agreed, and as we passed through an archway into the Egyptian sector, they all fell behind me as we veiled our faces. I watched the crowds carefully as we passed through. I saw that Horemheb was still feared by the people; they made way for him and bowed respectfully, but as he passed, I saw them watch Tut curiously, before their eyes fell on us. I knew by the way they looked at us they wondered what we had done to deserve Horemheb's attention, and whispered of a possible public execution in the near future.

We took a sudden turn, which caught me off guard. Instead of heading to the palace, Horemheb guided us toward the temples. It confused me, but didn't dare speak up to ask what he was doing, not with all eyes upon us.

He took us straight to the Temple of Amun-Ra. Horemheb demanded that we be taken to the high priest. We were led through the temple, which was being repaired and returned to its original glory. Reliefs were repainted, broken altars and statues replaced, and the chanting of priests filled the rooms.

Horemheb brought us into the central room. The high priest stood at his prayers, then turned to us. At first, he looked angry for being disturbed, but when he saw Horemheb, his expression became fearful. "Commander, what brings you here?"

"This boy." Horemheb pulled Tut forward to show him to the priest. "This is the son of Amenhotep the fourth."

The priest, shook his head, confused. "I'm sorry, I thought there wasn't one."

"There was. He is the son of the greatly beloved Queen Kiya."

"Tutankhaten?" The priest seemed even more confused. "But the boy is dead."

"No, he is standing right before you. After the assassin killed Queen Kiya, the boy was placed in hiding with his aunts by my orders so his life would be preserved."

The priest stared at Tut, who stood firm. Then he looked to us and recognized who we were instantly. "The daughters of Jorem are his aunts? But that would mean—"

"Kiya was a Hebrew, the eldest daughter of Jorem," Horemheb said tersely.

The priest looked disgusted. "He was always a foolish man. Whoever heard of making a Hebrew a royal wife?"

"He did as he pleased, priest, you know that. But you cannot deny his heir."

The priest looked Tut over closely before ruffling his hair. "He looks terribly Hebrew."

"So did Kiya before she was transformed. Even you didn't recognize her when she visited this city."

The priest withdrew his hand and examined Tut.

"No, I did not," he mumbled, remembering when I visited as Kiya. He reached over and tried to pull off Tut's robe.

Tut pushed him back and glared at him. "Don't touch me!"

I glanced at my sisters and saw them all raise their eyebrows, each of them clearly thinking the same thing as I did—that Tut was far too much like me. Anger flashed across the priest's face, but Horemheb laughed.

"The boy is a natural-born king."

The priest scowled at Horemheb. "Of course you would forgive his insolence. I have heard those rumors about you and his mother. The boy is probably not even the late king's—"

Horemheb grabbed the priest roughly by the sash. "What are you insinuating, priest?"

The priest gazed at him fearfully and backed down. "Nothing, Commander."

Horemheb let him go. "Good, because I'd hate to have to remove your head from your body."

The priest grasped his neck and swallowed hard.

Horemheb glanced back at me before he spoke again. "Now, shall we prepare the boy?"

"Yes, Commander." The priest bowed quickly and motioned toward a room to the side. We followed him, but at the doorway, he stopped my sisters and me. "You cannot enter."

"Yes, they can," Horemheb said.

"No, they are Hebrew women—"

"Yes, they can," Horemheb said, more forcefully.

The priest flinched, his eyes widening, and allowed us to pass.

The tight room had a window cut high above us to allow a small amount of light that bounced down from two mirrors. A tub sat in the center of the room, filled with hot water—like the one I had been placed into for my own cleansing ritual in Amarna—and the air smelled strongly of incense.

The priest removed Tut's clothes and had him climb into the tub where he blessed him. Once he finished the blessing, he grabbed a razor.

Horemheb stopped him. "I will take it from here. I know the ritual."

The priest didn't dare question him, but simply handed over the razor and departed.

Horemheb offered it to me. "I think you should do this."

I stepped forward and took the razor from him, then knelt down behind Tut. I sensed Tut trying to be brave as he stared fixedly ahead. I gently stroked his thick brown hair and kissed it, grieving for it, remembering how my own had been removed so harshly, and how his was just like mine. Then, I brought the razor up and began shaving.

The first lock of hair I took and tucked into my pouch on my belt, with the knife I kept there. With the next few strokes, my sisters came forward and also took a lock each. Horemheb stood back and watched solemnly as we tended to my son with reverence. Once he was completely bald, I ran my hand over his scalp to check it was smooth, before softly kissing the back of his head.

"You're a brave boy, Tut," I said.

His hand came up and ran over his head before it dropped back into the water. He didn't make a sound, but held his chin up as he struggled with his emotions.

119

Horemheb brought me oil and perfume. We helped Tut out of the water and rubbed him down with them. He never even flinched.

Once we finished, Horemheb knelt in front of him and showed him how to tie the Egyptian skirt around his hips, before attaching one of his own daggers to Tut's belt.

"Always keep this on you," he told him. "You never know when someone might try to hurt you."

"Is that why Mama carries her knife with her, because you told her to?" Tut asked.

Horemheb looked up at me and raised his eyebrows. "You still carry—"

"I do, yes," I said quickly, feeling caught off guard.

He seemed mildly impressed before he returned his focus to Tut. "Yes, Tut, that's exactly why."

He stood up and turned Tut around to face us.

I looked at my son, and for the first time I saw an Egyptian Prince.

"Oh, Tut," I said breathlessly. "Your father would be proud."

He shifted uncomfortably. "Maybe, but Papa would think I look silly."

Horemheb grunted with disgust while I stepped forward and held his shoulders.

"Tut, you're a prince. I have always told you that, and now is your time to be one. This is how you must look now. You may not like it, but it will grow on you as you become accustomed to it. Papa had to dress like this for many years, and he had some painful experiences during that time. That's the only reason why he doesn't like the way Egyptians dress."

He sighed. "At least I don't have to wear all that jewelry and makeup—"

"Yes, you do," Horemheb interrupted. "We just have to go elsewhere for that."

He signaled us to veil ourselves again, then led us out. He scanned the room for the high priest before motioning him to come over.

The priest rushed to obey, and as he bowed, Horemheb said, "I need you to change his name."

"What's wrong with my name?" Tut asked, looking up at him.

"The Aten is not the god of the royal family," Horemheb answered shortly.

Tut opened his mouth to speak again, but was cut off by the priest anointing his head. "You will now be known as Tutankhamen."

As the priest stepped away from us, Tut muttered, "That's not so different, I guess."

Horemheb smiled with amusement before leading us out of the temple. As we entered the courtyard, he threw a shawl over Tut to shield him from prying eyes.

He led us to his estate, which I hadn't seen since we visited while I was queen. I gazed around with surprise at its transformation. The gardens were well groomed, the stone tiles no longer sprouted weeds and grass from between the cracks, and the walls and floors had been cleaned, painted, and polished. Statues had been replaced, curtains hung, and the wooden doors repaired.

As we passed through, we saw only an occasional servant working, but in general, the house was empty.

With no one else around, I felt safe enough to talk to him. "Horemheb, when will we be going to the palace?"

"Once the boy is ready," he answered as he led us upstairs and pushed open a door.

He walked in. I instantly knew the wide-open room was his bedchamber. It had an open wall leading to a balcony overlooking his gardens with heavy drapes he could pull across for privacy. In each corner of the room stood a potted palm, and to my right sat his dresser and mirror, his wigs and hats set out on it. By the left wall lay his large bed, a canopy hanging open over it.

I followed him in, but my sisters hesitated at the doorway. I looked back at them. "Come on."

"But…" Eliora looked conflicted, but Rena's eyes lock with mine as she lifted her chin and stepped in after me.

The other two quickly followed, and as Rena passed me she whispered, "I can do hard things, Naomi."

I felt a twinge of guilt, knowing her words stemmed from the day my baby died and I had snapped at her harshly. "I know you can, Rena."

Her eyes flashed at me angrily before she looked back at Tut. I felt nervous about her doing something rash to prove herself to me, but before I could say anything, Horemheb called me forward.

I hurried over and stood beside him as he sat Tut in front of his dresser, facing the mirror. We gave Tut a moment to stare at himself with amazement, having rarely seen mirrors in his lifetime, before Horemheb handed me some eyeliner. "Show him how it's done."

I knelt down beside Tut and demonstrated on myself first what he needed to do, then wiped it off and handed him the eyeliner.

He took it and turned to the mirror, carefully drawing the lines on himself. When he finished, I smiled at him proudly before touching him up ever so slightly, to even out the lines.

Horemheb then brought over some jewelry, which I recognized as my own from my days in the palace.

"These were your mother's," he told Tut. "I picked out the jewelry, which could be worn by a man as well as a woman, for you."

He rested one of my necklaces around Tut's neck, then clipped some armbands around his wrists, tightening them as much as he could.

As he did so, I couldn't help staring up at him, wondering how he managed to get hold of my jewelry.

He sensed my gaze on him, and he glanced at me before he tried to ignore me.

Suddenly Adina's voice cut through the silence. "You know, this is the first time in many years not one of us has been pregnant."

I looked across at her and my sisters as they stood side by side looking near identical, slender, and very beautiful. I smiled at her warmly, before glancing in the mirror, knowing I was the least pretty of us all. In the reflection, I caught Horemheb watching me momentarily before he looked away, focusing entirely on Tut. I stood, wanting to remove myself from the uncomfortable situation, and walked toward my sisters with my arms open.

They rushed forward and we held each other with our heads pressed together.

"It's nice to not have enlarged bellies in the way, isn't it?" I said. They giggled quickly before I looked up at Rena. "I'm sorry for what I said to you, Rena, when my son died."

She flushed. "Naomi, you were in pain—"

"No, Rena, it was unkind. You were young when I was taken away, but you're stronger now, I know that."

She sighed, looking relieved. "Thank you, Naomi. I value your opinion of me more than anything. You saved me, and because of that I never want to disappoint you."

"You never have."

She smiled joyously and a tear ran down her cheek.

Eliora giggled and wiped it away as we held each other tighter.

I heard Horemheb clear his throat behind me. I let go and turned to face him, but my gaze dropped to look at my son. For the first time in his life I saw his father in him. He held his head up nobly, and his dark eyes looked pointed and beady with the makeup on. He transformed as I had, from a humble Hebrew to an Egyptian royal.

"Oh, Tut," I gasped. "You really *do* look like a prince now."

He looked embarrassed as he twisted the wristband self-consciously. "I don't know if I am. What if my uncle is mean to me?"

I fell to my knees in front of him and held him by the waist. "Tut, he's going to hate you no matter what you do."

Tut's face fell, and he looked frightened, so I hurried on. "He's going to hate you because you are the true heir, not him. But Horemheb is going to watch over you. He will guide you and keep you safe, just like he did for me when I was in the palace. Don't let Smenkhkare bully you. Stand up for yourself and let him know you are the rightful Pharaoh and he is the thief, not you. He will see you as a small boy, weak and ignorant, but you must prove him wrong. He's a bad man, Tut, but you are a good one, with the heart of a lion, so you will be able to overcome him."

Tut nodded, and I saw in his eyes that he took courage in my words. "You'll be with us when we go to the palace, won't you, Mama?"

Horemheb turned away and grumbled something under his breath before he said, "Yes, Tut. She won't be leaving us until you are given a room in the palace."

Tut threw his arms around me. "I don't know when I'll be able to do this again."

I felt my tears coming, but I struggled to keep them back so he wouldn't see. "I won't let it be too long."

"I love you, Mama," he whispered.

"I know you do, Tut, and I love you too."

He slowly let go of me and kissed my cheek. He then looked to Horemheb and asked, "Am I ready?"

Horemheb gave a nod. "You are."

He rested his hand on Tut's shoulder and guided him out. My sisters and I fell behind again.

As we approached the palace, I felt afraid for Tut. So much could happen to him in that place, and being just a boy, he would be considered an easy target and subjected to all kinds of manipulation and intrigue. I stared at the back of Horemheb's head and prayed that he would be able to protect my son from the people who would try to harm him.

We arrived at the gates; the guards opened it for Horemheb to enter. As my sisters and I passed through behind him, I felt their eyes on us. They might have considered Hebrews a lower race, but the Egyptian men did covet our women for our stronger builds and healthier appearance. That, coupled with how beautiful my sisters were, made me certain they lusted after us.

Eyes followed us as we swept through the palace behind Horemheb. The palace of Thebes differed drastically from the one in Amarna. For a start, it had a roof. The roof was held up by tall, cylindrical columns covered in reliefs and hieroglyphs. Statues of the various gods stared down from everywhere, some small, but the more important gods towered over us.

As we approached the throne room, Horemheb spoke softly to Tut.

"Don't let them see fear in you, boy. If they do, you will be considered weak and unfit to take the crown."

"I will be brave," Tut answered fervently.

I couldn't help smiling behind my veil.

We turned around a corner and came face to face with the tall, heavily decorated doors to the throne room. The guards saw Horemheb and, as one dashed inside to announce his arrival, the other opened the door wide for him to enter. Horemheb didn't break his stride for one moment as he turned into the room, and we followed.

The throne room took my breath away, a wide and open room, huge windows stretching along opposite sides with long, white linens hanging down and flowing gently in the slight breeze. The floor was marble, the walls and pillars layered with gold, ivory, and copper, and at the far end of the room stood the oversized thrones for the Pharaoh and his queen.

Courtiers and noblemen filled the room and watched us curiously as we walked straight toward the thrones.

Suddenly, Horemheb stopped and bowed. I quickly fell to my knees, and felt glad to hear my sisters each do the same, and not stubbornly resist.

Then, a voice that gave me chills spoke.

"Commander." Smenkhkare's voice seemed to slither, and reminded me of a snake. "What is this? Have you finally decided to take a wife, or maybe four? You've had a soft spot for the Hebrews since Kiya, but I don't think this is the wisest of unions."

"That is not my intention." Horemheb straightened his pose.

I glanced up and saw Smenkhkare walk over to him and meet his eyes.

"What is your purpose in bringing them here, then? Are they for me?"

His gaze turned to us and I felt sick at the lust in his eyes.

"No, Smenkhkare," Horemheb answered.

Smenkhkare's head snapped back to Horemheb, and he glared at him.

"How dare you address me so informally. I am Pharaoh."

"Not anymore."

Loud gasps arose from all around before I heard a woman's voice call out, "What is the meaning of this, Commander?"

"I have brought the true Pharaoh," Horemheb answered.

"The what?" Smenkhkare spat at him.

"I have brought Amenhotep's son, the boy once known as Tutankhaten, but now named Tutankhamen."

Smenkhkare finally noticed Tut standing beside Horemheb. He snarled at Tut and snapped, "That boy is dead, along with his foul slave mother."

"No, he is not. He stands before you this very moment."

"Lies!" the woman's voice rung out again. "My mother made sure that horrible woman and her son had been done away with."

I dared to glance up again and saw Mayati standing with her hand on her hip, looking down at Tut.

"Who are these women, then?" Smenkhkare asked, staring down at us.

"They are the women whom I tasked with raising him; the boy's aunts," Horemheb answered calmly.

"Aunts?" Mayati stepped over and grabbed Rena by the arm, pulling her to her feet and removing her veil. "Disgusting! She does look awfully like Kiya."

Smenkhkare's interest piqued at Mayati's words. He rushed at Eliora, yanked her up and tore off her veil.

"Kiya was very beautiful, and strong, too."

He leaned closer to Eliora's face until his breath moved her hair.

"Tell me, do you still have the daughter of Mordad?"

"No," Rena answered.

I bit my lip as Smenkhkare turned to her with interest, and shoved Eliora back. He stepped over to Rena and grabbed her by the jaw. "You are defiant, like your sister. I might enjoy you—"

"Mordad's daughter eloped," Horemheb spoke loudly to draw attention to himself. "When she heard we were returning to the city, she became fearful, so found herself a husband and fled the land."

Smenkhkare pushed Rena back as he turned to Horemheb. "Pity."

Another woman stepped in front of me and said, "Stand, Hebrew."

I quickly obeyed, and found myself looking down at a grown Ankhesenpaaten. I held my breath as she looked into my eyes, but didn't remove my veil.

"You said these were his aunts, Commander?"

"They are," Horemheb answered with a quick bow.

"They do look like her," she muttered as she continued to stare into my eyes. "Right down to those hazel eyes."

She turned and looked Tut over. "And I see her in him also, as well as my father. I believe he is indeed who you say. Kiya was a clever woman, which was why my father loved her. Surely she would have provided a way to protect her son from harm."

"Ankhe!" Mayati yelled. "Do you dare turn against me?"

She sighed and folded her arms. "I am not turning against you, Mayati. I'm just looking at the facts, and the facts are that this boy likely is our brother." She lowered her hand and gestured to Tut.

"You are wise, princess," Horemheb responded.

She scowled at him. "Be quiet, Horemheb. I do not need you trying to flatter me."

Tut let out a short laugh, which drew everyone's attention to him.

I held my breath fearfully, as Smenkhkare slowly moved across and towered over him with his arms folded. "What is funny, boy?"

Tut folded his arms and puffed his chest out in an attempt to match his uncle's size.

Smenkhkare scoffed. "Disgusting child. His mother was a whore and so are his aunts. Take them to my bedchambers."

Several guards advanced toward us, but stopped as Tut spoke up loudly. "Don't you dare touch them, and don't you dare talk about my mother that way!"

Everyone froze and stared at him. Then Smenkhkare said, "What did you say to me?"

"I said, don't you touch them," Tut repeated slowly. "I am speaking very clearly, surely you understand what I'm saying."

I bit my lip, trying to fight back a laugh, until Smenkhkare raised his hand up to strike him. "You horrible little…"

I became frightened as Tut stood, unflinching, but Horemheb caught Smenkhkare's arm and threw him back.

"You will not strike the king!"

"I am king!" Smenkhkare bellowed.

"I know how we can settle this," Ankhe said gently. "Bring forth Queen Gerlind."

Smenkhkare stared at her for a moment before waving his hand for it to be done. As the guards rushed to collect her, Smenkhkare walked over to his throne and leaned over it with his head hanging.

Meanwhile, Mayati grabbed Adina, who was the only one left kneeling. She pulled her to her feet and removed her veil. "Why do you have to be so pretty?"

Ankhe returned to me and slowly slid my veil down. I had a terrible feeling she knew exactly who I was, and would reveal me at any moment. But Ankhe had always been surprising, and with a sniff and a pat on my cheek, she turned away from me to look at Tut.

"Do you remember your mother?"

"I do," he answered.

"But you would have only been three years old when she died."

"I have a good memory," he said boldly. "And she was wonderful."

Ankhe glanced at Horemheb and said, "You're not the only one who thought that."

Horemheb scowled at her. "Princess, I never—"

She waved him off. "I was talking about my father. You're so touchy sometimes, Commander."

"Ankhe!" Mayati snapped. "Stop encouraging the boy. He is *not* our brother."

"I wouldn't want to be your brother," Tut grumbled. "You are awful."

Ankhe laughed. "He is like Kiya—brutally honest."

"Don't say her name!" Mayati snapped. "You dishonor me and our mother when you do."

127

Finally the guards returned, and Smenkhkare turned as they led Gerlind over to him.

My heart leaped with joy at the sight of her with her head held high and her shoulders back.

"You called for me, my lord?"

He waved his hand toward Tut. "Look at the boy and tell me what you see."

She walked over and gently lifted Tut's face so she could look into it. Her eyes narrowed briefly, before they widened in shock. She glanced at Horemheb and whispered so the king and queen wouldn't hear. "Is it possible? Is this Kiya's boy?"

"Yes, he is," Horemheb answered softly. "He has returned to take his place, but they are waiting for you to confirm that he is indeed Tut."

She pursed her lips and looked into Tut's face again, gently stroking his cheek. "Oh, how I miss your mother," she told him, before turning and looking at Smenkhkare. "Where did you find him?"

"Who is he, Gerlind?" Smenkhkare's voice raised a pitch in fear.

"He is Tutankhaten. I saw the boy be born and watched over him when Kiya was out doing our husband's bidding. I would know his face anywhere."

"No!" Smenkhkare bellowed furiously. He rushed forward and tossed Gerlind aside, reaching for Tut, but Horemheb was quick to react.

He drew his sword and pressed it against his neck. "Kare, step down."

"I won't!" he snarled. "I deserve to be king, I deserve to be Pharaoh!"

"My lord." The voice of Ay sent fear shooting through me and I struggled to remain composed. "Do not fear. The boy is young. He cannot lead on his own. Why not let him be co-regent—"

"I will not be co-regent again, uncle!" Smenkhkare spat. "It was bad enough having to do it with my brother, but sharing the crown with this *boy* insults me!"

"I feel the same," Tut responded. "I was born to be Pharaoh. It is my destiny."

Ay raised his eyebrows at Tut while Horemheb looked impressed. Horemheb gestured at Tut and said, "This boy is the rightful wearer of the crown. It's time for you to step down, Smenkhkare."

Smenkhkare turned red with rage and lunged toward Tut, but Ay and Mayati blocked him. Ay held him firmly and said, "The Commander is right. This boy is the heir, so it is time for you to step down."

Smenkhkare glared at Ay furiously, and a silent exchange passed between them. It made me nervous for my son, as I knew just how clever and calculating Ay could be. But, Smenkhkare reached up and removed the tall crown from his head and handed it to Ay. Ay then turned and looked to Horemheb. "I will arrange for a coronation ceremony for a week hence. Are you agreeable, Commander?"

"I am." Horemheb bowed.

"And how about you, young prince?"

Tut stood taller. "I am."

"Very good," Ay said before turning to Gerlind. "Take them to the northern bedchambers and give the boy a room overlooking the gardens on the third floor."

"Yes, my lord." She bowed and walked toward the doors.

Horemheb gestured for Tut to follow and he hurried after her with my sisters and me following behind.

Once we left the throne room, I felt a woman beside me. I glanced down to see Ankhe walking with us. I focused on remaining composed, and didn't react to her beside me until she said, "I was the first to be demoted below Kiya."

When I didn't respond, she continued. "My mother and sisters never liked her, but I secretly did. I thought she was so brave, and I saw that my father loved her very deeply, and she cared for him, also." She looked up at me. "You look almost identical to her, and you are about the right age, too—"

"Princess," Horemheb said, falling back. "Don't you think it's a bit below you to talk with Hebrews?"

"Aren't you the hypocrite?" she responded sharply, but she looked up at me again and sighed. "I'm bored of this, anyway."

She slapped me across the rump and departed from us.

Gerlind led us to Tut's new room, which was quite beautiful. The walls were white, and there was a large, square window, which allowed light into the room. We could see his large bed draped with colorful linens, the same way Akhenaten's had been, and of course, there was a mirror mounted to the wall with a lineup of stands on the dresser.

Once Horemheb shut the door, Gerlind wrapped her arms tightly around Tut.

"Oh, Tut! What a miracle it is to see you alive and well! For years, I believed you were dead, but here you are!"

I saw his confusion about the strange woman squeezing him as he glanced across at me.

I nodded and spoke gently to him. "She knew you as a small boy; let her hold you."

The sound of my voice caused her to let him go and stare at each of my sisters, confused. "Kiya?"

"Kiya is dead," I answered simply.

She looked at me and clasped her hands over her heart. "What is she known by now?"

I couldn't help smiling as I answered, "I am Naomi."

Tears burst from her eyes. She sobbed, "What a relief it is to see you alive! What a marvelous deception you created. Even now, they still believe you are dead, and you stood right before them!"

She rushed to me and wrapped her arms around me.

I pulled off her wig so I could stroke her light brown hair and kiss her head.

"How I've missed you, my little Gerlind, and how I have worried for you! Are you Smenkhkare's now?"

She shook her head. "No, he wouldn't have me. He thinks I'm cursed because I was friends with you, Abi, and most importantly, Mordad, and all three of you were gone before he could take you. He thinks I brought some kind of witchcraft with me from my people which destroyed his favorite wives who belonged to his brother."

"He's such a fool." Horemheb scoffed. "Gerlind belongs to Ay now, instead."

"Oh, how horrible!" I gasped with disgust. "He's so old, and cruel."

She sighed and nodded. "I may have been frightened by our husband, but every time I am brought to Ay, I find myself wishing for Akhenaten."

"Gerlind," Horemheb said firmly. "You know you should use his real name."

"I know, I'm sorry, I meant Amenhotep." She pressed her cheek against my chest. "I've missed you so much. Those days with Abi, Mordad, and you were the most glorious, and I remember them with fondness. There are

130

very few of us left now. Many wives were taken back to their homelands when Smenkhkare took the throne, and many more of the concubines fled, or were put to death. Smenkhkare has only twenty-two wives and fifty-six concubines, and most of them he refuses to lie with because he thinks them too old or too ugly."

I stroked her hair gently, feeling terrible for leaving her with that horrible family. "Gerlind, do you have enough freedom to go out into the city?"

"Yes, I do."

"Then find the guards named Enoch and Jared. Do you remember Mehaleb?"

"Yes. He was the nicest guard we ever had assigned to escort us." She grinned. "And I remember that you had feelings for him."

Horemheb grunted with disgust.

I ignored him and smiled down at her. "He's my husband now."

She squealed with delight and threw her arms around my neck. "Oh Kiya! That's such wonderful news—"

Then her head shot back and she looked at me as she remembered the most important detail of the conversation we had when she found out about Malachi. She quickly let go of me, being acutely aware of Horemheb standing not far from her. "So what about those guards?"

"They are his brothers, so they know where I live and can help you come see me."

Her smile returned. "That would be so wonderful."

"They're still guards here?" I heard Horemheb mumble to himself. "I wonder where I posted them?"

"Probably in the dungeons," Adina snapped. "To get back at Malachi."

I let go of Gerlind and hurried to intervene. "Let's get Tut settled in, shall we?"

As we prepared the room for Tut, he stayed close at my side and never spoke a word. Then, as we were about to leave, he grabbed onto me and held me tightly.

"I don't want you to go. I'm so afraid."

I looked up at Horemheb pleadingly, and he scowled at me. "No, Naomi. Today was more than enough."

"Then you stay with him," I said firmly.

He groaned. "Naomi, I don't want to babysit—"

131

"I will, then."

He glared at me before he stepped over and pulled Tut away from me. "Fine, I'll stay with him." He turned to Tut and spoke firmly, "But don't expect this to be a regular thing. I have my own home and bed to return to."

Tut nodded with wide eyes and looked across at me. "I'll be brave, Mama. I'll make you proud."

I smiled as my heart broke. "You already do, Tut."

My sisters, Gerlind, and I all turned and left.

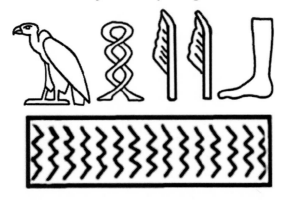

CHAPTER SIXTEEN

Gerlind led us through the most abandoned route out of the palace, while I introduced her to my sisters. She was very excited to meet them, and told them they were lucky to have a sister who would protect them so well. I couldn't help feeling humbled as they all agreed. When we reached the gates, she bid us farewell and promised me she would find Malachi's brothers, so she could visit.

We began our precarious journey through the city back to our sector. Evening had fallen, and the sun had set, leaving only a dim light. The streets looked nearly abandoned; we kept quiet and slipped by in the shadows, unnoticed.

Once we passed into our sector of the city, we all paused and took a deep sigh of relief, before we walked slowly toward our homes together. Rena linked her arm through mine and rested her head on my shoulder, while Eliora grabbed my hand and wove her fingers into mine. They did all they could to help comfort me, and I felt exceedingly grateful, but my heart still felt heavy.

My little boy was gone. He had grown up too quickly, and now I felt like he was being dangled above a pit of hungry crocodiles, and if he didn't hold on, he would be eaten alive. I prayed and hoped Horemheb would keep a tight grip on him and watch him closely. Horemheb was my only hope.

Adina sighed and I glanced across at her. She looked troubled, with her eyebrows furrowed and her arms folded.

"Adina?" I said gently.

Her gaze shot up to me, surprised. "Yes?"

"What's troubling you?"

She sighed again and looked away from me. "What happened between you and the Commander in Amarna, Naomi? The Egyptians all hinted at something, and Malachi is always so touchy about it, but you never talk much of your experiences there."

She pulled her arms tighter around her and huffed. "I feel like there's this great piece of time which has never been explained, and I want to understand. I spent those three years praying for you every day and worrying about you every moment. Then you came back to us and it was wonderful, but when I see you with the Egyptians and hear the way they talk about who you were, I feel like I just don't know you at all."

Eliora's hand tightened around mine, while Rena pressed closer to me. I knew they thought the same thing, but were too afraid to say anything. After all, I had stepped in for them, so they didn't want to appear ungrateful.

"So you want to know who the greatly beloved Queen Kiya was?" I asked Adina gently.

"I do," she replied. "And I want to know why there is such scandal associated with you and the Commander."

I sighed and changed direction. My sisters seemed surprised, but followed without question. I led them down to an abandoned irrigation pump by the river, where we wouldn't be heard. By then, darkness had fallen, and the stars and half-moon lit the sky. A gentle breeze lifted from the river, which felt cool and refreshing. I stepped up onto the stand for the pump, breathing in deeply, clearing my mind, and taking myself back to Amarna. Images flashed through my mind; people's voices rang in my ears again—voices I hadn't heard in years.

I pulled off my shawl, twisted my hair up in a bun, and wound my shawl around it. I removed my robe and tied my tunic belt tighter around my waist. I looked down at them as they watched me with confusion.

"Queen Kiya," I began, "was a gift given to Pharaoh Akhenaten from Aten himself. As Aten climbed the sky after his night-long journey through the underworld, he looked upon his son in Amarna and saw he did not have an heir to continue his great bloodline. So he reached down to the mountains, and molded the earth into a woman and breathed life into her. She was clever and virtuous, the perfect companion for a Pharaoh and mother for his heir. She was strong as an ox, so she could bear the child easily, and charmed the king with her grace and gift of tongues. Pharaoh loved her quickly, and she rapidly grew in favor and grace until she finally bore the son, and Pharaoh gave her the official title of Greatly Beloved Wife. A temple was built to honor her and the great gift she had given to the kingdom."

I paused to examine their stunned faces and smiled as I continued. "But not all loved her. The Great Royal Wife, Nefertiti, was jealous of the love Pharaoh showed Kiya, and with Nefertiti's father, Ay, and her vile daughters' assistance, they did everything they could to remove her from the palace. In the end, they would eventually kill her off and usurp all that was hers, but, while she was present, the Greatly Beloved had many supporters who guided and protected her, like her dear friends and fellow queens Abi, Gerlind, Halima, and…"

My voice caught as Mordad's face flooded into my mind. "And Mordad, the fair princess from Persia. How she loved Mordad, her dear sister, if not in blood, but in spirit."

I slumped and paused again, thinking of Mordad's strength and faith in me. I wondered if, wherever she was, she watched over me and missed me as much as I did her.

Rena rested her hand over her heart as a tear ran down her face, her empathy for me spilling over.

I took a deep breath and continued. "There was the handsome guard whom Kiya secretly loved, who swore to her he would wait fourteen years if he had to, like Jacob did for Rachel, and when she pleaded with him to let her go, he told her no, as his fourteen years were far from passed."

"Malachi," Eliora said wistfully, on a sigh.

"But, the one who was her greatest and most powerful ally was the Great Commander of the Army. He was assigned to tutor her and teach her foreign languages, so she could assist the king with his work, and after a violent fight between Kiya and Nefertiti, the king assigned Kiya to the Commander for him to be her guardian and caregiver.

"They became close friends, and despite the Commander's cruelty to others, he was always kind to Kiya, and found her the only tolerable person in the whole kingdom. He pushed her upward, and encouraged her to excel, and it was then the rumors began to fly; that the pair was in an adulterous relationship and the child she carried was not the king's, but in fact, the Commander's. But the rumors were not true. They came from the jealous

Queen Nefertiti, who wanted to cast doubt on Kiya's virtue. The problem was, despite being proved false, they never seemed to completely die. And then one day... one day..."

I hesitated, not sure if I wanted to admit to them what happened between Horemheb and me. But as I looked down at them—their eyes gazing up at me, riveted by my tale of things they had always wished to know and were now hearing—I felt I owed it to them to admit my weakness.

I took a deep breath, stepped down from off the pump, and pulled my hair out from the bun.

"Horemheb saw me with Malachi and heard him talking about his love for me, and he became angry. Once Malachi had gone, he grabbed me, pulled me into a room and began yelling at me in a jealous rage where he admitted that he loved me, before he grabbed me and he..."

I dropped my eyes. "Malachi must never know this, but he kissed me, and not just a small kiss, but a real, deep, passionate kiss, and I, I kissed him back. Compared to how my husband, the king, kissed me, it felt like magic and it excited me like nothing I had ever felt before."

I looked at my sisters, who showed a mixture of reactions to my revelation: shock, dismay, but also wonder.

"Did you love him?" Eliora whispered.

I folded my arms uncomfortably. "Not like I do Malachi, but yes, I believe I did. He was everything to me in that place. I spent almost every day with him, and you've seen him; he's strikingly handsome and powerful."

"But he's horrible." Adina scowled. "He's rude, irreverent, bloodthirsty..."

I raised my hand to stop her. "Not always, Adina. He's an Egyptian, don't forget, and a highly ranked one, too. He has to close himself off from those around him to survive. I'm not saying he's perfect, but he allowed me to see a different side of him, and he even allowed himself to trust me, which for him is quite an achievement in itself."

"He loves you still, Naomi," Rena said. "I can see it. I know you told me you think it's one of his tricks, but I don't think it is. I saw the way he watched you today, and the way he submitted to everything you said."

"But it doesn't matter anymore," I told her. "I love Malachi. He's my husband and the father of my children. I couldn't ask for a better partner in

136

life, and Horemheb, he's just the man who will watch over my Tut, nothing more."

"So *you* don't love *him* anymore?" Adina asked, her eyes narrowing on me suspiciously.

A small part of me screamed *yes, you do*, but I pushed it aside and answered, "That is in the past now."

"That's a fantastically romantic story," Eliora sighed.

Adina threw a nasty look at her, and she clamped her mouth shut.

"So there you go, that was Queen Kiya. I hope I was able to answer your questions," I said before turning to walk back toward our homes.

"Wait!" Adina called out. "So Malachi doesn't know that Horemheb kissed you?"

I turned to her. "No, and I'd prefer he doesn't find out. I'm afraid that if he were to discover it, he would find Horemheb and try to harm him, which would not end well, no matter what the outcome."

"For who exactly? Malachi or Horemheb?"

I tilted my head, feeling the anger behind her words. "Malachi, of course."

"Adina," Rena interrupted. "Naomi loves Malachi, we all know that. They were meant to be together."

Adina pushed Rena aside and advanced on me. She pointed at my chest and snapped, "You know, Naomi, you always got everything you wanted and you were always praised by everyone because you are so clever and so charming, and I hated it. When I was taken in marriage before you, I finally felt like I did something better than you, because for once, you weren't perfect, you weren't the one chosen, and I finally began to let myself love you. But this, this is *so* you, the you I despise. Malachi is so wonderful to you, but you have these secret feelings for Horemheb—"

"Adina, I don't—"

"Then why won't you tell him about that affair? You know, you are just like them. You keep secrets and twist the truth, so maybe you should leave Malachi and go to Horemheb. You would be better suited to him, and Malachi could find a wife who deserves him."

I felt like she slapped me across the face. That was how she had felt about me for years, and I hadn't known, and now I had disappointed her more than ever. I reached for her. "Adina…"

"Don't touch me, harlot!" she snarled, pulling back.

137

Rena and Eliora gasped in shock. My heart wrenched in my chest.

"Adina, you wanted me to be honest with you…"

She let out a cynical laugh.

"Oh, yes, Naomi, and I discovered how hard life really is for the spoiled favorite of our father, a king, a commander of an army, and a wonderful husband." She pushed passed me and marched across the field. "Don't visit me anymore, Naomi!" she called back.

I watched her go, feeling devastated that I hurt her so badly.

Rena rested her hand on my back. "Naomi, I don't think you're a harlot."

"In a way, I am," I mumbled.

Rena wrapped her arm around my waist and kissed my shoulder. "You made a mistake. We all make them."

I looked over my shoulder at her and touched her hand on my waist. "Do you think Malachi deserves better than the likes of me?"

"No!" both she and Eliora gasped.

I nodded solemnly and sighed. "I should get back to him. He's probably working himself into a frenzy thinking Horemheb has stolen me away."

Eliora's hand rested between my shoulder blades as we walked back toward our homes. "I'm glad you told us. I have always wondered what it was like for you there, and to be honest, I'm glad you had people who looked out for you, especially Mordad, who was a sister for you when we couldn't be."

I smiled at her, feeling my heart swell with love. "Thank you, Eliora."

We arrived at Rena's home first, then at Eliora's, before I continued on by myself to my home. As I approached, a lamp burned in the window and a dark figure sat outside on a stool. I smiled, delighted Malachi waited for me, but then felt a pang of guilt after my conversation with Adina. Maybe I should tell him. Maybe he would be reasonable and not seek out Horemheb to exact his revenge. He and I hadn't been married at the time, so he had no reason to be vengeful.

Malachi raised his head at the sound of my approach, and he stood. I quickened my pace, eager to have his arms around me after such a long and emotional day. He rushed toward me, and when we met, he lifted me up and kissed me. It was long, deep, and loving. I clung to him as the loss of my Tut sank in and tears streamed down my face.

He pulled away and kissed my cheek where the tears fell. "My dear Naomi."

"I'm so glad you're here," I said softly, looking into his eyes.

"I'm glad you came back to me."

He carried me into the house and laid me on our bed where he kissed me again. His tenderness as he made love to me was just what I needed to relieve my stress and ease the pain in my heart. Afterward, as we lay curled up together and I gently stroked his face, I knew I had to be truthful with him.

"Malachi?"

He looked into my eyes as he stroked my shoulder. "Yes, Naomi?"

"There's something that has been on my conscience for quite some time that I feel you need to know."

"You know you can tell me anything," he said in a hushed voice, kissing me on the lips.

I took a deep breath, trying to decide the gentlest way to break it to him. "Do you remember in Amarna, when you talked to me about when we would one day be married and have children of our own as you took me back to the women's wing?"

"Yes, of course."

"Well." I sighed, feeling hesitant. "A few weeks before we left, Horemheb overheard us, and after you left me, he came and grabbed me in a jealous rage..."

Malachi sat up and leaned over me with concern. "Did he hurt you? Did he...?"

I saw him growing angry as a horrible thought filled his mind.

"No, he didn't. But that was when he first told me he loved me, and it was also when he..." I paused, watching his face closely. "He kissed me."

Anger flashed across his face. "He... oh, I should—"

"No, Malachi, because the truth is, I kissed him back."

Malachi drew away from me in horror. "Naomi!"

"I'm sorry, Malachi!" I pleaded. "It was a mistake! I was swept away by him. You know how he is."

"I know how he is with *you!*" He snarled. "You kissed him?"

I flushed. "I regretted it right away."

"Naomi!" He groaned and grabbed his hair. "All this time and you never said anything?"

"I was afraid of how you would react," I said, my gaze falling. "I was afraid you would do something rash and get yourself into trouble, and I didn't want to hurt you—"

"Well, you have managed to do that!"

I looked away from him, ashamed.

He moaned. "I don't want you to see him anymore."

"But he's my only link to Tut."

"Tut?" He laughed. "Oh, he is so good! He uses the boy to keep you coming back. This is so infuriating! Has he tried to kiss you again?"

"No!" I gasped. "Malachi, I've made it very clear that I love you. He wouldn't dare!"

He looked down at me and raised his eyebrows, and I understood what he meant. He believed Horemheb would. "The worst part is that you may love me, but you crave him. He is your vice, your weakness. He's a poison of which you can't seem to get enough. He draws you in and keeps you hooked until someone finally pries you away."

I pulled the blankets around me and clutched them, feeling ashamed. Was he right about Horemheb? Was he my vice? I didn't want that, I wanted to be faithful to Malachi.

I looked up at Malachi and said determinedly, "Then I will speak to him only when I must, and with you present. I want to be faithful to you. I love you more than anything and I don't want to keep hurting you. So from now on, you are completely in control of this. When you say stop, I will stop; when you say no, I will obey."

He stared at me, and slowly, I saw him relax. He knelt down on the bed and leaned forward to kiss me. "Naomi, thank you."

I clasped his face and smiled at him lovingly. "No, thank you for being so wonderful."

CHAPTER SEVENTEEN

I had to try to make amends with Adina. I didn't want to fight with my sister. So I went to visit her, but she sent her eleven-year-old son to answer the door. He told me she wasn't home and he didn't know where she had gone.

When I told Rena about it, she insisted on going back with me the next day, and when we were again refused, Rena forced her way in. I heard her argue with Adina quietly. I couldn't make out what they said, but when Rena came back out, she was furious. She grabbed my arm and started dragging me away when I heard Adina call out, "Tell that harlot never to come back here again!"

When I told Malachi what happened, he huffed with frustration and marched us straight to Adina's house.

Uriyah answered and allowed him entry, but insisted I stay outside. I waited, with Zakkai on my hip and Itani dancing around in circles, until suddenly voices rose.

"You forgave her, Malachi? Are you completely mad?"

"Adina, she's my wife—"

"All the more reason why you shouldn't have! He is a loathsome Egyptian who would gladly do it again—"

"You think I don't know that?" Malachi said, his voice tense. "But *she* wouldn't."

"She wronged you, Malachi, and she has been lying to us for years. How can you just forgive that?"

"Because I love her, and I know you do, too."

She laughed sarcastically. "Oh, yes, everyone *loves* Naomi. Even the Egyptians who despise us somehow love *her.*"

"I'm done talking to you, Adina. You are being jealous and unreasonable."

The door burst open. Malachi rushed at me and grabbed my arm. As he turned me to leave, I saw Adina glare furiously at me before Uriyah shut the door.

We headed home, and as we walked Malachi said, "I thought you were supposed to be the fiery one and your sisters more docile. I have yet to see that! Your sisters are just as hardheaded as you are."

I tried not to smile.

Rena and I were drawing water at the well. We took our time, as we always did, so our children could play together and we could talk.

"Samuel said he is going to intervene," Rena told me. "He said if Malachi has forgiven you, then she has no right to be holding onto this."

"Is he upset at me, too?" I asked warily.

She sighed solemnly. "Not really. He's just disappointed that you didn't feel like you could tell us. He was actually more upset by the story of Aten creating you to give to the king. He said it belittles Papa and all he did for you."

I smiled, glad he wasn't angry with me. "It's quite farfetched. Most of the royals and nobility knew exactly what I was and just played along to keep their king satisfied."

"And satisfied he was."

We both jumped at Horemheb's voice and turned to see him enter the square. He smiled at me as he walked over and said, "No man was more contented with his wife." He looked across and saw Itani. "Is that the princess?"

"I can't talk to you any more, Horemheb, not without my husband present," I told him.

His eyebrow twitched, but that was the only sign of irritation he showed. "Very well. Send for him, then."

Rena called her oldest son over and told him to go find Malachi working in the fields.

Horemheb watched the boy dash away before he looked at Itani again. "She has Egyptian hair."

I looked at her long, straight black hair, but didn't respond.

"Itani, come here," he commanded.

She approached him nervously.

He lifted her chin to look at her. "You have your mother's eyes. It's a strange combination, with your darker complexion. Unlike your brother, you resemble your father more than your mother, except without the obvious deformities."

"Leave her alone, Horemheb," I said gently.

"There's no harm in looking, Naomi," he responded and gestured for her to keep playing. "I have no intention of ever taking her back to the palace. I'm just curious."

He glanced at Rena, who quickly turned away from him uncomfortably. His eyes narrowed on her, but he didn't comment. Instead, he spoke to me again. "You may not be able to speak to me, but I will speak to you until he arrives. I have conjured a plan for you to be able to visit with Tut on a regular basis without arousing suspicion."

I gasped and clutched at my heart, fighting back my impulse to gush excitedly.

He smiled at my obvious delight and continued. "I'm in need of a good servant in my house to prepare meals for me and repair clothes, blankets, do my laundry and so forth. They are simple tasks, but I will pay you well, and I can bring Tut into my house with me and not raise any questions about my motives. The few servants I do have in my house are loyal to me, and if they begin to suspect, they will not say a word about it. It also means I will be able to bring you to Tut's coronation in a few days, so you can see him officially become king."

"Naomi!" Rena gasped. "That's perfect! It would..."

She trailed off as she glanced at Horemheb and remembered what happened between us.

Horemheb's eyes narrowed on her again before he looked at me. He stepped toward me. "Naomi, did you—?"

"Don't you get any closer to her!" Malachi's voice rang out across the square. Before I could even look up, Malachi pulled me behind him and glared at Horemheb. "You will speak to me from now on, not her."

"Very well." Horemheb straightened and raised his chin to meet Malachi's eyes. "I wish to employ her as a servant in my household—"

"No," Malachi said firmly.

Horemheb's eyes darkened and his fists clenched. "She will be well paid and—"

"No!" Malachi snarled.

Horemheb fingered his sword as he tried to subdue his irritation. "You're being unreasonable—"

"I'm being unreasonable? You're in love with my wife! I think I am doing what I need to do to protect her from you."

A flash of pain registered on Horemheb's face for a moment; however, not enough for anyone but me to notice. "I am offering her the position to—"

"I said no!" Malachi bellowed, lunging toward him. "You will never touch her again, do you understand me?"

Horemheb looked at Rena as he suddenly realized why she had acted strangely. He knew by what Malachi said that I had confessed to my family what we had done back in Amarna.

Rena's gentle voice spoke next. "Malachi, he's offering her a chance to see Tut regularly. Don't you want that for her? He is her son."

Malachi turned on Rena as he stepped back and pulled me tighter against him. "Rena, you know what I know, surely you can't—"

"She survived in the palace under much worse circumstances for three years, you know that better than anyone. Let her do this, so she can see Tut." She looked across at her three sons. "I can't even begin to imagine how I would feel if someone took away one of my sons."

Her words seemed to hit Malachi; he winced. He stroked his beard as he stared off, thinking through what he should do next. Then, without looking at Horemheb, he said, "Will she be able to bring the other children with her?"

Horemheb nodded. "Of course."

"If I am to allow this, you must first agree to my terms."

Horemheb's chest rose, and he clenched his jaw, resenting being commanded by Malachi, a lowly Hebrew. But true to form, he controlled himself and answered, "And what are your terms?"

Malachi's hand tightened around my wrist. "She will be given a fair wage."

Horemheb scoffed. "That's not even a question."

Malachi ignored him and continued. "She will be allowed to see Tut whenever she wants. When she asks for him, you will bring him the next day. She will be treated fairly and kindly, especially when she is with child, when you must reduce her workload."

Horemheb scowled slightly, but Malachi didn't see it, and continued without missing a beat. "But most importantly, you must never be alone with her. If you need to speak with her, you will have someone else present at all times, no exceptions."

Horemheb glared up at him, but answered calmly. "Your terms are reasonable. I will accept them."

Malachi didn't seem relieved in the slightest as he turned to me. "Naomi, promise me you, too, will adhere to what I have asked."

"Without fail, Malachi," I answered fervently.

He gently clasped my face and looked into my eyes as he whispered, "I love you, Naomi, and I know you are a good and faithful wife. I trust you completely, but him, I do not. Be careful."

I rested my hands on his wrists and smiled up at him. "I will. I will keep the children with me as I work; that will prevent anything from happening."

He bent down and kissed me, mostly just to make the point clear that I belonged to him. He then turned back to Horemheb and negotiated a wage for me.

Horemheb told me to start the next day with breakfast for him just after dawn, and he departed.

Malachi watched him leave, never letting go of my arm. Once Horemheb was out of sight, Malachi turned back to me and softly kissed my forehead.

"It's time for you to be a queen again," he said quietly. "Look out for Tut. Tell him we still love him and to be brave."

I grabbed onto his robe as I gazed up at him lovingly. "I will, Malachi, and thank you. You are truly a wonderful husband."

His expression softened and he kissed me again. He then bid Rena and me goodbye. "Take care of my wife, Rena."

Rena laughed. "She's the one who takes care of me."

I smiled as he leaned over and kissed both Itani and Zakkai before returning to his work.

I arose early to make breakfast for my family, and also Horemheb. I left some on the table for Malachi before I woke the children. I lifted Zakkai onto my hip, coaxed Itani out the door, then rushed back into my room where Malachi still slept. I bent over him and kissed his cheek, which woke him and made him smile.

"Naomi, good morning."

I stroked his hair. "I will be back in time to make our supper tonight."

He grabbed my robe. "Kiss me properly."

I smiled and kissed him on the lips.

He sighed, satisfied, then sat up to get ready for the day. "I love you!" he called to me as I hurried Itani out the door.

I rushed through the city with Zakkai on one hip, a basket with Horemheb's breakfast on the other, and Itani clinging to my robe. As we entered the Egyptian sector, I pulled my shawl closer to my face and made Itani cover her hair. But no one paid us any heed. Servants were out everywhere, buying goods for their masters, and I blended in.

As we entered the gates to Horemheb's estate, Itani gasped in awe while Zakkai oohed and pointed at everything. The estate was the fanciest place either of them could ever recall.

A pleasant woman met me and led me on a tour of the estate. I couldn't help being amazed by the transformation it had gone through since I had wandered its hallways years earlier. The last place she took me to was the two small rooms I saw while I had explored the estate. But this time, I found the laundry room fully stocked with soaps and buckets, and a clothesline hung just outside the door.

The small food preparation room had a heavy wooden table just in front of a stove with a chimney, to channel the smoke out the window. The storage room was well stocked with the finest and most expensive foods available, along with the standard grain, barley, meats, and water jugs. These were the rooms where I would prepare food, do the laundry, maintain clothing and whatever else needed to be sewed or woven.

The maidservant seemed glad for the assistance. Apparently, Horemheb had cut his staff down to very few after the move from Amarna. He felt they lacked loyalty to him, and he needed to focus on things other than dealing with troublesome staff.

She took a shine to my children and told me I could let them run and play wherever they wanted and she would let the rest of the servants know to keep an eye out for them.

The first thing I did was set Horemheb's food out for him before I worked on his meal for that night.

Itani took Zakkai to explore the gardens, leaving me in peace to bake the bread. It was simple work, and I quickly knew that I would enjoy my time here. A few other servants entered to greet me, and it pleased me to find them all very friendly.

As I slipped the bread into the oven to bake, Itani squealed with delight from out in the garden.

I poked my head out the window. "Itani! None of that!"

"Yes, Mama!" she called back. I heard her giggle before she dashed across the garden with Zakkai trotting after her.

I turned back around and saw a manservant drop off a large cut of meat. I thanked him and sliced it up to salt and dry, but left a small part to cook for the meal that night.

Horemheb entered with the food I had left for him in his hand and sniffed the air. "That smells incredible."

I glanced around, knowing I shouldn't be alone with him.

"Calm down, Naomi," he said as he chewed his food. "The doors are all open; I can't do anything without someone hearing. Your husband won't have you thrown out."

He walked over and stood beside me, waving the lamb I had prepared for him in front of me. "This is very good. It's no surprise your husband has grown fatter since working at the palace. Although, just so you know, I prefer pork."

"I don't know how to prepare pork," I answered.

"That's right." He smiled. "Your people don't eat pigs. Well, I guess my diet is about to change."

"Why are you being like this?" I asked him shortly.

"Like what?"

I stopped working and looked at him. "Friendly."

He smirked. "Why, Naomi? We were friends once, or have you forgotten?"

"No, I haven't," I replied. "But that was before everything."

"Mmm." He turned away from me and looked out the window to watch Itani and Zakkai playing.

I saw a longing in his eyes and remembered how he had always wanted a child of his own. My heart filled with compassion for him as he slid off his hat and said softly, "It's nice to hear children playing in these gardens."

I stopped working and walked over to stand beside him. "Horemheb?"

He looked down at me.

"Why have you never remarried?"

He folded his arms and frowned. "Finding a tolerable woman with whom the union would be beneficial to me is nearly impossible. The only women who are of a standing which would assist my own are princesses, and none of them are trustworthy. It would be Amenia all over again."

I huffed. "Why don't you just find someone you like?"

He laughed. "You know I despise just about everyone, Naomi."

"That's true," I answered with a smile.

He turned and looked me over. "It's nice to talk with you again. You were always the only person I could have a conversation with."

I blushed and turned back to the meat. "I should get this done before it attracts too many flies."

I continued to work in silence as he watched my children play while he ate. I wondered what he was thinking, but as usual, he remained completely unreadable.

When he finished eating, he turned to me. "I will bring Tut here later to study some scrolls. It seems that despite my military training and position, I perpetually have to teach people foreign languages."

I couldn't help giggling.

He stepped closer to me and his hand rested on the small of my back. I held my breath nervously, not sure what he was doing, but unable to pull away from him.

"He is a very clever boy," he said softly as he touched the ends of my hair that hung over my shoulder. "He's very like his mother."

"I don't know what you're talking about," I said, pushing his hand away from my hair. "Kiya was dead before the Egyptians moved back here."

His other hand withdrew from me. "Yes, she was."

He stepped back and walked toward the door. "Have some food for us when we arrive. The boy hasn't been eating well. It seems he was spoiled with too much good food, and now what he is given in the palace he finds repulsive to the taste."

Despite being concerned that Tut hadn't been eating, I smiled to myself, flattered by Horemheb's compliment.

Horemheb's voice moved through the house and my heart skipped a beat. I hurried to find Itani and Zakkai and lead them upstairs to bring food to my son. Itani knocked on the door, and Horemheb answered it.

"Ah, good. I have been feeling hungry. How about you, Tut?"

"No," I heard him answer flatly, but as I entered, he glanced over and his whole face lit up. "Mama!"

I placed the food down on the table in front of him. He rushed around to me. I held him tightly and kissed his head. "Oh Tut! It's so wonderful to see you."

"What are you doing here?" he asked excitedly as he eyed the figs, cheese, and chickpeas I had brought up.

"Horemheb employed me to work here so I can see you."

He grinned as he reached over and took some food. "He didn't tell me! This is such a wonderful surprise. Oh Mama, the palace is awful. I'm not allowed to play with the other children, and Smenkhkare watches me all the time. I miss you and Papa terribly."

Itani wrapped her arms around him. He looked down at her.

"You brought her? Get off me, Itani." He pushed her away, which made her pout.

"Oh, Tut, she misses you. It's very quiet without you, and I know your Papa misses your company out with the herd."

He grabbed my hand and pulled me around to sit next to him. "I miss *being* out in the field with him. All this tutoring I get from sunrise to sunset is very boring." He ate greedily while he talked. "I don't know why you like it. I wish you could do it for me."

I laughed. "You know that would be pointless."

"Do you think I will be able to go out in the fields again sometime?" he asked.

I shook my head. "No, Tut, those days are over."

He sighed sadly. "I thought so."

"Maybe you could find something else you can enjoy just as much." I gestured to Horemheb. "The Commander is a master at many things. Maybe he could teach you something new."

Tut jumped to his feet excitedly. "Like sword fighting?"

Horemheb rested his hands on his hips. "I don't think you are quite old enough for that. How about I start you with dagger throwing or driving chariots?"

"Chariots?" Tut's eyes widened with delight. "Yes, I want to do that."

Horemheb chuckled. "Chariots it is, then."

149

Tut shoved the last of the chickpeas in his mouth. "I'm so hungry," he mumbled.

I laughed. "I'll go get more, but make sure you leave some for others this time. Your brother and sister need to eat, too, and so does Horemheb."

I stood to leave. Itani and Zakkai rushed over to him. As I passed Horemheb, he grabbed my arm and whispered, "Thank you. I have been concerned about his eating for days. This is a huge relief."

I looked up into his eyes and saw he was genuinely worried. I glanced back at Tut and muttered, "If he refuses to eat, bring him dates. He never refuses them."

"That's good to know." He let go of my arm and I hurried downstairs to bring back more food.

I returned home that afternoon feeling like a heavy load had been lifted from my shoulders. To see Tut had been so wonderful, and I knew his siblings had enjoyed seeing him again, also. As I prepared our humble meal for the night, I watched anxiously for Malachi to return home so I could tell him all that happened. But when I did see him coming, I saw that he wasn't alone. He had Samuel with him. I wondered what was going on, and hoped everyone was fine.

I stepped out of the house to meet them. They both barely acknowledged me. I stared, confused, as Itani and Zakkai rushed passed me to meet their father. Malachi lifted them both up happily as Itani kissed his cheek over and over and told him about seeing Tut.

Samuel came straight to me with a stern expression and took my hand. "Naomi, let's talk."

I looked at Malachi, who watched me steadily. I felt confused, but agreed. I handed Malachi my payment for the day's work and told him to pull out the food when it finished cooking. Samuel then led me away.

We walked along the riverbank as he said, "Naomi, I spoke with Adina today."

"Oh." I dropped my gaze as my heart sank, remembering again her anger at me.

He looked down at me, then wrapped my arm through his, patting my hand. "I think I have found the heart of her anger. It took me quite some time, and listening to her yell for over an hour, but she eventually opened up to me.

"She has always been terribly jealous of you, but after hearing and seeing how all those Egyptians spoke of you, and how that wife loved you like you were *her* sister, something inside her just snapped. The sacrifice you made by going to Amarna was never for her, and she felt like you traded her for your fellow wives and forgot about her. She feels like you loved Mordad more than you ever loved her, and she is envious of the love Mordad gave to you in return.

"She was also completely thrown off guard by the apparent fear that the royal family still feels for you, even now when they think you are dead. She wonders what you are capable of, to provoke such feelings within them. There is no denying you had to be a different person in that place, and I'm glad they gave you a different name so you are able to separate yourself from it all now, but with Tut stepping up to take the crown, she is afraid Kiya will return and the sister she admires will disappear.

"The Commander is a symbol of that. He's the one who came here with Kiya, he was the one who offered her to the king and pushed her upward. Finding out that you did, at one point, have feelings for him made her fear that maybe he would be able to bring Kiya back at the expense of Naomi."

"That's surprising," I said breathlessly, and we fell silent.

We walked up and down the riverbank while I processed what he had told me. How could I convince Adina that Kiya was dead and would never come back? I glanced up at Samuel and squeezed his arm tighter. "What should I do?"

He took a moment to form his answer in his mind before he said, "Show her that you love her, above all those wives, and that you never forgot her. Show her that Kiya is never coming back."

"But how?" I asked desperately. "She won't see me."

"Dana is with child again, and so, since her own sister died a few months ago, she will need all of you more than before. I will arrange for you to all come and speak with her, and you can talk to Adina then."

I nodded. "Thank you, Samuel."

He sighed and wrapped his arm around my shoulders. "I just wish for this to pass."

He walked me back to the house where the meal was cooked and my family waited for me. I kissed him on the cheek as I said goodbye, then stepped inside.

Itani talked excitedly about her day. She told Malachi about the gardens, and the steep stairs in the house, and all the secret rooms she and Zakkai discovered together. I sat next to Malachi and gently asked her to pause so we could pray over the food, but once the food was blessed, she instantly started up again.

After dinner, we put the children to bed and I cleaned up for the night. Malachi wrapped his arms around my waist and kissed my neck. "It seems like the children have found a wonderful new playground."

I smiled. "It seems so, and I am grateful that it is completely enclosed so they can run around without me having to watch them every second."

"You should buy yourself something nice tomorrow," he said gently as he replaced the coins into the pouch on my belt.

I turned around so I could look into his eyes. "Thank you, Malachi, for everything." I took his hand and guided him to our bed.

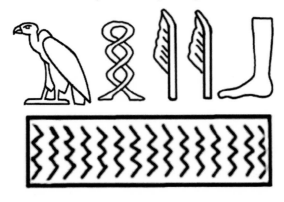

CHAPTER EIGHTEEN

I kept myself veiled as I followed Horemheb behind the procession through the city. Tut sat up on a throne, carried through the streets from the palace to the temple of Amun-Ra. Dressed in a skirt and plenty of gold and fine jewelry, he kept his head exposed in preparation for the crown to be placed upon it.

He seemed nervous as he prepared to leave, but when he saw me with Horemheb, he took courage, climbed right onto the throne, and announced that he was ready and everyone else needed to hurry up.

As we passed through the gates to the temple, the crowd fell back, and only the most elite were allowed to enter. Horemheb grabbed my hand and pulled me forward, claiming I was essential to him because he felt unwell and needed me to administer medicine if he felt weak.

I entered behind Horemheb, and found the temple transformed. I stared around in awe. The Egyptians were true masters of magic and trickery, and the priests of Amun were no exception; they, in fact, excelled above many others at the art. The wide-open room was smoky and dark with one pillar of sunlight following Tut as he was carried to the raised platform where he would be crowned. The priests, dressed from head to toe in white, chanted and amidst all the smoke, they seemed to be more like shadows as they faded in and out of sight.

I felt a little frightened. Aten's worship had always been in clear daylight and lacked the priests' elaborate efforts to appear mystical. As I gazed around nervously, I accidentally walked into Horemheb, who had stopped.

He pushed me back to maintain the appearance of superiority, but he glanced back at me in a way that told me not to worry.

I watched as the priests brought Tut forward and recited his royal heritage, to prove him the literal offspring of Amun-Ra on Earth, making him the rightful king and Pharaoh over all of Egypt. I watched Tut as he remained composed and responded perfectly to everything he needed to do.

When the priests finished and turned him to present him to the people as they crowned him, I saw him scan the onlooking crowd before his gaze locked on me. As the priest lowered the crown onto his head and handed him the staff and crook of the Pharaoh, Tut's eyes never left me for one moment.

The feast was in full swing, and Horemheb kept himself close to his new young Pharaoh to ensure his safety. I was expected to stay back by the walls with the other servants and watch, but occasionally Horemheb swung by and discreetly handed me food.

I could tell Tut desperately wanted to approach and throw his arms around me, but he knew he couldn't, so he glanced at me every so often, instead, to make sure I hadn't left the room.

I watched my son proudly while Horemheb guided him around to introduce him to foreign dignitaries. Suddenly, I felt a presence beside me. I looked down and saw Ankhe standing there, watching Tut as well.

"He is a handsome boy," she said, tilting her head. "I believe he will grow into a very handsome man, but that doesn't seem surprising, considering how lovely his mother was."

My stomach did a flip, and I became nervous that she would expose me. I felt grateful in that moment for being a servant, so obligated to keep silent and not respond to her.

Ankhe turned to me and removed my veil.

"You are one of his aunts, aren't you? It's not really a surprise the Commander would keep you around. He has had a soft spot for Hebrew women for as long as I can remember. I blame Kiya for that. She had a presence about her that brought great men to their knees: my father, Smenkhkare, Horemheb, and probably many others, too. As her kin, you understand what I'm talking about, don't you?" She stared at me fixedly, and when I didn't respond, she snapped, "Answer me, slave!"

I kept my eyes averted as I spoke softly. "No, I don't."

A smile spread across her face as she rested a hand on her hip. "Wasn't she beloved by her father even above his own son?"

I hesitated, but as she leaned closer, I knew I had to answer. "Yes."

She stretched out her hand and touched my hair. "She was very beautiful. My mother told me she had lovely hair, worth coveting, so she had it removed. If it looked anything like yours, I can completely understand what she meant. It's not really a surprise Horemheb had feelings for her. Even with her hair gone, she had smooth skin and light eyes, just like you."

She ran her hand over my cheek. "Horemheb probably keeps you around because you remind him of her. I tried to convince him to marry me, you know, but he wasn't interested. He likes the taller, stronger build of you Hebrews, perfect for childbearing. That's one of the reasons why my father brought Kiya in, because you Hebrews breed like rabbits and the women carry children with ease.

"My family, on the other hand, seems to be unable to bear heirs. My mother could not conceive a single son, Mayati is yet to have one of her children live, Meketaten died giving birth, and I, well I was never able to conceive for my father and now I am not married."

She turned and looked over at Horemheb. "I would love to marry him. He is handsome, strong, and has a keen mind, but he finds me frivolous and is repulsed by me. Why do you think he doesn't like me?"

I kept my eyes fixed ahead as I answered her. "He doesn't like anyone."

She laughed lightly. "This is true. If I was as clever as he, I would probably find everyone else dull as well."

She grabbed me by the neck and pushed me back against the wall. "Tell me something. Is Tut truly Kiya's son?"

"Yes," I answered quickly.

"And who are you, then? Are you Kiya? Is that why the Commander keeps you around, because he still loves his queen, and so he can secretly lie with you whenever he desires?"

"No."

Her hand tightened, cutting me off. "I don't like people who want to hurt my family. Kiya hurt my father when she died, *if* she died. He loved her so deeply—"

"Princess," Horemheb's voice interrupted. "Why are you handling my servant in such a manner? What has she done to offend you?"

Ankhe let go of me and turned to face him with a smile. "I was just talking to her. I've been curious about Hebrews since I met Kiya."

He glared down at her as she stroked his arm.

"How about you, Commander? In what manner do you handle her?"

"You are vile," he muttered.

"Oh, Commander, you have no wife, where else could you possibly relieve your stress?" She ran her hand over his bare back. "It's not that I haven't offered…"

He pulled away from her with disgust. "Leave me and my household alone, Princess, and have some decency."

He grabbed my arm and pulled me away. He hurried me over to Tut and had him announce the feast over, then he led us to Tut's bedchambers.

Once in the room and the door shut behind us, Tut turned and wrapped his arms around my waist, yawning. "I'm tired, Mama."

I stroked his head, having wanted to hold him in my arms all day. "You've had a long day, Tut. You should get some rest."

"Will you stay with me?" he asked, looking up at me earnestly. "I get so lonely here."

"She cannot," Horemheb interrupted as he slipped the crown off Tut's head. "If she's caught, she will be in great danger."

"But I miss you so much when you are gone, Mama." He pressed his face into my chest and held me tighter. "I don't want to be Pharaoh anymore. I just want to go home with you. Please stay with me, just this once."

"I can't, Tut," I said gently. "You know I love you and I wish I could, but Horemheb is right. I'm supposed to be dead, and if I'm caught, I could be forced to marry Smenkhkare and I would never be allowed to see your Papa or your siblings again. I will try to see you as soon as I can, but until then, take this." I pulled my knife out and sliced off some of my hair for him. "This way I will always be with you."

He stretched out his hand and, as I lowered my long, thick tress onto his palm, his fingers closed around it.

"Thank you, Mama."

"Tut," Horemheb said in a firm voice. "You're a man now, so you must be brave. You have your mother's strength, so it's time for you to use it. I have told you stories of her courage when she lived as a queen, so use her example when you feel afraid."

He looked across at Horemheb and nodded. "I will." Then he dashed across to him and wrapped his arms around his waist.

It surprised both Horemheb and me, and after my initial shock, I found myself smirking at Horemheb's baffled expression. He patted Tut's back in an awkward manner, not being accustomed to affection, and said, "Good boy. Now you should go to bed."

Tut let go of Horemheb and pulled off the last of his jewelry. He handed it to Horemheb before he moved slowly toward his bed.

Horemheb turned and placed the jewelry on the table.

I followed Tut, made sure he was comfortable in his bed, then kissed him softly on the head. "I love you, son."

He smiled warmly up at me. "I love you too, Mama."

Horemheb came up behind me and touched my elbow, signaling that the time had come to leave. I turned and blew out the lamps before following Horemheb. I felt relieved to see two guards posted at his door, but was startled when one said, "Naomi?"

I turned and saw Jared staring at me with surprise.

"Jared!" I gasped and grabbed his arm. "You watch over my Tut?"

"Yes. I was given this assignment right after he moved into here."

"Oh, what a relief!" I breathed. Then I turned to Horemheb with a knowing smile. "You did this."

He nodded. "Who better to watch over the boy than his own family?"

I laughed. I turned to Jared again and patted his cheek. "See? He's not all bad—"

"Naomi." Horemheb groaned.

"Sorry, I'm not supposed to make him look soft in front of his men—"

"Naomi!" he said, more forcefully.

Jared smirked quickly before he muttered, "Does my brother know you are here with him?"

I nodded. "He knows I have been with him all day."

He raised his eyebrows. "And he is fine with it?"

"Well, no." I sighed and folded my arms. "But he knows I'm here for Tut, and that is it."

"Malachi has always been the brave one," I heard the other guard say, and I turned to see Enoch on the other side of Tut's door. "I wouldn't leave you alone with *him*."

"You know, you are both still under my command," Horemheb said as he stepped closer and looked them over. "So I would watch what I say, if I were you. You know what I am capable of."

They both fell silent and gazed ahead.

Horemheb gave them another look before he nodded. "Good men."

He turned and took my arm to lead me away.

He took me first to his estate where he had me prepare his food for the morning, so I would not have to come until the middle of the day. As I cooked, he leaned against the table watching me. It made me feel uneasy, so I tried to focus entirely on cooking.

Finally, he said, "Naomi, I will be leading some troops to go to battle in two days, so I will probably be gone for several weeks. I'm afraid that means you will be unable to see Tut while I'm away."

I paused as I thought about all the implications of his statement. Tut would be left unprotected in the palace with Smenkhkare, and of course, my old adversary, Ay. They could take advantage of Horemheb's absence and have my son assassinated.

I turned to him and spoke in a tense voice, "Take him with you."

He raised his eyebrows. "What?"

"Take him with you. You can't leave him here with that horrible Smenkhkare and Ay. They will kill him, just like they tried to kill me."

"You know what it will mean if I took him, don't you? He will see bloodshed."

"I know, but it is less likely to be his own. I know you will protect him, and as the new Pharaoh, the men will be inspired to see him leading them into battle with you at his side."

He smirked. "Very clever, Naomi, using my pride to make me bend to your will. It seems Kiya is not completely dead after all."

He stepped up to me and leaned over my shoulder to smell my cooking. His hands rested on my waist, and although I wanted to, I couldn't bring myself to pull away.

"You should pack some extra food for Tut and me when we leave," he said. "If I'd known you made food this good, I would have forgotten about the scrolls and dragged you down to fatten me up every day, instead."

He stepped back from me, and I breathed a silent sigh of relief.

"I'm going to retire now. Have my guards at the gate take you home when you're done."

I couldn't help watching him leave. I realized that what Malachi had said to me was true. Horemheb was my vice; I couldn't say no to him, and I couldn't get enough of him. When he came up to me and I felt his closeness, my heart pounded in my chest, and flashes of him kissing me passed through my mind. I tried to convince myself that he was toying with me, that he wanted to push Malachi over the edge so he could fight a worthy opponent.

As I walked home, I felt grateful he would soon be gone so I could distance myself from him again. It would give me time to build up a resistance to him, now that I knew he was my weakness.

CHAPTER NINETEEN

W eeks had passed since Tut and Horemheb's departure, and I felt very glad for it. A few days after they had gone, I began feeling sick, and since then I had spent every day vomiting. I hadn't been that violently ill with a pregnancy since Tut, and I hoped it would mean that the child would survive.

Malachi rarely left my side. He saw how weak the pregnancy made me, so he employed men to cover for him in the fields and around our small farm. Hepsati and Joshua brought us food, and helped where they could. Somehow, Hepsati remained blind to my sickness and talked endlessly about how she too wanted to be with child so she could share the joy of it with me. I told her she was mad.

Soon, the sickness passed and things returned to normal. Samuel sent for me then, so I could talk with Adina. I found myself afraid to face her. I last had seen her quite some time ago, and I felt uncertain how she would react when she saw me. So Malachi came as emotional support and to show we were truly and completely committed to each other, no matter what.

Not long after our father died, Samuel had moved his family into our old house and given his home to Malachi's brother, Jared, and his family. I was glad he had decided to retain our old family home, and I smiled fondly as we approached.

My sisters were already present, and they all looked at me. Rena and Eliora greeted me excitedly, not having seen me since I had fallen ill, and Dana touched my abdomen and kissed my cheek. But Adina hung back and turned away from me. I knew if we were going to resolve our differences, I would have to initiate the conversation. So, as we all moved to sit together, I sat down beside her. She folded her arms and scowled, half turning away from me. I sighed sadly, but listened as Dana spoke about how she wanted us to assist her when the time came for the child to arrive.

When she stood to show Rena and Eliora where she kept her sheets and stool, I grabbed Adina's arm and held her down. She tried to pull away, but Samuel entered the room and gave her a fierce glare that told her to stay seated.

Once the others had gone, I spoke to her softly.

"Adina, I know I have disappointed you." She scoffed and turned away from me, but I continued. "I want you to know that I love Malachi. I chose him from the very beginning and remain completely committed to him. I will never go back to that life I had to lead in the palace. I lived a daily struggle just to stay alive, and I spent hours secretly praying for my life. Adina, how I longed for you in that place; even the night I met Malachi, I thought of you and how we would talk and play together, and was grateful that it was not you in my place. Knowing you were safe gave my heart solace, and knowing I had protected you from the horrific things I had to face brought me the peace I needed to keep going."

Her shoulders hunched as she slowly turned to me with tears in her eyes. "But you loved Hepsati's mother more than you ever did me. Even to this day, you still silently grieve for her."

"I grieve for her because of her tragic life. She never knew the freedom we have to marry goodly men. She ached to see her homeland again, but she never would. I owe her my life, Adina. She threw me aside so the viper that was placed among my belongings would not strike me. She gave me her daughter so the child could be free, where she had never been, despite being a princess. I did love her like a sister, but you *are* my sister and everything I did, I'd do it all again for you."

Tears burst from her eyes. "Oh, Naomi, please don't go back to that place! I know you love Tut, but I'm so afraid they will discover you. I saw how that princess examined your face like she suspected you, and I almost screamed at her to leave you alone. I don't like how that Commander looks at you, either, and how since he discovered you are alive, he always seems to be waiting in the background. When you told me about what happened, I just…"

She paused and fell onto her knees, resting her head in my lap. "I had a sick feeling that he would take you away from me. That he would turn you back into Kiya and use you to overthrow all those perverted royals."

I stroked her hair, feeling compassion for her. "Adina, I could never go back there. Having to check my food and drink every time I wish to eat, checking my bed for poisonous creatures, having to keep a latch on my door so I am not attacked in my sleep, that is not a life I would choose. I worry for Tut every day, and am grateful for those who watch over him, but that isn't my life anymore. I have more than one child to raise, and I have a husband who has proven he would protect me with his very life. I owe it to them to stay here, and I owe it to you and our sisters as well because I love you each more than I do myself."

I reached down and pulled her up into a warm embrace. She clung to me as we both wept tears of relief onto each other's shoulders.

The annual festival brought our sector to life. Music played on every corner, and people sang loudly while tossing grain everywhere. The scent of roasting meat filled the air, and as we converged onto the festival square, where we would dance and sing praises. The aroma of a great bonfire surrounded us, and its light shone above the buildings in front of us.

My sisters and I were expected to dance and sing, being the daughters of the direct line of Ephraim, and as we entered, the daughters of the other direct lines linked arms and formed a circle around the fire. Samuel's daughter was not yet old enough to join us, but the other daughters had some younger girls with them.

My sisters and I exchanged grins. We knew we would be able to dominate that year, with each of us now being veterans at the dance. The six daughters of Levi lined up next to us to the left, while the seven daughters of Zebulun lined up to our right. Directly across from us were the ten daughters of Judah, whom we loved to taunt. The oldest daughter was almost ten years older than I was, but we had been rivals since I had first started dancing, when I was eight years old. Then, as my sisters joined me and my aunts passed, she grew fiercer with her rivalry as I rapidly became the most popular dancer with my charming taunts and flirtatious ways. But I hadn't participated in many years, being in Amarna, then in disgrace, and more recently, too pregnant to be able to dance competitively.

I knew I must have looked impressive with my sisters, having retained some of my jewelry from my time as a queen, and borrowed some from Horemheb's house. We were all heavily adorned in gold and brightly colored garments. I was not showing yet, so we all looked strong and healthy and wore our hair free of the shawls to show that not one of us had begun to gray. We were the smallest group, but the most threatening.

The crowd gathered as the musicians set up. I met the stare of the oldest daughter from Judah, and smiled at her mischievously. She smirked back, accepting my challenge, and the music began.

We danced barefoot in the dirt, my sisters and I staying close at first as we moved around to examine our opponents.

"The daughters of Asher are weak this year," Rena said as I spun her under my arm. "The age gap is too wide, the girls are too young, and the women too old. They will be the first to step out."

And they were. As the music kicked up a notch and the twelve groups finished assessing one another, the daughters of Asher knew they stood no chance and bowed out.

"Manasseh look good this year," Eliora said to us as we all pulled in close. "They are all in their teens, none are heavy with child, and they are easily as pretty as we are."

"But we have Naomi back." Adina smiled. "She was always the best at pleasing a crowd."

I laughed and twirled. "I'm a little out of practice, but I will see what I can do."

We spun out from each other and danced around in search of our husbands.

I felt a little nervous about how well Malachi would perform. I had never seen him dance before, so I hoped his sheer size would be threatening enough to intimidate the other husbands and young men.

I spotted him with his brothers and danced over. The three wives of his brothers looked delighted to see me coming. I danced into Malachi's arms and he burst out laughing. "Naomi, why don't you go find your brother instead?"

"No." I smiled as I held his hands and danced in front of him.

"Naomi is the best." Miriam laughed. "She used to hold the whole crowd in the palm of her hand. She may not have performed the fanciest moves, but she drew everyone's attention."

163

"But this is the first time I've had a husband." I grinned. "So I don't have to frighten some poor boy."

Tobiah shoved Malachi hard and he stumbled forward into me. "Go on, little brother. Don't leave your wife to have to find some poor boy."

I looked across the square and saw I would be the last one back out. "Come on, Malachi!"

He finally relented and followed me out to meet my sisters. He stood beside Uriyah, who had never liked the dance, and they both looked at each other uncomfortably.

"What am I supposed to do?" Malachi asked him.

"Just follow Naomi, she is very good. That's how I met her. She plucked me out of the crowd."

Malachi chuckled. "I'm very sorry."

I shoved Uriyah away and danced with Malachi. My sisters and I spun around our husbands as we quickly examined the situation.

"We have the strongest man out here," I told them, patting Malachi's shoulder. "Let's use that to our advantage..."

I trailed off as several of the daughters of Judah launched into the air and twirled around. I turned Malachi so he could see, and said, "Like that!"

"No, Naomi."

"Yes, Malachi!"

"But you're pregnant."

I huffed. "It won't harm the child."

My sisters and I prepared ourselves, then all together, we had our husbands toss and twirl us in the air. The crowd responded exactly as I wanted them to; I looked down at Malachi and saw it excited him, too. So, as he lowered me, he swung my feet up and dipped me down low. No one had ever done that before, and the crowd cheered. He thrived on the attention and rapidly became the best partner I ever had. The more confident he became, the faster the other groups dropped out. They saw we pleased the crowd with his strength and my charm. Even my sisters were impressed by how well Malachi took to the dance.

The last three tribes remained; the men were expected to step out. But before he left, Malachi spun me and bent me backward, kissing me just under my chin as my head dropped back. It caused a great cheer to arise, with such public displays of affection being so rare and almost scandalous.

As he lifted me back up, even my sisters were astounded by his move, and I knew we had put on a show to be reckoned with.

As the men departed, I took Rena and Adina's hands and we danced together again. The other two tribes left were Judah and Manasseh. I decided it was time to get in their way. The daughters of Manasseh would be the easiest to throw, as none of them were accustomed to this tactic of mine, so I led my sisters toward them. Within moments, we had them pushed back against the crowd, who laughed at the trick that hadn't been used in years.

I spun away and left my sisters so I could win the crowd over completely. I twirled and twisted along the edge of the spectators, who would take my hand and begin to dance as I passed them. Everyone seemed to suddenly remember how I had once been, and the crowd came to life with dancing and singing.

The noise rose in volume, and I spun around to see Manasseh stepping down. I rushed back to my sisters, and the four of us turned to Judah. There were ten of them, versus four of us, but the smaller girls and older women were tiring, so we managed to frighten them off quickly, leaving only the best five.

I faced my rival from Judah. We grinned at each other. She seemed pleased to have someone to challenge her again as we whirled and twisted to the music.

Suddenly, the feeling of the noise from the crowd shifted. It became fearful, and the music cut short. I turned toward the source and saw Egyptian soldiers shoving through. My rival from Judah grabbed my arm and pulled me back behind her, and my sisters converged around me. Fear coiled my stomach. Had the Egyptians discovered me alive and come for me?

As the soldiers pushed into the square, Smenkhkare emerged from among them. The soldiers pushed the crowd back as he bellowed, "This festival has not been sanctioned by me! Disperse immediately!"

The crowd rushed out of the square fearfully, but we were caught in the middle, near the fire. The women shoved me into the center of the group as we stood together, unable to escape.

Smenkhkare noticed us and smirked. "Is this some kind of offering?"

He walked slowly over to us and, stroking his long, straight beard on his chin, looked us over. "You look very beautiful tonight."

165

"Disperse!" I heard Ay call out. I looked across to see him enter with the soldiers as well. "Your god is not recognized here! How dare you worship him in our city!"

One of the young women from Judah squealed and I glanced across to see Smenkhkare pull her away from the others. He wrapped his arm around her waist and held her against him. "You're a pretty little thing."

She tried to push him away, but he held her tighter and kissed her. I watched in horror as she struggled against him, and when he finally pulled away, he laughed at her distress. "You are nice and strong. I think I will take you."

I tried to push through to stop him, but Adina and Rena grabbed me.

"No, Naomi!" Adina hissed. I looked at her and saw terror in her eyes. "Please, if he recognizes you—"

"We have to do something!" I tried to pull away from her.

My rival from Judah turned to me and grabbed my wrist. "You've already made this sacrifice once before; you don't have to do it again."

As I gazed up into her face, I saw a tear fall as the girl screamed. The girl had to be her niece, and she struggled within herself not to fight back. Another woman screamed and I looked across the square to see the girl's parents trying to plead with the guards, but the guards held them back.

I struggled against my sisters, more determined than ever to stop what was happening. "He will take me," I said desperately. "He will see me and want me more than her."

A stone flew across the square and hit Smenkhkare in the side of the head. A terrified silence fell. We watched him turn and gaze in the direction the stone came from, as blood ran down the side of his face.

"Who did that?" he bellowed, before tossing the girl aside. He marched toward the crowd, which pushed back in fear, and I saw, among them, Malachi and his brothers with their families and my children. I became fearful when I saw the expression on Malachi's face. I knew he had thrown the stone.

"Malachi!" I breathed. "No Malachi, don't...."

But as the crowd pushed back, he remained firm. Tobiah grabbed at his arm, but he shook him off, and gave Zakkai and Itani to Miriam.

Smenkhkare stood in front of him and rested his hands on his hips in an attempt to match his size. "You, slave, dare to stand against me? I am Pharaoh—"

"You are not Pharaoh. King Tutankhamen is Pharaoh."

I grabbed onto Adina and Rena's arms. I felt sick. I couldn't believe Malachi was standing up against Smenkhkare. He could easily be put to death for such defiance.

Ay rushed over and said loudly, "Make an example of him, my lord. Let these people know where they belong and what will happen if they dare try to rise against us."

Then Malachi did something that made me want to fall to my knees and sob because I knew it would be the end for him. "You, Lord Ay, are the cruelest of them all. I know what you did and how your hand was in the assassination attempts and final end of Queen Kiya. You were even part of trying to kill the heir, Tutankhamen, himself."

Smenkhkare drew his sword and held it to Malachi's neck.

I twisted to Adina and covered my face, unable to watch. She held me tightly as I waited for the sound of the final blow, but it didn't come. Instead I heard Ay say, "Take him to the dungeons. We will make an example of him in a public execution tomorrow, where we will burn him to death."

Smenkhkare chuckled. "You should have just let me take the girl."

I turned back around to see the soldiers bind him before leading him away.

"No, Malachi!" I screamed.

He turned to look at me, but just as our gaze met, he was shoved forward.

I struggled desperately against the women around me. They held me back until the soldiers had all gone, and the square was almost empty. Then they let me go; I fell to my knees and sobbed uncontrollably. I couldn't believe he had done that. I couldn't believe he would be gone by morning.

I felt Adina squat beside me and touch my shoulder. "Naomi—"

I pushed her off. "Leave me."

From the other side, Eliora took hold of my elbow. "Naomi, we—"

"I said leave me!" I yelled at her with venom in my voice.

My hair fell over my face as I watched my tears fall to the earth and make small puddles in the dirt. The women slowly left as I cried, my heart breaking. I stayed there, unable to understand why he would do such a mad act of suicide. My wonderful husband, whom I loved so deeply, would soon be dead, but why did he do it? I didn't know what to do, how I could save

167

him. I rubbed at my tears, when I suddenly saw someone kneel in front of me.

I started, having thought I was alone, when Rena's soft voice sounded. "Naomi, you know where the dungeons are; go find him. I will take your children tonight."

Her hand reached out and brushed my hair back over my shoulder. "He loves you, Naomi. Let him see the woman he loves in his last few hours."

I rubbed my eyes with the heel of my hands and looked at her. "I can't believe he did it."

"I can," she said, stroking my cheek. "You are in everything he sees, and he saw you in that girl. He saw you being taken to the palace in Amarna and given to the king. He couldn't let it happen again, not to the likes of Smenkhkare."

"I should have done something," I said softly. "I should have revealed myself to him."

"Oh, Naomi, you know that would have only made matters worse. He would have taken you *and* killed Malachi, because Malachi would have fought him to the death to free you."

I didn't want her to be right, but I hated that she was. I reached out for her hand and she helped me to my feet.

"I will go to him. I must see him for myself anyway. I cannot bear the thought of never seeing him again."

She softly brushed my tears from my cheek before kissing it. "Go, dear sister, but be cautious."

I turned and ran through the abandoned city. I occasionally had to pause and duck into the shadows to hide from the night patrols, but I made it to the dungeons swiftly, and without being caught.

I walked briskly around the walls whispering for Malachi. Then suddenly, near my feet, someone said my name.

I fell to my knees and tried to peer through the tiny window.

"Malachi, is that you?"

A hand reached out, and I caught it.

"Yes, my dear. Why are you here? It's not safe for you."

"Oh, Malachi!" I lay down in the dust and kissed his hand. "Why did you do that?"

"It was the right thing to do," he whispered as his other hand came up and touched my cheek.

"But I'm going to lose you! I can't lose you!"

He let go of me for a moment as I heard him move things around. Then he climbed up and I was able to see his face. I touched his cheek; seeing a dark shadow over his right eye, I began to cry again.

"Naomi, don't cry," he said gently and kissed my hand. "Knowing you are safe brings me peace, so don't feel badly for me."

"But we were supposed to have many children and live long lives together. You won't even have a chance to see the child I carry now."

He sighed sadly. "You are strong, and our families will take care of you."

"But I want you. All I ever wanted was you."

He kissed my hand again as I saw a tear fall. "I love you, Naomi, but you should go now before you are caught."

"No," I said defiantly. "I will fall asleep in the dust if I must, but I will not leave you, especially not tonight."

He sighed again. "All right, it will be nice to know you are here. But take this." He bent down, then handed me a thin sheet. "It's the best I can do. You mustn't sleep on the dirt."

I placed it underneath me and saw him smile. I reached back through the window and touched his face.

"I love you, Malachi. I love how you always give, even when you have nothing left *to* give."

"I have to live up to the standard my wife has set." He stroked my arm, then he touched my face. "Sleep, Naomi. You need your strength. I'm not going anywhere."

"But—"

"Naomi, you are with child. Sleep."

I sighed. "Very well. But you must wake me if anything happens, or when the sun rises."

"I will, my beloved. I won't go without saying goodbye."

I rested my head and shut my eyes as he softly kissed my hand.

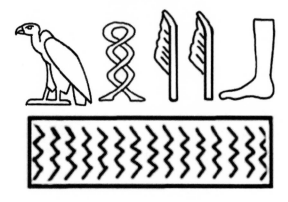

CHAPTER TWENTY

S omeone woke me by nudging me with their foot. I opened my eyes, but the sunlight behind the man blinded me. I shuffled up into a sitting position, but as he squatted in front of me, I saw Horemheb. "What are you doing here?" he snarled.

"Horemheb?" I said, dazed, then I came to my senses and I remembered the night before. "Horemheb!" I grabbed him by the collar of his loose tunic. "They—a girl—he's…"

I shook my head, frustrated by being unable to form a sentence.

He pulled me up to my feet. "Go home before someone finds you here."

"No!" I gasped and grabbed onto him tighter. "When did you get back?"

"Less than an hour ago. I haven't even gone home yet."

I pointed down at the dungeon window. "They're going to kill him! You have to do something!"

"Who?" He bent down and Malachi appeared, looking up at us. Horemheb scowled and turned to me. "What did you do?"

"Nothing!" I gasped. "We were holding an annual festival and Smenkhkare and Ay came with soldiers and forced us to stop."

"They tried to take a girl," Malachi said, snarling. "But I couldn't let them do that again. I will gladly die for doing what I did."

Horemheb grunted. "I'd gladly watch you die."

I shoved his chest. "Don't say that!"

He caught my arms and glared at me. "You are very good at causing me trouble, you know that? Let me go find out what's going on and I'll see what I can do."

Tears of relief filled my eyes. "Thank you, Horemheb."

He gazed steadily into my eyes. "You can't be out in the open like this. Go and wait for me at my estate where I will either bring you your husband, or collect you so you can watch his trial."

I felt elated as I dashed away, and as I went to turn the corner, I glanced around to see Horemheb kneel down to talk to Malachi.

An hour later Horemheb came to collect me. I had replaced all the jewelry I'd borrowed, and found myself a shawl and veil to cover my hair and face, if need be.

He scowled as he entered and grabbed my arm.

"Your husband is a fool." He tugged me to the front of the house. "Throwing a stone at Smenkhkare? Accusing Ay of conspiracy to murder? Just because we all want to do or say those things doesn't mean we should."

"What's happening?" I asked fearfully.

He groaned. "He will appear before Smenkhkare, Ay, Tut, and myself. Tut is your only hope because I would love to see him dead—"

"Horemheb, please!"

"But I wouldn't worry. Tut has the superior authority and I doubt he will let his father figure die."

We approached the palace. He had me veil my face before we entered. He led me through to the throne room where Tut sat, with Ay and Smenkhkare standing to his right.

They turned as we entered, and Ay frowned at Horemheb. "You brought your slave with you? Was that really necessary?"

"This is not my slave. She is the wife of the accused. I found her outside and she begged me to come see her husband before he died." He tossed me to the floor. "She clung onto me desperately until I agreed. She is lucky I am feeling compassionate today, as I have had my blood lust quenched for the time being."

Horemheb marched up and bowed quickly to Tut before taking a place at his left.

I looked up at the four most powerful men in the kingdom, and wondered; what if I stood and announced that Kiya was not dead, and I was she? Tut would be glad of it. It would mean he would have his mother back. Horemheb would thrust me into the position of Queen Mother instantly. But Ay and Smenkhkare, they were something else entirely. Smenkhkare would probably force me to be his wife, while Ay would try to kill me. It would cause division and an internal war that could bring about the loss of many lives, including my son's and mine. So, I remained silent, and didn't bother lifting myself up from the ground.

Tut watched me, and as he realized who I was, it dawned on him who was about to be brought before him.

Just then, a door opened and two women entered. I looked at them and saw Mayati and Ankhe. Mayati went straight to Smenkhkare and rested her hand on his shoulder, but Ankhe noticed me on the floor. She changed her course and stood over me.

"You again?" she said softly. "You seem to keep showing up. The Commander must really like you."

Finally, the doors burst open. Two guards dragged in Malachi. He was bound, but he held his chin up defiantly, and even when he was forced to his knees, he remained dignified.

Ankhe turned slightly; I looked up at her. She stared at Malachi with her eyes narrowed. She walked over to him and I heard her whisper, "Why are you familiar?"

"Ankhesenpaaten!" Mayati snapped. "We wish to proceed. Stop playing with the slaves."

Malachi suddenly noticed me in the room. "Naomi!" He gasped and tried to lunge toward me, but the guards held him back. He glared up at Horemheb.

"Why is my wife here?"

"Silence!" Ay bellowed. "Or we will have her executed as well."

Malachi fell silent, and Tut and Horemheb both glanced at me. I wasn't the only one who noticed the subtle gesture; Ankhe turned quickly and stared down at me fixedly.

"My lord," Horemheb said gently to Tut. "You are to lead these proceedings."

"Yes, of course." Tut sat up straighter and cleared his throat. "Hebrew, you have been charged with assault on Smenkhkare and slander against Ay. What say you in your defense?"

I could tell Horemheb had run through what Tut needed to say by the way he spoke. It definitely sounded more like the words of Horemheb than my nine-year-old son.

The guards pulled Malachi onto his feet so he could answer.

"We were holding an annual festival in our sector of the city when we were attacked by the soldiers of these men. They told us we were not to worship our own god—"

"Ay," Tut said, looking up at him. "I thought we were trying to give religious freedom back to the people. How is attacking the Hebrews for worshiping their own god doing that?"

Ay's face tightened. "Their god is not recognized—"

"But it's their god, they recognize him. They will be allowed to worship as they please, so anything this man is accused of cannot be held against him because he was being denied that right and was defending himself and his family."

I smiled and looked to Horemheb, who remained stone-faced. He really was a very good teacher.

"But what about me?" Smenkhkare snarled. "Look at me!" He pointed at the gash on the side of his head.

Horemheb responded, "Why did you throw the stone, Hebrew?"

"To protect the virtue of a young maiden. We all fear a repeat of our beloved Kiya and the tragic life she led, and the end she was given."

"Kiya!" Mayati gasped. "Smenkhkare, you are never to touch a Hebrew woman, I have told you this! You deserve what you got if you tried, and I will not feel pity for you."

She stepped in front of Tut and bowed. "My lord, let my husband suffer for his foolishness, but do not punish this man for doing what he believed was right."

I looked across at Malachi. He had a gleam in his eye. The whole thing had been well staged, I could see that now. Horemheb had coached not only Tut with what to say, but Malachi also, having known Mayati would not react well to the mention of Kiya.

Tut raised his hand, and she stepped away from him. He stood and spoke to Malachi. "It seems you will live today, Hebrew. But from now on, be careful with the choices you make. We may not be so forgiving a second time."

"My lord is merciful and understanding," Malachi said and bowed deeply.

"Take your wife with you." Horemheb gestured to me. "The sight of her offends me."

"Wife…" I heard Ankhe mumble, and as Malachi rushed to me and helped me to my feet, she stared at us with wide eyes. We didn't give her a chance to register what that might have meant as we dashed out the doors.

We hurried through the palace, but as we passed through a garden, Ankhe appeared beside us.

"I know now why you are familiar. You were the guard who escorted us to my father, and whom he sent to protect Kiya. I know what you look like with a beard because you returned to tell him of her death, and I thought you looked strange with facial hair."

Malachi pulled me back behind him as he responded, "You're father was a great king. I had a deep respect for him—"

"So how did you meet your wife? I know she is kin to our young Pharaoh."

Malachi bowed quickly. "I am sorry, Princess, but we cannot stay here. I am afraid they may change their minds and kill me."

He pulled my arm, keeping himself between Ankhe and me as he walked out of the garden.

"She broke my father's heart, slave!" she called after us. "You make sure she knows that if she still lives."

We hurried out of the palace into the streets and back to our sector, where we both breathed a sigh of relief. He wrapped his arms tightly around me.

"Oh, Naomi, my prayers were answered! All night, I sat up, pleading with the Lord to deliver me, and He did! That son of ours truly is a gift from heaven. Again and again, he has blessed us and preserved our lives so we could remain together."

I grabbed his face and kissed him, not caring who saw. As I drew away, I said, "Don't you ever scare me like that again! We truly were blessed this time, but you cannot risk your life like that! I need you, Malachi."

He sighed as he brushed my hair back from my face and stared into my eyes. "I'm glad you need me, and I'm so grateful you stayed with me last night. You kept me from sinking into despair and losing hope."

"And if I hadn't, Horemheb would never have noticed you locked away and you would be dead."

His eyebrows twitched and his smile became forced.

I huffed. "Malachi, he was the one who saved you. I could tell he not only told Tut what to say, but you, also. He's a master at his game. I've seen it up close and participated with him many times—"

"Please, Naomi, I don't want to talk about him. I'm grateful for what he did, but I know he didn't do it so my life would be preserved, and you know that, too."

I stared at him silently, unable to contradict him. I rested my head against his chest.

"It doesn't matter. You are here and you didn't die. Let's go collect our children from Rena and spend the day together at our farm."

He kissed my head. "That sounds perfect."

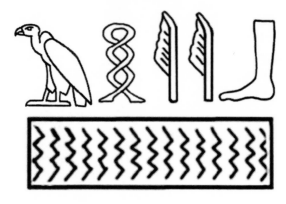

CHAPTER TWENTY-ONE

I worked on hanging Horemheb's laundry out to dry. I spent several hours washing blood out of his clothes and blankets, and incinerating the items I couldn't save. Everything smelled foul, and made me sick on several occasions, but he reassured me I would be paid extra for the work. I hated to think what Tut saw out there, and hoped Horemheb had kept him well away from the fray.

A bang sounded inside the house, and I looked up to see what was going on, hoping my children hadn't broken something, but I was surprised by one of Horemheb's menservants rushing to me.

"Naomi, the master requires your presence immediately, but he needs you to remain discreet."

"Where is he?" I asked, placing the wet laundry to the side and drying my hands.

"In the palace. He will meet you in the entryway. I will show you to the servant's entrance so that you can enter without being noticed."

"Wait, someone needs to watch my children."

I glanced around and saw, in an upstairs window, one of the maidservants. I called to her, and she agreed to keep an eye on Itani and Zakkai.

The manservant took my arm and led me out of the estate, to the palace servant's entry. He showed me where I needed to go, then left me to return to his own responsibilities.

I moved silently through the entryway. There, I made my way around the pillars of the wide room where voices filtered to me. Pulling back, I hid until Horemheb and a captain passed by. I stood in the shadows watching Horemheb as he finished his conversation. Then, as the captain departed, Horemheb glanced around and walked slowly toward me. As he passed, he muttered, "Follow me at a distance."

I obeyed and kept my eyes lowered, to remain discreet. I followed him out of the palace, along several streets, and down to the river. We walked along the farmland on the banks until we reached some reeds and he stepped into them. I turned in and found myself face to face with him. He grabbed my hand, and signaled for me to be quiet. He led me through the reeds to a small island. The tall stalks surrounded it, and during the flooding months, completely cut off the island, making it perfect place for a secret meeting.

He quickly scanned the area and came back to me. "Naomi, Tut is to marry."

"Marry?" I gasped. "But he's only nine years old."

"That doesn't matter to these people, you know that. But I feel it's something that will assist him with keeping his crown."

"Why?"

"Smenkhkare still threatens Tut's authority. He still says he is not the true son of Amenhotep, that the real Tut died several years ago along with his mother. All they have is my word that his death was a deception conjured up to protect his life, and my word is weakening of late. If he marries, he will have the claim through marriage, as well as his blood, to the throne. Ankhesenamun—"

"Ankhe?" I hissed. "She's twice his age, she must be almost twenty by now! And she cannot be trusted, she is a daughter of Nefertiti."

"Naomi, she wants this. She believes that Tut is who I say he is, and she wants to help keep him on the throne. She was the only one of Amenhotep's daughters who actually loved him and understood that he wanted your son to be his heir. At the end of his life, she began to see her mother and grandfather's scheming. Her loyalty to them wavered. This is for the best."

"And you support this?" I said, my voice quaking.

"I do. Already Smenkhkare has tried to assassinate Tut—"

"Oh, Horemheb!" I gasped in horror. "We ran to avoid these attempts on his life!"

"I know, Naomi. Please, stay calm. You have to trust me."

I dropped my gaze and nodded. "Can I see him?"

He straightened and looked steadily down at me. "No, you can't."

My gaze flashed up to him, my anger rising. "What? You promised I could see him whenever I wanted."

"It's not safe for you right now. If someone sees you and recognizes who you are, you will be in danger."

"That's always been a risk and it's never stopped you before."

He huffed. "Tut is in a delicate state emotionally. After what happened with your husband, he feels shaken. If you are caught, and he has to watch you die, it will ruin him."

I turned away so he wouldn't see the tears in my eyes.

"You promised me you would take care of him."

"And I am. He's the king and I am loyal to the crown. You know I will do anything to protect the crown. Tut is the direct line. No one can take that away from him. You did your duty to your king well, and now his line is preserved. Tut will ensure the continuation of the line with Ankhe. Amenhotep's only good decision was to marry you."

"You talk about Akhenaten like you never cared for him." I spun and gazed up at him. "But you were always his most loyal subject."

He raised his chin slightly. "I am loyal to the crown."

I stared up at him, confused, but then it dawned on me what he meant and had always meant. It wasn't the king as an individual to whom he gave his devotion, but the crown.

"You deceived me! I always thought you loved Akhenaten."

He grabbed my arms and bent down to look into my face. "You need to stop speaking his name or the priests of Amun-Ra will kill you. He has been declared a heretic—"

"You never cared about him at all!" I said, pushing him off me. "He was just one in the line-up for you, someone you had to tolerate for a brief period of your life."

He scoffed. "How could I love the man who turned our world upside-down? Aten as the only god? That was madness."

I wrapped my arms around myself and took a step back in shock. "And what is Tut to you, then? My son is his son, also. And what about me? You used me to keep him right where you wanted him. You told me to make him love me and I did, and you told me his happiness was your happiness, but that was a lie. You just wanted to keep Nefertiti and Ay in check while keeping a tight grasp over the king. What else did you lie to me about? Will you protect my son only until someone with purer blood comes along?"

He looked down at me with a stern expression. "Tut is different."

"Why? Because he's my son?"

"Exactly. He's the true heir."

"I'm a Hebrew, Horemheb. My blood runs through him as well as Akhenaten's—"

"Stop saying that name!" he yelled. "Tut will never do the things his father did. He is not insane! He understands the importance of our people being able to worship all the gods, even at his young age. For years, I have had to worship Horus in secret and now, finally, I am free."

"Horus!" I gasped in shock. "All that time, you told me not to worship my god and you were worshiping Horus! I trusted you, I listened to you because I believed you were honest with me and we had no secrets between us, but apparently we do and always have. What else have you lied to me about? Your claims of love? Were they just to soften me up to keep me where you wanted me?"

He winced at my words and pulled back from me, but he quickly recovered and pointed at me accusingly.

"I thought the same about you, *Kiya!*" he snarled with venom. "I thought you were honest with me as well, but then I find you having a secret love affair with *that* guard."

"I never once committed adultery," I growled defensively.

"No, but you didn't have to, did you? You are married to him now. But when did you intend to give me that piece of information, that you loved *him*? Never, I presume. I had to find it out by seeing you with him."

He reached out and grabbed me by the hair on the back of my head, pulling me up against him. "That was a lie far worse than any of mine. That seared my heart because I didn't lie when I said I was in love with you, and every day my love still burns. I watch your son not only because he is the rightful heir, but because he is a part of you, the only part I can have."

He let go of me and pushed past, heading toward the reeds. Just before he entered them, he called back to me, "Tut will be married in three days."

Then he parted the reeds and disappeared.

I stared at the place where he had disappeared in complete shock. Tut was to marry? My little boy? I couldn't believe it, I couldn't believe the perversion of the Egyptians, and I wondered what Ankhe was thinking. I knew she suspected me, and I wondered if she was marrying my son in an attempt to draw me out.

I didn't know what to do. I wanted to go to Tut and talk with him, see what he thought and felt about all of it, but I couldn't; Horemheb had put him off limits to me. I remembered that Malachi's brothers were his guards, and I decided I would send a note with them. That would have to suffice.

I thought about all Horemheb said to me. He was a follower of Horus; he had always been one, I had no doubt about that. I thought back to my time in Amarna and remembered the rumors that he was, and I realized he had never confirmed or denied those rumors. He had always been ambiguous; he was always so ambiguous.

He let his wife worship Isis and Hathor and never turned her in, even though he despised her. She had been caught only because she had an affair.

I remembered the day we searched Thebes for spies in the abandoned temples, and we entered the Temple of Horus. He stopped the soldiers before they destroyed the statue of Horus, and it suddenly became clear why. I felt so naive for not noticing.

But I was angry at him for the way he deceived me with his feelings for Akhenaten. I truly thought he loved my husband and served him loyally. I believed that he wanted to help him in every way possible. He had done nothing to make me doubt his loyalty. I had watched him ease Akhenaten's pain when his body failed him; I saw him speak peace into Akhenaten's ears, and inform him of deceit among his subjects.

But there was one thing that should have raised doubt in my mind—me. Despite the king's love for me, Horemheb coveted me, loved me. He wanted me to have a son so he could have me, once the king was gone, just like Malachi. He tried to have me while I was still married to the king, which should have been my biggest clue. I couldn't believe he loved me so much he would risk it all for a moment's satisfaction.

I suddenly found myself hurrying through the reeds after him. As I burst out, I glanced around and found him nowhere in sight, so I ran back to his estate. I rushed in and searched the house until I found him in his room overlooking the garden, watching my children play.

"Horemheb."

He turned, surprised. "Naomi, you're out of breath, sit down."

He took my arm and led me to a chair as I caught my breath. "I don't know what to make of you anymore," I said. "You worship Horus?"

He nodded with a stern expression. "I always have."

"Why didn't you ever tell me? You've known all along I worship Elohim."

"It was different for me," he said as he leaned against his bed. "I'm an Egyptian nobleman. I was right at the top, by the king's side. But you're a Hebrew; everyone expects you to worship your people's god. Even the king himself knew that in your heart, you remained true to your own faith."

"I suspected that he knew," I muttered, standing back up and looking out to the gardens. "But I can't believe that you didn't love him. You were so devoted; you knew exactly what to do when he had his attacks."

His gaze dropped. "I had to preserve the crown. At first, he had no heir, and when you did finally give him one, I needed to keep him alive as long as possible to give you time to raise the boy. As much as I didn't approve of his methods, he was better than Smenkhkare, and he was far better than Nefertiti and Ay."

"Why didn't you tell me these things sooner?" I asked, turning to face him. "Do you think I wouldn't have understood?"

He smiled and nodded. "I knew you would understand. But I didn't want to put you in more danger than you needed to be, and, I needed you to see the king the way *you* wanted to see him. If I had tainted that, he would have sensed your integrity faltering."

I leaned back against the arched doorway onto the balcony and sighed.

"What am I to do, Horemheb?"

"About what?"

"Tut. He's just a boy; he can't marry. He can't lie with Ankhe at his age. The very thought repulses me and makes me want to tear him away from that place."

I rubbed my temples, fighting back my emotions.

Horemheb pushed off his bed and walked over to stand in front of me. "Naomi, you are a wonderful mother. You love your children with your whole heart, and they know it, and return your love to you. But this is something which you must let go. Kings, princes and princess in Egypt marry young, you know that. You saw that Ankhe was not even ten years old when you arrived in Amarna, and she was already married to her father. Tut knows his duty. I have talked with him in great detail about what this

181

would mean, and he agreed. It's crucial he marry her now, because soon, our neighbors will send him their daughters for wives and Ankhe needs to be his first and Great Royal Wife."

"And they are both agreeable to this?" I asked softly with my gaze low.

He touched my chin so I would look up at him. "Yes, they are."

I stared into his eyes, feeling myself being drawn in by him again. I touched his waist, trying to control my impulse to grab him and pull him closer.

"Horemheb, don't..." I whispered as he drew nearer. His nose brushed against mine and his breath grazed my lips. I held my breath, unable to move.

Then his hand rested on my waist and he paused before running it over my slightly swollen abdomen. He pulled back and twisted away from me.

I exhaled, relieved that the child within me ended what I couldn't.

"I can't believe you're with child *again*," he muttered. "How many do you intend to have with that man?"

I stroked my abdomen. "As many as I can."

He made a strange choking sound and turned back to me. "Get out, Naomi. I can't look at you right now."

I hurried out, feeling guilty for what just happened, but so grateful for my fertility and the protection it gave me from my own weakness.

As soon as I shut the door, I heard him wail in frustration and break something. I jumped, startled by his intensity, and as he sobbed, I found my feet stuck to the ground. I'd never seen or heard him cry. He was the master of his emotions; he never let them overpower him. I stood there, completely mesmerized by his sudden outburst, and wondered what he had done when he'd heard I died.

The head maidservant startled me as she rushed around the corner. "What happened?"

"I don't... he's..." I pointed to the door and asked, "Has he ever done that before?"

She grunted. "Just once, when Queen Kiya died. That went on for days and he tore his room to shreds. Do you know what provoked this?"

I hesitated, not sure if I should expose myself or him. "He told me the king is to marry."

She rested her hand on her hip and sighed. "Queen Kiya's son, of course. Anything to do with that woman makes him mad." She glanced at the doorway. "At least he doesn't sound like he's tearing the place apart this time. Come now, dear, let's give him his privacy."

As she led me down the stairs, I felt bad for all the pain I unwittingly gave Horemheb. I wished he could let me go, and I wished, more than anything, I had remained dead to him.

I hadn't intended to go to the wedding feast, but when I didn't show up at Horemheb's estate, he came looking for me. As I made my way back to the house from washing clothes by the river, I saw him waiting by the small garden, watching what appeared to be a slave boy tending to the plants. As I drew nearer, I gasped in shock as I realized the boy was Tut. I lifted Zakkai onto my hip and ran toward them.

"Tut!"

He stood and turned to face me. A wide grin spread across his face. "Mama!"

He climbed over the small fence and ran to me. We reached each other and he held me tight. "It feels like it has been so long since I could talk to you!"

"I know, son. Things have been very busy for you." I kissed his head as he stepped back from me.

"How is Papa? I was so frightened when I saw the man I had to judge was him. I didn't want him to die." His eyes fell to my abdomen as he ran his hand over it.

"Your Papa is fine. He's very grateful for what you did for him."

Tut grinned up at me mischievously. "I can do some pretty amazing things as Pharaoh, and everyone has to listen to what I say. I love bossing the priests of Amun-Ra around the most. They react so well."

I laughed. "You always enjoyed telling people what to do."

"It's great!" He beamed as he stroked my belly. "You better be a boy, I don't want any more sisters."

"You can't tell the baby what to do, Tut." I smiled and stroked his head.

"Why not?" He pressed his face against me. "I command you to be a boy."

I shook my head. "Tutankhamen, don't you start bossing your siblings around."

"Why not?"

"Because I said so."

He huffed. "Fine."

Itani came up beside him and grabbed his hand, beaming up at him adoringly. He pulled away from her, disgusted. "Don't touch me."

I flicked his ear. "Don't be mean to your sister," I scolded, before turning to Itani. "Run and get Hepsati. She will want to see your brother as well."

Itani spun on her heel and ran toward Hepsati's farm.

When I looked back to Tut, I saw him bending over for Zakkai to rub Tut's smooth-shaven head. I frowned, missing Tut's hair, which had been so much like my own. I sighed, and touched his back to coax him into the house.

When I looked up, I was startled to see Horemheb waiting for us by the door, having forgotten he was there. Tut ran straight over to him and grabbed his hand, pulling him into the house. I wasn't quite sure what to do. I had been avoiding him since we almost kissed, but I knew, with Tut and the other children around, he wouldn't dare try anything. So I led Zakkai back into the house and gave them a cup each and put out a jug of water. I felt Horemheb watching me, but I didn't dare look back at him.

"Mama, did you know Uncle Enoch and Uncle Jared are my guards at night?" Tut asked me.

I smiled at him as I put a dish full of dates on the table. "I did. I was glad to see them there the night of your coronation. They will take good care of you."

"They're great," Tut said excitedly as he took a handful of dates. "They already killed an assassin who tried to break in to kill me, just like Papa did when I was little. I was only a bit scared; mostly it was very exciting."

My stomach knotted with concern for him and I couldn't help glancing at Horemheb.

Horemheb's gaze met mine, but he didn't react.

"Oh, Tut, that..." I hesitated, not wanting to frighten him. "Tut, you just be careful."

"Of course, Mama, but I won't get hurt. Horemheb always has someone watching me if he isn't, plus, I'm learning how to be a warrior."

The door burst open and Hepsati threw herself at Tut. "Tut! I have missed you so much!"

Tut flushed and patted her back. "Yeah, you too, Hepsati."

184

She squeezed him tighter. "I'm so glad you're here. I can tell you and Mama in person my news." She grinned at us both. "I am with child."

Tut pulled a revolted face. "No, you're not."

I laughed and wrapped my arm around her. "How wonderful! You've been wishing for this."

"Urgh! Hepsati!" Tut grumbled.

She slapped his shoulder. "Be happy for me."

"No, it's disgusting." He looked over to Joshua who stood by the door. "Don't touch my sister again."

Both Hepsati and I slapped him.

He glared up at us. "Hey! I'm the Pharaoh. Stop hitting me!"

"I'm your mother, and I will do as I like to you," I snapped, before turning my attention to Horemheb. "You went into *that* much detail when you told him what being married would involve?"

He shrugged. "The boy has to know at some point."

The door flew open again and Itani shoved Joshua out of the way, pulling Malachi in behind her. His gaze fell on Tut and he smiled happily before he saw Horemheb sitting across from him. He consciously tried to ignore him.

"Tut!" He beamed and reached his arms out for him.

Tut leaped to his feet and ran over.

"Papa, let's go to the fields and tend to the sheep together."

Malachi wrapped his arms around him and lifted him over his shoulder.

"I don't think so. But you can try and beat me. You look bigger than I remember, so you might stand a chance."

Tut wriggled to try and wrestle him. "I'm Pharaoh! I command you to let me win!"

"That's not going to work on me!" Malachi laughed.

Tut's legs flailed around and he almost kicked Joshua in the face.

I grabbed Joshua and pulled him out of the way. "I'm sorry, my children are a little wild."

Joshua smiled nervously while watching Tut. I could tell he didn't quite know what to do now that Tut was king, so I encouraged Hepsati to stay with him to ease his discomfort.

Malachi and Tut went outside. Zakkai rushed after them to try to join in on the fun, while Itani stared up at Horemheb. Horemheb glanced at her out of the corner of his eye before lifting his chin and talking to Hepsati. "Princess, how are you faring?"

She giggled. "Princess? I haven't been called that in a very long time."

She moved and sat down where Tut had vacated and said, "Just to clarify, you're the Commander Horemheb my mother despised, aren't you?"

He nodded. "I am."

"I can't believe you're still around." She rested her elbows on the table and looked at him. "The things she would tell me about you! Did you really kill a whole tribe of nomads on your own for stealing from a granary?"

"It wasn't quite like that," he answered, folding his arms. "They had come to negotiate a trade, and while they were leaving, they decided to take more than the share which we had agreed upon. The amount they tried to take would have caused a food shortage. I tried to stop them without bloodshed, but they resisted. I did what I had to do, and I didn't do it by myself, I had three guards with me."

"But there were fifty of them," Hepsati said.

"No, there were only thirty." Horemheb scowled and folded his arms.

"Less than ten apiece," Hepsati smiled.

"No, it was more like ten for me and the rest for the guards."

I heard Joshua stumble back into the wall, and I turned to see him looking extremely agitated. Horemheb glanced up at him and grinned, drawing his sword and resting it on the table.

"This sword, in fact, did the deed. It's my favorite weapon."

"Horemheb," I said sternly and shook my head, knowing he was enjoying taunting poor Joshua.

He leaned back, leaving the sword resting on the table.

Tut burst back into the house, and seeing the sword, his face lit up. "Mama! Horemheb has let me use that sword."

I glared at Horemheb. "He's too young—"

"He never used it against anyone," he said, raising his hands. "He just ran some drills and waved it around in front of the soldiers to make himself look powerful."

Tut rushed over and stood beside Horemheb, running his hand over the blade. "One day, I'm going to be a mighty warrior like Horemheb. Everyone will fear me, and run from me like they do from him."

He looked up at me, wide eyed and excited. "You should have seen him, Mama! He could kill five men with one strike! Those Hittites were terrified of him! When they heard he was in command, they began to tremble, and their spirits fell, which won us the battle."

Malachi wrapped his arm around my waist. I glanced up at him, relieved to see he, too, seemed disturbed by the story, and the implications of the bloodshed to which Tut had been exposed.

Horemheb suddenly launched to his feet. "Well, our time has run out. The boy must prepare to be married."

Malachi's arm tightened around me, and Tut's face fell. "Oh, yeah."

"Tut," I said gently. "If you don't want to…"

He looked at me. "No, it's not that, Mama. I just forgot that I had to go back. I miss being here."

"Oh, Tut." I walked over to him and held him against me. "We miss you, too."

He squeezed me tightly before he looked up and said, "Are you going to come with us, Mama? I want you there."

"I don't think I can." I sighed. "I believe Ankhe suspects me of being your mother and I don't want her to expose me."

Tut spun to Horemheb. "Make her come."

"I can't make her—"

But Tut cut him off. "Yes, you can. I command you to."

"Tut!" I snapped.

"Tut," Malachi began gently. "I too believe she suspects your mother. She recognized me that day I was on trial and followed us out of the palace."

"Well, she will be with me, won't she?" Tut said defiantly. "So she won't be able to go near Mama."

I looked across at Horemheb for help. He shook his head. "He's *your* son. I blame you."

Tut grabbed my hand. "You're coming as Horemheb's servant like you did to the coronation."

I looked at Malachi to see what he thought. He touched my hair and sighed. "The Commander is right; he *is* your son."

Tut grinned, knowing he was about to get his way.

"Very well," I sighed. I walked into my room to collect my shawl and veil.

I could barely see the signing of the contracts from back among the crowd that had gathered. I stood on my toes, but could only see Tut and Ankhe's heads tilt down as they both signed. Once it was complete, a great cheer rose up, and we were all ushered into a grand hall overlooking the river for the feast.

I stood by the wall behind Horemheb and watched my son in silence. Ankhe was not a very large woman, small even by Egyptian standards, so she didn't look that strange beside him. I could tell she was trying to be kind to him, which gave me some relief, but a twinge of fear shot through me, knowing she was Nefertiti's daughter.

Tut, on the other hand, didn't have any concerns and took a liking to her. He showed off, and I felt a little embarrassed by it. But Ankhe laughed with him, which only made my emotional conflict worse.

As the crowd stood to mingle, Horemheb slipped back to me and handed me some food. "Here, you need to eat if you hope to keep your strength while carrying your child."

"Thank you," I said quietly as I took it.

He watched me as I removed my veil to eat. "Good. Now keep out of sight. I must attend to my obligations."

As he walked away, I scanned the room and saw Gerlind. I stared at her fixedly, trying to draw her attention, until finally she sensed my gaze and looked over. Our eyes met, and she made her way discreetly over to me.

She stood beside me, watching the crowd, and whispered, "I have discovered your brothers-in-law, but I haven't been able to leave the palace. Ay has been pressing me for information on your son and has brought me in to be with him almost every night for the last two months."

I glanced at her and responded softly, "I'm sorry, Gerlind. That must be awful."

She smiled and nodded. "He is vile, but I cannot flee like Abi did. My homeland is too far, and with my paler complexion, I stand out everywhere I go around here."

I glanced around before softly squeezing her hand. "Be brave. Maybe soon you will be given to my son instead."

She sneered. "No, Ay has no desire to give me up. He is far too pleased with me for that. I'm stuck with him, and my only hope is he will soon die."

She tilted her head closer to me and whispered, "I know he wishes Tut dead, but he is biding his time. He knows the Commander watches your son closely, and he stands no chance while he's around. When he took Tut with him to battle, Ay was furious. He had arranged an assassination during that time, but instead, the boy went to war and came back with basic military training."

She squeezed my hand. "He is loyal to you—the Commander. I was right, wasn't I? He wasn't trying to trick you that day, he was—"

"Gerlind," I said firmly, cutting her off. "I married Malachi. I am carrying his child. I do not wish to discuss my youthful follies."

But she smiled up at me pleasantly. "Oh my dear, you may have moved on, but he has not. He loves your son as his own because he loves you."

I stared across the room uneasily, and saw Ankhe staring at us.

"Gerlind, go," I mumbled, trying not to move my lips.

Her gaze followed mine and her hand pulled away before she withdrew from me.

The evening drew near, and the hall was lit by torches as the party began to break up. I watched Horemheb, wondering when he would return to me and release me from my duties. I wanted to go home and attend to my family. Suddenly, someone grabbed me from behind and pulled me into a dark corridor. Whoever it was pinned me against the wall and a hand flew over my mouth. Another hand touched my abdomen, feeling the child there. As my eyes adjusted to the dim moonlight, I saw my assailant—Ankhe.

She glared at me as her hand lifted from my belly and squeezed my earlobe.

"Pierced," she muttered, before squeezing the other one. "Both of them. That's not normal for Hebrews."

I tried to struggle against her, but her fist pressed against my abdomen. "Be still, slave!"

I froze, fearful that she would strike my child and cause it harm. Once she seemed satisfied I wouldn't fight against her, she said calmly, "There are certain physical attributes that I know Kiya had, like scars."

Her hand ran up my sleeve and her fingertips found the scar which her mother gave me. Her hand wrapped around my arm tightly and she shoved me hard against the wall.

"Kiya! I knew it! That's why you are here for everything Tutankhamen does, because he's your son!"

"Let me go!" I growled.

"No!" She slapped me across the face. "You broke my father's heart, you whore! I will never forgive you for deceiving him. You made him believe you were dead so you could marry that guard."

"He knew I wasn't dead!" I replied, glaring down at her. "It was all an act. Your mother and Ay kept sending assassins after Tut and me, so we faked our death. But I made sure your father knew. I couldn't deceive him; he was a good husband. He even made it look convincing by sealing my tomb."

"Liar!" She snarled. "He mourned for you all his days."

"Because he knew I couldn't return to him!" I answered. "But that was not my fault. I was driven from the city long before my pretended death."

She grunted and dug her nails into my arm. "My mother."

Her gaze shot up to meet mine as she grabbed my throat. "But you married the guard he sent away with you. You were not faithful—"

"I did not marry him until I was widowed," I answered calmly. "I am no adulterer."

She sneered. "What of the Commander, then? Why does he keep you so close? Were the rumors true, that he seduced you? Is Tut really his?"

"No," I said firmly.

She stared at me, waiting for a more detailed response. When I was not forthcoming, she raised her hand and grabbed my hair by the roots, pulling my head back.

"I have hated you for years, but once I did admire you, secretly. I wanted to be strong like you. I wanted to please my father like you did. I wanted him to love me like he did you. He was the gentlest man I have ever met." She let go of my hair and ran her hand down my cheek. "What makes you so special?"

"I gave him Tut—"

Her hand squeezed my jaw. "It was more than that! You are not the prettiest of all his wives. You are lovely, yes, but not compared to so many others."

"I don't know why he favored me. I tried to be a good wife, that's all."

Her fist opened as she ran her hand over my abdomen. "A good wife bears sons."

"A good wife is loyal to her husband and lends him her ear in the strictest confidence. She is a woman of integrity and virtue so her husband's heart is secure in her."

"Hmm." She turned my head to study my face. "Queen Kiya, mother of my new husband."

She stepped back from me and let go. "I will not turn you in. My vile uncle would have you for his own, which would drive my sister mad. Instead, I will promise you this, my dear Kiya: I will take care of your son. My father wanted him to be Pharaoh and I will see my father's wishes are fulfilled, but you should not return to the palace. My family may not pay much attention to Hebrews, but eventually they might start noticing a pattern."

She stepped away from me, and pulled open a door to return to the feast. I waited a moment, feeling stunned, but relieved before I too followed.

Back inside, Horemheb noticed me reenter. He had a fleeting moment of alarm as he glanced across at Ankhe, but I shook my head and gestured not to worry. I returned to my place by the wall and watched Ankhe as she returned to Tut's side. She took his hand and softly kissed it, which caused him to look alarmed, but he didn't pull away. I pulled my veil back across my face to hide my revulsion as my tears fell. My little boy was no longer my little boy, but was being thrust into manhood before my very eyes.

Suddenly, I was grabbed a second time. I was pulled behind a pillar and pinned against it by Smenkhkare. He sniffed me, which made me twist away with disgust. He sneered and whispered in my ear, "I like Hebrew women; they are strong and fertile."

He pulled at my skirts and I fought against him, my panic rising. He was much stronger than when I had fended him off in the palace, so my attempts to push him away were futile. He laughed to himself greedily in anticipation, and only paused for one moment when he felt my belly.

"Oh, there's already one in there." He sneered. "Well, we will just have to fix that."

"No!" I struggled harder as he pushed his hand against me.

Then, out of nowhere, Horemheb thrust him off me and stood between us. "How dare you assault my servant! Why do you dishonor me so?"

"Oh, Commander, don't be so dramatic. She's just a slave." He pushed forward, but Horemheb held him back.

"She may be, but she is mine." He glared at Smenkhkare. "Do you wish to steal from me?"

I knew by the way he spoke that he wanted to imply that my child belonged to him so Smenkhkare would leave me alone.

Smenkhkare looked at me with a disgusting smirk across his face. "All right, Horemheb. I will leave her be."

He stepped back and slowly walked away from us to Mayati.

Horemheb grabbed my arm. "I think it's time to get you out of here."

"I agree," I responded as he pulled me away. I looked across at Tut, who watched us leave with a hint of sadness in his eyes, but Ankhe rested her arm around his shoulder and nodded to me.

Horemheb hurried me through the city straight to my home where, as usual when I stayed out later than normal, Malachi waited for me. He stood, looking tense as he saw us approach, and walked toward us.

When we reached him, Horemheb pulled me back and said with a snarl, "Be grateful she's in one piece and unharmed. She is never going back to the palace again, so don't you dare do something that could force her to go there."

Malachi reached for me angrily. "Give me my wife."

"She can't go back, do you understand? Ankhe knows who she is now, and Smenkhkare tried to rape her. You have to protect her. They are too dangerous." He looked down at me. "There's only so much I can do without raising suspicion, and practically claiming this child as mine was pushing my limits—"

"You what?" Malachi shoved him.

Horemheb drew his sword. "I will kill you—"

"No, stop, please!" I stood in front of Malachi, blocking Horemheb. "I can't do this anymore. Horemheb, you have to let me go. Pretend I am dead again, do whatever you need to do to forget me. Please, please."

He stared at me, stunned, and his sword slowly lowered. "Kiya, I can't—"

"I'm not Kiya anymore," I said softly.

His hand tightened around the handle of his sword as he glared at Malachi. "Well, then, Naomi, I will cut your work hours back to once a week, and you must never be there when you know I will be, which means you won't get to see your son!"

"Horemheb, don't—"

"No, Naomi!" He lifted his sword and pointed it at me. "I have not reached my position through being merciful, and I have gladly cut men down for less than this."

He pointed his sword at Malachi. "And you! I should have killed you years ago, or I should have let Ay and Smenkhkare have you. If I ever see your face again, I won't be forgiving, I *will* kill you."

He marched away.

I watched him go, feeling a deep pain in my heart. I clung onto Malachi's arms for some relief. Once Horemheb disappeared into the darkness, Malachi gave me a long, loving kiss.

"What was that for?" I asked as he pulled away.

"For finally cutting him off," he answered, pushing off my shawl before he led me back to the house.

"Oh." I squeezed his waist affectionately, but couldn't bring myself to feel good about what I had done.

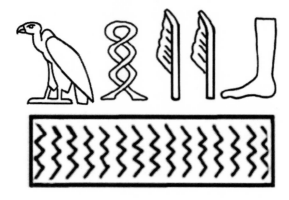

CHAPTER TWENTY-TWO

S everal weeks passed, and I hadn't been able to see Tut. Horemheb, true to his word, had not been around when he knew I would be at the house, and so, neither was Tut. I would instead find notes for me under pots in the food storage room.

Tut would tell me what he was doing, and said he liked Ankhe very much and found her to be a lot of fun. She took him out into the gardens and played hiding and tag games with him. I felt happy for him because I knew how much he missed playing with his siblings and cousins, and was grateful Ankhe let him be a boy still.

This continued for months. When Dana had her baby and it was a boy, I grieved that I had not seen my son in such a long time. Then, when his birthday passed, I spent the day crying.

A few weeks after his birthday, I was with my sisters drawing water at the well when we heard the sound of horses' hooves and chariots rushing toward us. We collected our children, and a moment later, several chariots swept around the corner and into the square. I looked up at the men, annoyed by their recklessness, and saw staring back down at me as he passed, my Tut. He grinned as he flew by, and was gone again. I looked to my sisters stunned, who all turned to me.

"Was that Tut?" Rena asked.

"Yes," I answered. "That was very reckless. He should know better."

A few days later, while we were in the market, the same thing happened. But with the busier street, people panicked. His opponents had to slow down, but when he saw me again, he grinned before pushing his horses harder. I rolled my eyes, knowing he was showing off for me.

Later, as I returned home, a chariot rumbled behind me. I stepped to the side to clear the road, but it pulled up beside me and matched my pace. "Hello, Mama."

I looked up surprised. "Tut!"

He grinned excitedly. "Look at me! I've gotten very good, haven't I?"

"Tut, you put a lot of people in danger today."

He grunted. "Mama, don't be boring. I wasn't going to hurt anyone, I'm in perfect control."

"You sound like the Commander."

He pulled up his horses and jumped out in front of me. "The Commander is a great man. If I could be just a little like him, I would be very pleased."

I sighed and looked him over. He wore a skirt and had two gold sashes crossed over his chest. He also wore a tall hat with a gold band along its rim to hold it onto his head.

I touched his face and smiled at him warmly. "I've missed you."

He grinned excitedly and touched my belly. "When's he going to come out?"

"Any day." I sighed. "I wish it was yesterday."

He laughed. "I want to see Hepsati. I bet she looks strange."

I looked at his chariot. "Why don't you visit us for a while?"

"Can I?" he asked excitedly.

"Of course, you are always welcome."

He laughed, grabbed Zakkai, and pulled him onto the chariot with him.

"I'll beat you there." He flicked the reigns and the horses lunged forward.

"Tut, you be careful with Zakkai!" I called after him. I looked down at Itani who held my hand as she stared after him with a surprised look on her face.

When we reached the house, the chariot was out the front, but no one in sight. As we approached, voices mumbled inside, and realized Tut had already brought Hepsati over.

Itani and I entered to see Hepsati and Tut sat facing each other by the table while Zakkai knelt on the floor playing with his toys. Itani rushed over to sit beside Tut, and for the first time I could recall he put his arm around her.

"Itani, have you been good for Mama?"

"Of course I have!" she replied indignantly. "I help with the cooking and laundry now, and Papa—"

He clamped her mouth shut. "Good, because someone needs to take care of Mama. Look at her, she can barely walk."

"Thank you, Tut, that really makes me feel wonderful," I said as I sat beside Hepsati, who rubbed my back.

He visited with us for a long time, filling us in with everything he had been doing.

When Joshua entered looking for Hepsati, Tut greeted him excitedly. Soon, Malachi burst in.

"Tut!" he exclaimed. "I knew it had to be you by that chariot."

He rushed toward him, but Tut backed away and raised his hand angrily. "Don't come near me!"

Malachi drew back, startled. "Tut—"

"I am Pharaoh to you!" Tut bellowed.

"Tutankhamen!" I gasped. "Don't talk to your father like that."

"He's not my father." Tut turned to me. "Amenhotep was my father. *He* was just a thieving guard."

Hepsati stood. "Tut, Malachi may not be our real father, but he has always looked out for us. He has risked his life for you."

"He didn't do it for me, he just wanted to steal Mama." He turned and glared at Malachi, who stood frozen stiff with shock. "You never really loved me."

Malachi looked wounded by his words. I jumped up, grabbed Tut's arm and spun him to face me.

"Who has been telling you these lies?"

He grabbed my arm tightly and stared up into my eyes. "They are not lies. You belong in the palace. You are a queen, you are my mother. You don't belong here in this dirty place."

"Tut!" I gasped horrified. "Who has been telling you these things? Was it Ankhe or Horemheb?"

His grip on my arm tightened. "Come back to the palace with me."

"I can't; you know that." I looked across at Malachi with concern.

"Don't look at him!" Tut bellowed. "I should have let him die when he was accused—"

I slapped him across the face. He grabbed at his cheek, surprised, and stared at me.

"Don't even say such things, Tutankhamen!" I said, my voice quivering with emotion. "I don't know what you have been told, but I love Malachi. I married him by choice. He didn't force me or steal me away, and he does love you like his own son; he always has. I will not have you speaking ill of him in my home."

Tut pulled away from me angrily and snarled, "You should have married the Commander."

He pushed by and spat at Malachi's feet as he passed him. He slammed the door shut, which made us all jump.

We stood frozen, until my anger got the better of me and I rushed after him.

"You are not getting away with this," I muttered to myself as I flung the door open. I hurried over to him as he climbed into his chariot. "Tutankhamen! You listen to me!"

"Mama, no, you listen to me! I am Pharaoh!" he yelled.

"You are still my son and you will heed what I say!"

He grabbed the reins, trying to ignore me.

"Tut, listen to me. There are things you don't understand, things that are complicated."

He threw an icy stare at me. "Nothing is complicated here. It's Malachi's fault I can't see you anymore!"

He whipped his horses into a trot, but as the chariot turned, it knocked me over. I stumbled and hit the ground. I yelped in pain.

Tut glanced around, pulling his horses up hard.

"Mama! I'm sorry, I didn't—"

But then my waters broke. I grabbed at my belly as a cramp came on.

Tut leaped off his chariot and ran to me.

"Mama! What's wrong? Did I hurt you?"

He grabbed for my arm, but I pushed him away. "Go fetch your aunts."

"Is it the baby? Did I hurt it?"

"No, Tut! It's just time. Go get your aunts!" I turned and called out, "Malachi!"

Within an instant, Malachi rush to my side. Tut backed off, staring at him, obviously conflicted.

"Tut! I need you to go get your aunts!" I said again desperately.

He stumbled back to his chariot, unable to take his eyes from me as Malachi helped me to my feet. As he climbed on, he yelled, "Don't you touch my Mama! If you hurt her, I'll kill you!"

He whipped his horses and raced away.

I looked up at Malachi as he led me back into the house.

"I don't know what has gotten into him, but I'm sorry that he blames you."

I saw a pained expression on Malachi's face, but he didn't show any contempt.

"He's just a boy. He doesn't understand anything more than what he has been told."

Back inside, Hepsati took me into my room to help me change out of my soiled clothes, while Joshua took Zakkai and Itani back to his house, and Malachi boiled water.

"Mama," Hepsati said softly. "I'm glad I can stay with you this time." She gently stroked my hair as I winced from a cramp. "Don't worry about Tut. He's just hurt because he hasn't been able to see you in so long."

I smiled at her, loving her more than ever. "Oh, my dear, you grow lovelier every day. Your mother would be so proud."

She smiled and giggled. "Why do you always seem to think of my mother when you are giving birth?"

"Because I wish her to be with me when I give birth."

She gently encouraged me to lie down before she whispered, "Is Papa upset?"

I lifted my knees to ease the pain a little as I muttered, "I believe so. He loves Tut."

"I know. He loves all of us." She stroked my hair again.

We fell silent as Malachi entered, placed the hot water beside me, then kissed my head. "How are you doing?"

"Oh, I've definitely had worse." I smiled through the pain.

"I will stay until your sisters arrive," he said softly.

I took his hand and held it tightly. "Thank you, Malachi."

"Papa," Hepsati said gently. "You're a good father. I love you."

He smiled, but obviously felt wounded by Tut's reaction to him. He touched her face. "You make it easy for me, Hepsati."

His attention returned to me as I grunted, a wave of pain suddenly hitting me.

It wasn't long before my sisters arrived. We heard them all in the chariot as it pulled up, and they rushed in to me, each smiling excitedly. They checked my progress before Eliora said with enthusiasm, "We rode a chariot! It was terribly exciting! Oh, and how surprised the children were to see their cousin dressed up as a king!"

I looked up at Malachi, who avoided my eyes. He stood and spoke softly. "I will leave you ladies to it. I will go and watch over the children with Joshua."

"Malachi," I said. "Send me Tut."

He nodded and stepped out. A few moments later, we heard Tut yelling at him again. Hepsati's face turned stone cold as she climbed to her feet and rushed out.

"What's going on?" Rena asked.

"Tut has been turned against Malachi," I answered hurriedly as my pain rose. I wailed, this being the worst one yet. As it died down, Hepsati and Tut were arguing loudly.

"Tut, you are being ridiculous!"

"Don't you dare talk to me like that!"

"I will, you brat. You're still my brother, after all!"

"Tutankhamen!" I bellowed. "You get yourself in here this second!"

The argument fell silent, and a moment later Tut's timid voice came through the blanket over the doorway. "I'm here, Mama."

"You listen to me." I gasped from another cramp, but forced myself to talk to him despite my pain. "I am in the middle of giving birth and you are making me miserable! You be kind to your family, do you hear me? Now you go talk to your Papa and have him explain his side of things."

"No, Mama, he's a liar. He only married you so he could claim royalty. You were supposed to marry the Commander, my *real* father wanted that—"

"Stop it, Tut!" I said angrily. "You go talk to him this instant."

He muttered under his breath as he left the house.

Hepsati reentered after he had gone and sat beside me. "He's being awful. I can't believe him!"

Adina pulled me forward so Eliora could rub my back and said, "Has he forgotten everything Malachi has done for him?"

"I don't know," I answered, breathing deeply.

"Malachi is the best father in the world!" Hepsati said defensively. "I remember when he pulled us free from the lions, and when he came back from the fields with an arrow in his back when he blocked it from hitting Tut! Oh, it makes me so mad he is being this ungrateful!"

"Don't you get yourself worked up," Rena said, touching her knee. "I'd prefer to just do one delivery at a time."

Our conversation fell quiet as we all focused on getting the child out of me. The labor progressed steadily, but thankfully not too quickly like Zakkai's had. As my pains drew so close together, they felt like they weren't subsiding at all. My sisters pulled me up onto the birthing stool and began talking me through the delivery.

Suddenly, loud arguing started outside again, but I realized there was a new voice. My head shot up.

"Horemheb!" I wailed. "Don't you take my son!"

The arguing fell silent, but then, "Naomi, he is Pharaoh. We are leaving!"

I grabbed Rena's arm. "Go out there and stop him."

"Why me?" she asked fearfully.

"Because you are the most like me, so he is more likely to listen to you than anyone else." I then screamed as the child pressed down on me.

Rena hurried to obey, and was out the door in an instant.

The pain became unbearable and I sobbed.

"Come on, Naomi," Adina said as she moved around in front of me to catch the child. I took courage from her action and bore down as hard as I could. Rena burst back into the room and grabbed my arm just as I heard my baby's cry. Adina laughed. "Oh, it's a girl!"

Eliora and Rena held me up while Adina cleaned her, and once Adina cut the cord, they lowered me to wash me up while she nursed. Hepsati rushed outside and I heard her call out, "It's a girl, Papa! What shall we name her?"

My sisters all fell silent to hear his response.

"Rachel," he answered. "Because I had to wait for her mother like Jacob did for Rachel."

My sisters all looked at me with tears in their eyes. I blushed and looked down at my new daughter. "Rachel."

When she fell asleep, Eliora gently lifted and wrapped her up so she could take her out to show Malachi. I rested my head back, grateful for another strong, healthy child and an uncomplicated delivery.

Suddenly, Tut's voice rang out. "Give her to me!"

I groaned and tears well up in my eyes.

Adina noticed my distress. She climbed to her feet and burst out of the house.

"Tutankhamen, you awful boy! Your mother has just given birth and you are behaving in a manner which is distressing for her! You selfish child, you were not raised this way."

She quickly redirected her wrath. "And you, *Commander*, I know this is your fault. You take my sister's son away from her and fill his mind with your jealous contempt for her husband. I don't care how fearsome and how highly ranked you are in the palace, you are nothing in my eyes, and you will undo the damage you have done."

A long silence followed. Then, Horemheb broke it. "Tut, go say goodbye to your mother. You have been gone for hours and must return."

The door banged open and Adina burst back in to help cover me before Tut's head appeared in the doorway. "Mama?"

"Come here, Tut," I said gently.

He rushed over to me and climbed onto my lap, snuggling up to me. "Mama, did I really upset you?"

I sighed and stroked his head. "Yes, Tut."

"I'm sorry," he said softly. "I just miss you so much. Ankhe is nice to me, but she's not like you. I'm just so angry that Malachi lied to you and keeps you away from me—"

"Tut," I said sternly. "Do you remember the scar on Malachi's shoulder?"

"Yes, he says he was shot by an arrow."

"He was. Do you remember why?"

He thought for a moment then frowned. "To stop it hitting me."

"Yes, and you know the scar on Hepsati's arm?"

"A lion bit her," he said quickly, and his frown deepened. "But Papa saved her and me so we wouldn't get eaten."

I smiled. "Tut, why would he do those things if he didn't love you? Why would he have spent hours out in the fields with you if he didn't enjoy your company? He did those things before he married me. He's loved you all along."

He stared off, looking confused. "Mama, why does he stop you from seeing me then?"

"He doesn't." I stroked his head. "There are just some things that are more complicated than you know."

"Like that you were supposed to marry Commander Horemheb after my father died?"

I sighed. "That's how he would see it, yes."

"Hmm." His arms tightened around me. "Promise me you will start seeing me again. I've missed you."

"I will try. I do still work at the estate and receive your letters. Ask Horemheb if you can come and see me while I'm there."

"I will."

"And, Tut?"

"Yes, Mama?"

"Go apologize to your Papa. He's still the same man you always loved."

He gave a long, drawn-out sigh. "Very well, Mama."

"Always remember there are two sides to every story," I told him. "Horemheb sees things one way and Malachi sees them another. Neither are right or wrong, just different."

He smiled at me happily. "This is why I miss you. You know how to make me feel better."

I laughed, relieved he seemed to be responding to me like my Tut always had.

He gave me another tight squeeze and kissed my cheek. "I have to go. I've been gone too long."

"I know." I touched his cheek and smiled at him.

"I will see you soon, won't I, Mama?"

"I will do all that I can."

"Good." He grinned and left me with Rena as she let out a sigh of relief and stroked my hair.

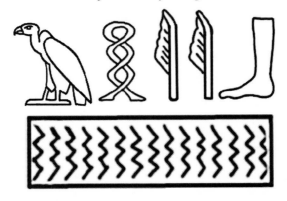

CHAPTER TWENTY-THREE

I didn't go to the estate for a few weeks while I recovered from the delivery, but when I did, all the servants were excited to see my new baby. Itani and Zakkai were happy to be back, as well, and played and hid from each other all over the estate.

In the kitchen, I found the food disorganized, and half of it had rotted. I placed Rachel in a bed I made from blankets on the floor, and began to clean. The smell made me feel sick as I cleaned out the bad food, and wondered how Horemheb ate in my absence.

I soon found a few notes for me from Tut. I opened each of them and read them slowly, smiling to myself, but the last note surprised me as it was from Horemheb.

It said simply, *I will bring the boy to see you.*

I rested my hand on my hip and sighed. So this was how it would be from now on: one-sentence notes and pretending I didn't exist. Even though I had asked for it, I didn't feel good about losing him as a friend.

Once I disposed of all the bad food, I began cooking, and soon the whole household kept passing by the doors and windows to smell the aroma of fresh bread and fried fish. At one point, I heard Horemheb enter with some dignitaries and one said, "Commander, what is that divine smell?"

"I have a gifted cook. Can we get on with business?" he responded shortly.

I knew I needed to bring them food, but I felt nervous, having not actually *seen* Horemheb in months. I gathered together what I could and walked slowly to the room they sat in, and, before I pushed open the door, I took a deep breath to compose myself.

I entered the room. At the far end of the long table sat Tut. His face lit up at the sight of me, and he leaped to his feet. Horemheb give him a subtle warning look, so he covered his enthusiasm smoothly. "Horemheb has the best cook. Bring the food straight to me."

I obeyed swiftly and he took handfuls and shoved them into his mouth.

"My lord." Horemheb scowled.

"Be quiet, I'm hungry," Tut murmured with his mouth full.

A laugh echoed in the room that almost made me coil back in fear. I glanced across the table to see Ay as he said, "Commander, he's just a boy. He needs to eat to grow. Let him be."

Horemheb walked around to stand beside me and said quietly, "Put the food down and get out."

I placed the food in front of Tut and hurried out of the room. The coolness in Horemheb's tone frightened me; I had no desire to push his patience. But I could not leave. Curious to know what had brought the likes of Ay into Horemheb's house, I left the door open a crack to listen.

"This is very good food," Ay said. "Maybe I should arrange for her to be placed among the servants at the palace."

Tut laughed. "No! I don't want to share her with everyone else. She is why I come here all the time."

"Greedy boy," Ay teased playfully.

I clenched my fists, wanting to wring his neck for his hypocrisy.

"Let's get on with things, shall we?" Horemheb said sharply. "I have no desire to spend the whole day dwelling on this."

"Very well," Ay said. "Captain, give us your report."

The man's voice who had spoken earlier began. "The Hebrews are booming in number. They have taken up the whole southern third of the city on the east side of the river, and their farms cover some of the most fertile land for miles. During our absence, they appear to have taken many liberties in usurping land and privileges not previously allotted to them. I believe we should perform a culling. Send men down and kill all children under the age of two. It will not only reduce their numbers, but will break their spirits."

I gasped and clamped my hand over my mouth. That would include Rachel, and most likely Hepsati's soon-to-be-born child, along with several of my nieces and nephews.

"That's horrible!" Tut exclaimed.

"My lord," Ay said. "As a boy yourself, your sentiments are understandable, but they are a lower race, barely above beasts in intelligence."

"You forget my mother was a Hebrew," Tut said with a haughty tone. "And you feared her because she was so clever."

I smiled and dared to peek through the crack to see Ay's reaction. He gritted his teeth, but did not respond.

Horemheb spoke instead. "Maybe we could conscript more men into the army. I'm planning a campaign soon, and the extra numbers would be helpful. They would likely sustain many losses, which would reduce their ability to breed. I don't think the slaughter of children is quite necessary at this point."

"I like that better," Tut said. "That way they stand a fighting chance, while subduing our enemies."

"So what is your decision, my lord?" Ay asked.

"Conscript all men between twenty and twenty-five." Tut said firmly.

I quickly thought of Joshua, and wondered if Tut remembered he would fit into that age bracket.

"Is that enough?" Ay said. "Surely all men up to thirty—"

"It should be enough," Horemheb said. "When we get the numbers in, I will know for sure."

Suddenly Itani came screeching through the house with Zakkai hot on her tail. I winced and rushed to silence her. Just as I grabbed her I heard Ay say, "What is the meaning of this?"

I whipped Itani's shawl over her head to cover her Egyptian hair and pulled her behind me. "I'm sorry, my lord. They are just children."

He scoffed. "Foul Hebrew offspring. Silence them before I do it for you permanently."

Horemheb stepped behind him and grasped his shoulder. "It is the price I pay for good food. Leave them be."

But Ay stared at Itani. "Let me see that girl."

I pulled her closer to me without thinking. "I'm sorry she offends you. I will take her away—"

"I said, show me the girl!"

I trembled as I glanced at Horemheb, who watched with a stone cold expression. I looked down at Itani and gently grabbed her hand to pull her out, knowing he would instantly see her father in her.

"That's my sister!" Tut suddenly pushed through and pointed at her. "No one tried to kill her, so of course she lives and resides with my aunts. I have this servant bring her here so I can see her." He grabbed Itani's arm and pulled her out. "See? She looks like my father and my wife."

"We should take her to the palace," Ay said, reaching for her.

Tut pulled her out of his reach. "No, I don't want her to marry Smenkhkare. She will continue to live with my aunts and her existence will remain hidden. She is no threat to you or anyone else."

Tut impressed me. He spoke like a true king and a man twice his age. I couldn't help glancing at Horemheb and feeling grateful he taught my son so well.

"But, my lord, if she is anything like your mother, she will breed well."

Tut looked furious and was about to speak when Horemheb interrupted. "I thought you did not approve of their mother."

Ay looked at him, alarmed, before he snorted. "Let's get back to business." He pointed at me. "Keep these children under control, slave."

I bowed and snatched Itani's hand as they returned into the room. I pulled her and Zakkai into the kitchen where Rachel slept soundly and snapped at Itani. "I've told you not to screech like that!"

She looked like she was about to cry. "I'm sorry, Mama. I didn't know."

"We are not in our home here, Itani, and as you just saw, you could be taken away if someone realizes who you are. Do you want to be taken away?"

"No, Mama." A tear ran down her cheek.

I grabbed her and pulled her against me. "Oh, Itani, you gave me such a fright. I don't want you taken away, either. It's bad enough we no longer have Tut, but if they took you too, I would be devastated."

She clung to me as she sobbed into my chest. Zakkai sat down and stared up at us, looking confused, with his large, dark eyes. I loved how much he looked like Malachi. It made me feel like he was always with me.

As Itani's tears slowly subsided, she let go and looked up at me. "Mama, would they really make me marry the man who tried to kill Papa?"

"Probably yes," I answered with a frown.

"But I'm just a little girl."

"It doesn't matter to these people, Itani. Look at Tut. He's not much older than you and he is married."

She sighed. "I don't want to be married yet. I will be good from now on. I won't scream."

I sighed, feeling relieved knowing she was frightened enough to really mean it. "Thank you, Itani. Now go play *quietly* with Zakkai."

She let go of me and reached for Zakkai's hand. He stood and took it and the two of them went out into the garden. I sighed again and glanced around, making sure the room was cleaned satisfactorily, before I picked up Rachel and took her into the next room to do the laundry, which had piled up.

An hour later Tut came in quietly and sat beside me. I smiled at him as I fixed one of Horemheb's tunics, and he huffed. "Hepsati is going to be angry with me, isn't she?"

"About what?" I asked.

"About Joshua. He's going to have to go to war."

I placed my work down on my lap and looked into his eyes. "Tut, no matter what you did, it would have affected someone in our family, and sending full-grown men to war is much better than the slaughtering of children."

He grimaced. "You heard all that?"

"Yes, I'm ashamed to say I was eavesdropping."

"I feel so terrible!" He groaned. "If Joshua dies, Hepsati will never forgive me."

I reached across and squeezed his knee. "I will explain everything to her. She will know that it is better for her husband to risk his life than have her soon-to-be-born child slaughtered."

Tut nodded slowly and looked down at Rachel. "When he said that, I thought of Rachel and I knew I couldn't let my sister die."

"You did the right thing, Tut."

He looked into my eyes and I saw that he looked distraught. "Did I?"

"Yes. Sometimes we are faced with hard decisions, and no matter what path we choose, something bad will happen. It's in those moments our character is tested; we have to know how to choose the lesser evil. You did that today."

He smiled at me proudly.

"Well-spoken, Naomi," Horemheb's voice muttered from the door. "So you do still have your own mind. Tell me then; was your husband the lesser of two evils?"

"Stop it, Horemheb." I sat back and folded my arms.

"I know I am evil, and I know you know it too, as I have told you my past sins, but I know for a fact that your beloved husband has killed men also. You know, he's still technically part of the royal guard, as he was never officially released. I should call him up for duty."

I turned and glared at him. "I said stop it."

He clamped his mouth shut. After a few moments his eyes fell on Tut and he said, "Tut, go check on your sister."

I watched Tut nervously as he slipped out of the room, wishing he would stay. Then Horemheb rushed at me and grabbed me by the arm, pulling me to my feet. "Don't talk to me like that!"

I pulled away from him. "Then don't threaten my husband!"

He raised his hand to hit me, but he stopped himself. "No more, Naomi! You want me to pretend you're dead, so when I have to speak to you, you will treat me like your master, not your old friend, do you hear me?"

I stared at him for a moment, then slowly bowed. "Yes, master."

He grunted as he looked me over before he walked out. Rachel fussed from the noise, so I lifted her to nurse. I gazed down at her and hummed to soothe her while she ate, then I leaned back against the wall and closed my eyes. Things were changing fast, and the Egyptians were growing concerned with our swelling numbers and strength. I knew I had to tell Samuel about what I had heard so he could convince some families to move to one of the smaller cities up north, or maybe establish a settlement in the declining city of Amarna.

I opened my eyes again, and was startled by a reflection in the small mirror opposite me. Horemheb had not left at all, but stood just outside the door, watching me with a pained expression. Careful not to react, as I knew it would only cause a fight, I shifted to make sure my breast was obstructed from his view and allowed Rachel to finish. Once she'd eaten her fill and dozed off, I covered myself and placed her down on the small bed of blankets. Then, I slipped just outside the door which led to the clothesline with a basket of clothes and waited.

It didn't take long for him to enter the room and gently lift Rachel. He caressed her in his arms and softly stroked her cheek with his finger.

"Hello there, little one," he whispered. "You are a beautiful girl, just like you're mother, aren't you?"

He smiled before glancing around to make sure no one was watching. I pulled back quickly, and when he started talking again I knew he hadn't seen me.

"I wish you were mine. I wish Tut was mine, and Itani. I feel like I am your and your siblings' father sometimes. I watched you mother carry each of you and took care of her when I could." He sighed and softly kissed her head. "Maybe one day. Your mother is the most incredible woman. I wouldn't want anyone else raising my children, so you are a very lucky girl. I wish she would give me just one child, just one, and I think I would be capable of accepting not being able to have her. No one is like her."

He held her close to him and kissed her again.

I stood frozen, completely stunned by the man I saw before me. He was not the hardened, unfeeling Horemheb I knew; he was a man more like Malachi than he would care to admit. I found myself wishing he had shown me that side of him sooner, back in Amarna, because maybe I would have waited for him. But I couldn't think like that. Malachi was the best thing in my life, and just because I saw one moment of tenderness in Horemheb, that shouldn't take away from the years of tenderness and sacrifice Malachi had given me.

As he gently lowered Rachel, I decided to try to talk to him again, but as I entered the room, he stiffened and rushed to the door.

"Horemheb, wait."

His fists clenched, but he didn't turn back around. "What is it?"

I found myself unsure what to say. I couldn't admit to him that I had been watching; he would be embarrassed and become angry that I had spied. So instead, I said, "Thank for all you do for Tut. He sees you like a father now and admires you greatly."

He laughed sarcastically, but cut himself short. Slowly he turned to look at me. "Naomi, don't flatter me." He then left me again.

Malachi and I had just finished putting the children to bed and I sat nursing Rachel, when we heard a soft tapping at our door. We exchanged confused looks, and he stood to answer. He opened the door and laughed. "Enoch, what are you doing here?"

"I brought a guest, someone who wanted to see your wife," his brother responded.

A moment later, I heard a woman say, "Hello, Mehaleb. It has been quite a while."

"Gerlind!" Malachi exclaimed and pulled the door wider to allow them to enter.

Gerlind locked her gaze on me and gave me a quick smile, but I knew something bothered her. She rushed over and embraced me as I covered myself for Enoch.

"Oh, Naomi, this is the first chance I have had to come to you, but I wish I could come under more pleasant circumstances."

"What's wrong?" I asked, staring into her distressed face.

"It's Tut. There's an assassination plot being schemed as we speak."

I grabbed her arm. "Is it Ay? Did he tell you—?"

She shook her head. "No, he knows better than to try and contend with Horemheb. It's Smenkhkare and Mayati. They want the throne back. I heard an assassin will be sent three nights hence."

I stared at her with alarm and squeezed her arm tighter. "Are you sure?"

"Yes, I heard Mayati herself talking about it. She doesn't care if Ankhe is with him and dies also, she just wants her place back as queen."

"And she didn't know you were listening?"

She shook her head. "I was returning from my husband's chambers and she was hiding in a room with Smenkhkare discussing the details with the assassin. I had to come to you as soon as I could."

I glanced across at Malachi, who stood by the window talking happily with his brother, neither of them aware of our discussion.

"Tell no one," I told her. "I will solve this."

"What are you going to do?"

"I will tell Horemheb, of course. He will know what to do."

She let out a long sigh and glanced over at Malachi. "Oh Naomi, let's not talk about this any longer, then. If Horemheb is to know, everything will be fine. Let's talk about your husband. He is far more handsome than I remember."

I smiled and giggled softly. "It's the beard; it really suits him."

"These past eight years have been kind to him. He has aged very well indeed."

I grinned as I looked Malachi over. He was very handsome with his warm smile and gentle eyes. My heart skipped as he laughed at something Enoch said, and I felt like I had been given the most wonderful man in the world. I knew that no matter what, no one could ever take his place in my heart.

"Would he be interested in taking up polygamy?"

I looked at her a little surprised, but when I saw the gleam in her eyes, I laughed. "You want to share another husband?"

"Malachi would be far better than Ay," she said, looking him over. "At least he would be kind to me."

I touched her shoulder. "I'm so sorry, Gerlind. I wish I could help you escape that place."

She shrugged. "This is my lot in life and I have come to accept it. I'm just grateful for my children and try to focus on them."

"How many do you have now?"

She held two fingers up and shrugged. "Both Amenhotep's. I think Ay is all dried up."

I couldn't help laughing loudly.

I stood outside Horemheb's door. I could hear him inside, getting ready for the day. I had his food prepared for him as an excuse to enter, but I found myself unable move. I knew I needed to; I had to tell him of the assassination plot against my son, but my nerves and our history got the better of me. I closed my eyes and took a deep breath to compose myself. I had to do it, for Tut. I stretched out my hand and knocked.

The door flew open, which startled me. Horemheb glared down at me. "It's about time. I heard you come up quite a while ago. Come, put my food down and leave."

I felt embarrassed. Of *course* he heard me. I rushed over and placed his food on his dresser before I turned to face him.

He walked over and picked up an egg while watching me. "Well, get out."

"I have to tell you something," I said softly.

"Not right now, I'm in a hurry."

"Please, it's important."

He paused and looked me over. "Very well, what is it?"

"You probably already know, but I just want to be sure."

"What, Naomi?"

"Smenkhkare and Meritaten have an assassination planned for two nights hence," I blurted out.

He tensed, and stared at me. "How do you know this?"

"Gerlind came to me. She overheard them making the arrangements with the assassin."

"And you trust a wife of Ay?"

I glared at him. "She is not just a wife of Ay. We were sisters when we were the wives of Akhen—"

He grabbed my mouth to cut me off. "You really need to stop using that name."

He slowly let go and stared into my eyes. "I had not heard of this conspiracy. Thank you for bringing it to my attention." He stepped around me and grabbed his hat. "Tell me something, Naomi, are you still tenderhearted?"

"What do you mean?"

"I mean, how do you feel about watching men die?"

I caught my breath fearfully. "Why would you ask me that?"

He chuckled. "Because I think I will need your help to confront Smenkhkare and Mayati. I think if they see the mother of their king, the woman whom they fear, I will be able to subdue them."

I gasped. "You want me to reveal myself to them?"

"Oh yes, I think it will work wonders."

"What does that have to do with watching men die?" I asked.

He laughed and ran his hand down my arm. "Oh, Kiya, you are a naïve one, aren't you?"

I looked over my shoulder and glared at him. "Don't say that. I am *Naomi*, and I am not naïve."

He smiled and leaned closer to me, enjoying teasing me. "Naomi, coming with me means I will have to kill men loyal to Smenkhkare and Mayati."

I tensed, dreading the thought of watching him kill. But I thought of Tut and the risk to his life, and I took courage. "For Tut, I will do anything."

He stepped in front of me and rested his hands on his hips. "You were always brave."

He lifted his hand and covered my eyes. "But I won't let you see anything. I don't want to taint you."

He then softly kissed me on the lips.

I pulled away, startled, but he dropped his hand, smiling. He was toying with me.

"I will come and collect you in two nights. I will signal with a bird call." He stepped back, placed his hat on his head, and checked himself in the mirror. "Now get out."

CHAPTER TWENTY-FOUR

Midnight had fallen by the time Horemheb whistled for me to come outside. I looked at Malachi, who lay sound asleep, and carefully slipped out of bed so he wouldn't awaken. I glanced back at him, feeling guilty for betraying his trust. But Tut, I had to protect Tut, even if it meant being alone with Horemheb. I tiptoed through the house and silently shut the door behind me.

Before I had a chance to turn, Horemheb grabbed me and covered my mouth. "It's crucial you do not make a sound unless I tell you otherwise, do you understand?"

I nodded fervently.

He released me and took my hand. "Naomi, this will be very dangerous, and when I tell you to close your eyes, you must obey immediately."

I nodded again, too afraid to speak. He pulled my shawl around me to hide my face and glanced down the street.

"We must move swiftly." And with a sharp tug of my arm, we ran through the dark streets toward the palace.

We reached the gates. He pulled us up hard, pinning me against the wall. He looked around, saw the guards on duty, and sighed with relief.

"These men will let me pass. They know I am the guardian of your son and will not question my motives." He looked down at me. "Act like a slave."

I hung my head and let my shoulders slump.

"That's better," he muttered, then stepped out, beckoning me to follow.

I hung back behind him, like a slave would, as we approached the guards. They saw Horemheb and stood straighter at attention.

"Let me pass," he said in a commanding tone. "I have heard rumors of a possible assassination attempt tonight and I must go to watch over Pharaoh Tutankhamen."

The guards immediately obeyed and opened one of the gates. We made it all the way to Tut's room without anyone stopping us, where I was surprised to find Enoch and Jared absent. I pulled at Horemheb's arm and gestured toward the door.

He stepped closer to me and whispered, "They are Hebrew. They have been moved to the infantry."

I held his arm tightly and froze with alarm, which made him look irritated as he pulled at me.

"Naomi, not now." He opened the door and we entered.

Tut lay asleep in his bed and I felt grateful to see he wasn't with Ankhe. Our noise roused him as we entered, and he spoke in a nervous voice. "Who's there?"

"It's just me," Horemheb answered. "And I brought your mother."

"Mama!" He gasped. I heard him feel around for a lamp.

Horemheb managed to find one first, and lit it so I could see my son clearly.

"Oh, my Tut!" I hurried to him and held him in my arms. "How are you faring?"

"Most of the time, when I'm alone at night like this, I'm frightened," he answered honestly. "But Commander Horemheb rarely leaves my side, like he promised."

"My son," I said softly. "It's all right to be frightened. I used to be frightened all the time when I lived in the palace, but you can't be brave unless you are afraid first. You are lucky to have the Commander watching over you, as he did for me. He will protect you with his very life."

"I know, Mama." He squeezed me tighter before he let me go. "But I want to go home again, even just for a short while..."

"No, Tut. Not now, it's too dangerous. You must stay here and do your duty as king like we always talked about."

"But you always said I'd be old like you, not still a boy."

"I know, but things change." I sighed and stroked his cheek. "I love you, Tut. You know that, don't you?"

"Of course, Mama, and I love you, too."

Tears welled in my eyes and I quickly kissed his forehead before he noticed them.

"Tut, you must listen to me now because what I'm about to say to you is very important. Do not stay in your bed tonight. Take your blanket and sleep under your dresser or someplace where you will be hidden, and don't come out until I or the Commander return for you. Do you understand?"

"Someone is planning to hurt me, aren't they?" he said in a hushed tone.

My voice caught. "Yes, Tut, but we're going to stop them. I promise you that after tonight, you will be safe."

Tut nodded, wrapped his arms around his blanket, and slipped off his bed. "I will sleep on the roof just outside my window. They're not likely to look there."

"Good boy." I smiled and watched him swing his legs over the windowsill and disappear.

Horemheb grabbed my arm. "Quickly! If we are caught here, they will know he is still close by."

He pulled the door open a crack to check the corridor, then we slipped out and dashed away.

Silence filled the palace. I could hear my own heart pounding and the soft tapping of my feet as they hit the stone floor. Occasionally, Horemheb pulled us up to watch as someone passed, before he hurried us onward. Eventually, he slowed down and grew more cautious. Then he stopped abruptly by the end of a wide room that had a high ceiling held up by thick, round stone pillars.

He turned and looked down at me.

"From here on, these people are loyal to Smenkhkare and Meritaten, so we must be vigilant. Most importantly, you must obey me unconditionally."

I gave him a quick nod.

He looked around again before tugging me into a sprint. Just as we were about to reach the corridor leading to their bedchambers, we saw the soft glow of a torch. Horemheb swung around and pinned me against a pillar. "Naomi, scream like I'm trying to ravage you."

I gazed at him, confused for a moment, then he sank his teeth into my neck and held my arms back against the pillar.

"Ouch!"

He glared at me. "Obey me, Naomi. If they hear you screaming, they will want to join in."

He grabbed my waist, shoved me harder against the pillar, and nibbled on my ear.

I took a deep breath and screeched, "Stop! Somebody help me!"

Despite the tense situation, I couldn't help feeling that Horemheb enjoyed himself as he kissed my neck and pressed up against me. I tried to pull away, but he held me tighter.

Suddenly, a torch behind him blinded me. A man sneered. "Are you going to let us join in?"

Horemheb's right arm let go of me and he whispered in my ear, "Close your eyes."

I shut them tightly as he pushed away and swung around. I heard four men start to say his name before the sound of a blade cut them off in one swift movement. The sounds of a tussle and swords clinking filled my ears before Horemheb said, "Duck!"

I bent down and heard, right where my head had been, the sound of a sword impact against stone. I turned around, opened my eyes, and saw a guard trying to pull his sword free of the crevice in the stone. I whipped out my knife and stabbed him in the arm. He pulled back from me and wailed, then I felt someone behind me and Horemheb's voice command, "Close your eyes."

I shut them again a moment before I felt a sword lunge past me. The man gasped in pain as he fell to the ground. I then felt Horemheb spin back around, and I heard him kill two more men. The fighting fell silent, except for the sound of him panting heavily as he caught his breath.

I didn't dare move or open my eyes, just focused on his hot body pressed against me, and how alive he felt. Suddenly, his hand reached back and wrapped around mine, but I felt disturbed by the wet stickiness on it. I whimpered softly, but fought to stay quiet and not panic.

"Come, Naomi," he said quietly, and began leading the way. "Keep your eyes shut until I say you can look."

He led me slowly out of the room, weaving every so often, and once he even lifted me into his arms and carried me.

"How many were there?" I asked softly, my voice quivering.

"Twelve," he answered calmly.

"Twelve?" I gasped.

"Hush, I told you, not a sound. You're a hopeless assassin."

I clamped my mouth shut as he placed me back on the ground and took my hand. As we rounded a corner, he told me I could open my eyes again. In the dimness, I saw dark marks on him, but it wasn't until we passed by a moonlit window that I saw he was covered in wounds and bleeding in several places. I also saw he hadn't sheathed his sword again, and the blade was slick with blood. Up until that point, I had never seen how fearsome he could be, or how powerful. I felt as if I was staring at a completely different person, a demon, even, and for the first time I understood the fear I saw in people's eyes when they heard his name or saw him approach.

As we headed around a corner, two more guards stood outside a door and Horemheb said, "Close your eyes again."

I obeyed as his hand pulled away from me and I heard him cut the guards down instantly. He then grabbed my hand and pulled me forward. I heard the door slowly open.

Inside, Horemheb pressed against me and whispered in my ear, "Naomi, shut the door, but don't look into the corridor."

I hurried to obey, moving as silently as I could. As I turned, I saw him walk soundlessly to the bed where two figures lay asleep. He waved me over, then pinned my hair back so he could place one of Mayati's wigs on my head, and pulled off my robe so I stood in my plain tunic. He then ducked behind the bed to hide.

It was up to me. I moved forward and, after taking a deep breath, I said boldly, "Arise, Smenkhkare!"

Both Smenkhkare and Mayati jumped with surprise, and upon seeing me, Mayati screamed.

"Kiya! She has come back for me!"

"Kiya!" Smenkhkare flailed around wildly in his bed, then fell onto the floor.

"You have tried to destroy my son," I said with a hiss. "He is the heir, the true king."

"I am King!" Smenkhkare snarled as he gazed up at me. "You're dead, you have no say in this world! Unless..."

He suddenly seemed to realize I was not a spirit and launched himself at me. I dodged him, but as he stumbled to the floor he caught my wrist and pulled me down on top of him. He flipped me underneath him, his eyes narrowing on my face. "You!"

He held my throat tightly, making me gag. "You almost ruined everything for me! Oh, I will bring you to shame if it's the last thing I do."

Mayati, who had stayed back until that point, surged forward to look down at me. "But this is impossible! Kiya has been dead for years!"

Smenkhkare loosened his grip so I could speak.

I sneered at her. "Yes, Mayati, Kiya has, but Naomi the Hebrew lives on, and I have come to make sure my son receives his birthright and is not killed by you."

Smenkhkare laughed. "What are you going to do, kill me? I am Pharaoh."

"Tutankhamen is the rightful wearer of the crown."

"That boy? He's probably dead by now—" But Horemheb cut him off as he pressed his sword against Smenkhkare's throat, making him freeze.

"Let her go," Horemheb said with a snarl.

Mayati cowered in the far corner of the room as Smenkhkare slowly released me and stood to face Horemheb.

"Commander, you dare betray me?"

"I serve the crown, and you are not its rightful wearer."

Smenkhkare laughed, then pulled me up against him, holding me between Horemheb and himself. "And her half-breed son is?"

He pulled off the wig and stroked my hair, inhaling deeply to smell it. "She smells good. I expected her to smell like a farm."

He groped my breast. In retaliation, I elbowed him in the stomach, causing him to release me. I swung around, slapping him across the face.

He grabbed where I struck him as he bent over, and scowled up at me. "Why, you vile little... Hebrew women are such trouble."

"I am the only Hebrew woman who has ever given you trouble," I responded and raised my chin to look him in the eyes defiantly.

He scoffed. "What does that mean?"

"When you disrupted our festival you took *my* husband, which was why Tut refused to have him killed. At the feast after Tut's marriage, you tried to rape a woman; again, that was me. When Tut was brought to you, you looked right at me with my sisters and didn't even see me. Kiya has haunted you for years, Kare; you have desired her, you have lusted for her, but never once did you think she was within your grasp."

Anger flared in his eyes. "You torment me! I will have you."

He reached for me, but Horemheb's blade stopped him.

"Not one step closer," Horemheb said in a smooth voice.

Smenkhkare looked down his nose at the blade pressed against his chest. "Commander Horemheb, ever faithful, aren't we? My brother would love to see how well you have protected his favorite wife, but I bet you have other motives."

Horemheb covered my face a second before I heard him plunge his sword through Smenkhkare's throat. Mayati screamed as Horemheb muttered, "Your voice was bothering me, Kare. You should have learned when to shut your mouth."

"Kare!" Mayati screeched. I heard her run across and catch him as he fell to his knees. "You killed him!"

I heard Horemheb withdraw his sword and Smenkhkare made a strangling sound as he tried to breathe.

"Oh, little princess," Horemheb said calmly. "You were always your mother's daughter."

He whirled me around so I couldn't see Smenkhkare take his last strained breaths and die.

"Now, Mayati," he said coolly. "We have a few choices here."

I heard her leap to her feet and back away from him. "Please, don't kill me!"

"Oh no, that's not one of the options."

I saw him, out of the corner of my eye, wipe his sword clean.

"But you can choose how to leave this world."

"Kiya!" she said in a pleading voice. "Kiya, talk to him! He listens to you, he's always listened to you! That's why my mother spread those rumors about you having an affair. They were completely plausible because no one had his ear the way you did!"

I turned around to look at her. "Mayati, you have been scheming to kill my son."

"No, please!" She rushed at me desperately and grabbed my shoulders. "I don't want to die! Demote me, banish me, do anything, but please spare my life!"

"You never would have spared mine under the same circumstances."

The blood drained from her face in fear. "Please, Kiya, I know you are right, but you were always compassionate. Please, have mercy on me now. Please forgive me for my foolishness. I will do better, I promise."

I grabbed her arms and met her eyes, indeed feeling compassion for her because I knew that no matter what, Horemheb would kill her.

"Dear little Mayati, you were a horrible girl, but I will forgive you for all you did and all your scheming."

Her face lit up. "Really?"

"Yes. But I'm not the one who wants you dead tonight."

Her face fell as the meaning of my words sank in. Then I heard the sound of a sword plunging through her. She gasped in shock and let go of me, looking down at herself. My eyes followed, and for an instant I saw the tip of the blade protruding from her abdomen.

"Naomi, shut your eyes!" Horemheb commanded.

I instantly obeyed, feeling utterly terrified. I heard him pull her back toward him, followed by the sound of a second blade plunging into her heart. She moaned in pain before she cried for a few moments, then, she fell silent and collapsed onto the floor.

I stood motionless, unable to even breathe as I listened to Horemheb wipe off his weapons and walk over to me. "The deed is done. Let us go check on your son."

He took my hand and I clutched at it tightly, unable to move. He pulled at me gently, but when I whimpered, he stepped over and lifted me up in his arms. "Keep your eyes closed, Naomi, all the way. I don't want you to see me right now."

He carried me to the door, checked the corridor was clear, then carried me out. As we turned a corner, he gently placed my feet on the floor and led me back through the palace. Suddenly, he stopped and whispered, "Tut's door is open."

"Oh no!" I gasped quietly.

"Stay here," he commanded and let go of my hand.

A few moments later, I heard the sound of a tussle; then, Horemheb groaned in pain. I gasped, terrified that he had been beaten as the struggle fell silent. I held my breath, waiting for a sign when I heard Horemheb say, "Tut, are you alive?"

There was a pause, then Tut's soft voice said, "Is that you, Commander?"

"Yes, boy, stay where you are."

The sound of Horemheb dragging a body into the corridor made me shudder, and he grunted as he tossed it out a window. His footsteps then came straight for me, and I felt his hand touch my face before he softly kissed my forehead.

"Naomi, would you like to see your son?"

I nodded fervently.

"All right, open your eyes."

I opened my eyes to see him heading into Tut's room. I rushed after him and saw Tut climbing back in his window.

"Oh, Tut!" I ran to him and held him tightly.

"Mama." He blushed and grinned.

"How are you? Did he find you?" I asked checking him over.

"No," he answered. "I heard him come in and start searching my room. I felt a little scared but I remembered what you said, so I made myself be brave."

"Good boy, Tut." I kissed his head. "But where is your wife tonight?"

He shrugged. "She was supposed to be here, but someone came and took her back to where the wives reside. Her sister had to tell her something important."

I looked to Horemheb, who nodded and rushed away. I guided Tut to his bed and had him lie down to sleep.

"Stay with me, Mama." He tugged at my sleeve.

I climbed onto the bed and lay beside him as he snuggled up to me in a way which reminded me of his father. "I was so proud of you tonight, Tut."

He clung onto me and sighed. "I'll be safe now?"

"I hope so," I answered.

He relaxed beside me. Soon, his breathing deepened and I knew he had fallen asleep. I closed my eyes, feeling tired, but the sounds of men dying filled my ears and prevented me from falling asleep.

After a while I heard two pairs of footsteps rushing toward us, so I rolled over to see who was coming. The door burst open and I saw Ankhe's anguished face rush toward us.

"Tut!" she said with fear in her voice.

Tut woke and sat up, startled, but when he saw her, he smiled. "Hello Ankhe. I'm glad you came back."

"Oh, Tut!" She wrapped her arms around him and squeezed him tightly. "If I had known my sister was out to get you, I never would have left." She clasped his face and softly kissed his head. "I'm so glad you are unharmed!"

"Of course I am," he said confidently. "The Commander and my mama came. Plus, I'm Pharaoh."

She laughed and climbed into the bed beside him. "Oh Tut, you are a brave young man."

I slid to the edge of the bed to stand up, but Tut caught my arm. "Mama, stay with me."

"I can't," I said, gently stroking his face. "I must return to your siblings and Malachi. Let Ankhe take care of you."

He scowled, but said, "All right. I love you."

"I love you too, son," I answered, but turned away in disgust as Ankhe lowered him down beside her and kissed his cheek.

I hurried out the door, mortified, and Horemheb followed. He rushed after me and caught my arm. "Naomi, decorum."

"I have to get as far away from *that* as possible," I said, feeling sick.

"Hush, Naomi." He pulled me behind him. "Now is not the time to be getting emotional."

I relented, and fell back behind him. We silently made our way out of the palace and to his estate. There, he led me to a small washroom and said, "I'll need you to help me tend to my wounds."

I nodded, and averted my eyes as he peeled off his clothes and covered himself with a rag. He sat down and handed me another rag so I could wash the wounds on his back while he washed away the blood splattered on his feet and legs.

As I carefully tended to a deep wound over his right shoulder blade, I whispered, "How does it feel?"

"You have very gentle hands," he muttered.

"No, I mean, to kill someone."

He dipped the cloth in water to rinse it off before he continued wiping at the blood. "Why would you ask me that?"

"I remember once, you told me you enjoyed the rush of battle. Is it the same thing?"

He paused and turned his head toward me slightly. "No, that's a different kind of killing. Battle is exciting and you never know what will happen next, but this, this has the satisfaction of justice being served."

I slowed, pondering what he meant. I wasn't sure if I agreed with him, but I could see his perspective: to get rid of those who will destroy you, before they have a chance.

"It helps that you never liked Smenkhkare in the first place."

He scoffed. "He was a horrible boy who grew into a horrible man."

"I wonder what Mordad would think if she knew we..." I stopped and pulled away from him.

He turned and looked at me. "Naomi?"

"She would be upset with me for doing this with you. She wanted me free of all of this, and free of you."

He sighed and turned away from me again. "You are still tenderhearted, Naomi, but think of it like this; I know he raped her at least three times."

"What?" I gasped in shock at the revelation.

"Oh, yes, Naomi. He lusted after Mordad like no other. But don't worry. Hepsati is the daughter of the late king. She was conceived when Smenkhkare lived in Memphis for a year."

"That horrible pervert!" I snarled. "Oh, now I wish *I* had plunged your sword into his throat!"

"No, you don't," he responded. "You would have felt terrible afterward and I couldn't live with that."

He leaned over and dumped out the bloody water. "Go fetch some clean water and the honey."

I took the bowl from him. I refilled it from the small pond in the garden, then detoured by the food storage to collect the honey. When I returned, he had dressed in a clean skirt and stood examining a gash on his shoulder. He glanced up at me and said, "Help me with this."

I sat him back down, carefully rubbed honey over the wound, then began to bind it. As I did, I felt him staring up at me, examining my face carefully.

"Naomi," he whispered. "Do you fear me?"

"No," I answered without looking away from my task.

"Even after everything that happened tonight? Are you not afraid I will come to your home and slit your and your husband's throats because I can't have you?"

I stopped and looked down into his eyes. It felt like a strange question to ask me because even though I knew he was ruthless and a killer, I also knew he could never hurt me. He had always protected me, he had always fought for me, and even if he did hate Malachi for being in his way, he couldn't harm him because he knew it would break my heart.

"Horemheb," I said softly and gently stroked his cheek. "You're not heartless, so I know I am safe with you."

He stood in front of me and clasped my face. "Naomi, you have so much faith in me, but yet you claim that you don't love me. Tell me the truth; do you feel anything for me?"

I looked up into his eyes, my heart pounding hard within my chest. I couldn't help my hand running over his strong, smooth-shaven chest as I bit my lip. I knew my answer, but I was afraid to admit it to myself, let alone him. I pushed back from him and turned away, ashamed.

"I can't do this."

"Naomi, tell me," he said firmly. "You know that for me there has only ever been you, but you have never given me anything, just a stolen kiss or long glances. I told you I would wait twenty years for you if I must, and Naomi, I swear to you I will."

"Sometimes you can be so much like Malachi," I whispered.

"Tell me, Naomi."

I looked back up into his eyes and caught my breath, dazzled by how strong and handsome he was. "Oh, Horemheb, I think I have always loved you."

His face lit up, but as he leaned toward me, I held up my hand to stop him. "But not like I do Malachi."

His jaw clenched and he turned away from me. "Very well. I am glad I have some closure. Thank you for being honest with me, but I think it's time you went home. The sun will rise in an hour or so. Don't worry, I won't expect you to come in and work today; you get some rest."

I turned slowly toward the door, but just before I left, I whispered, "I'm sorry, Horemheb."

I ran all the way home, and as I silently entered the house, I felt relieved to find Malachi still asleep. I carefully slid down under the blanket and dozed off. What felt like only a few minutes later, he rolled on top of me and kissed my cheek and neck. I smiled, feeling the sorrow and fear of the night melt away at his touch, and I knew without any shadow of doubt he was the best choice I had ever made.

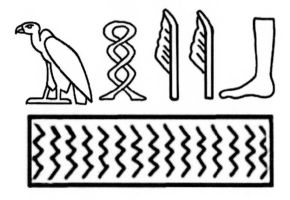

CHAPTER TWENTY-FIVE

S menkhkare and Meritaten were buried in their tombs quickly and without much attention. It seemed their murders were far too scandalous to be made public, but I also believed Horemheb had a hand in the cover-up.

Tut took sole possession of the crown, with Ankhesenamun at his side as queen. It wasn't long after that that he and Horemheb led an army, boosted with all our young men, including Joshua, to push the Hittites back over our borders. Many lives were lost, and there was much sorrow throughout the city, but all knew why it had been done and were grateful it had not been grief for their small children.

As the army returned, we waited to see if Joshua and Malachi's brothers, Enoch and Jared, would return with it. Enoch did not, and Joshua returned with one less leg. But the loss and sacrifices seemed to appease those who pushed for a resolution to the *Hebrew issue*, and a fragile peace between us and the Egyptians fell again.

I conceived and bore another son while they were gone, whom we named Aaron, and Tut greeted him excitedly upon his return.

As time passed, Tut began to realize Ankhe struggled to conceive and carry children full term. He sent out for treaty wives, and took many of the wives Smenkhkare had left behind, but none seemed to be able to carry for him. He didn't let it bother him. He would say, "I am young. My father was a man in his thirties when I was conceived. I have twenty years before I'm that age!"

And so, I watched my son grow and blossom into a confident young king whom all felt was a great hope for our future. My only worry was Ay, whom Horemheb and Gerlind both told me still wanted Tutankhamen dead.

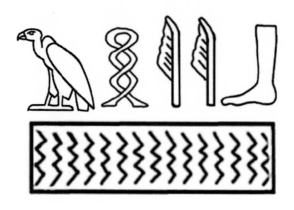

ACKNOWLEDGEMENTS

Thank you…

To you; for continuing reading the trilogy and loving Naomi as much as I do. Your support has been overwhelming and wonderful. You made my dreams come true.

And to Curiosity Quills, for all the support they continue to give. I love that I can be open and honest with each and every person involved and know my voice is heard.

I look forward to sharing the final installment, *Kiya: Rise of a New Dynasty* with you soon!

~Katie

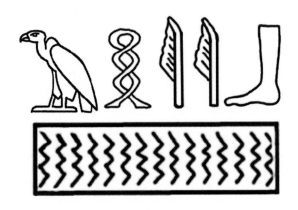

THANK YOU FOR READING

© 2013 **Katie Hamstead**
http://kjhstories.blogspot.com

Curiosity Quills Press
http://curiosityquills.com

Please visit http://curiosityquills.com/reader-survey/ to share your
reading experience with the author of this book!

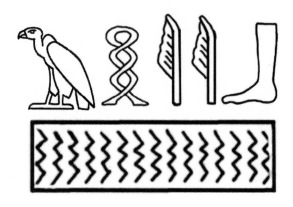

ABOUT THE AUTHOR

Born and raised in Australia, Katie's early years of day dreaming in the "bush", and having her father tell her wild bedtime stories, inspired her passion for writing.

After graduating High School, she became a foreign exchange student where she met a young man who several years later she married. Now she lives in Arizona with her husband, daughter and their dog.

She has a diploma in travel and tourism which helps inspire her writing. She is currently at school studying English and Creative Writing.

Katie loves to out sing her friends and family, play sports and be a good wife and mother. She now works as a Clerk with a lien company in Arizona to help support her family and her schooling. She loves to write, and takes the few spare moments in her day to work on her novels.